THE
OCEAN
IN OUR
BLOOD

TARA PYFROM

AOS Publishing, 2024

Tara Pyfrom

ISBN: 978-1-990496-91-2

Cover Design: Chanelle Poupart

Visit AOS Publishing's website:
www.aospublishing.com

For Catherine

Without you, surviving would
not have been worth it.

For Hazel

Now you will know why we
are the way we are.

For Charlotte

Fifteen years was not long
enough, sister.

Acknowledgements

Thank you to my wife, Catherine, for believing in me long before I believed in myself. For years before our ordeal, you told me to write a book, and I refused to listen. It turns out you were right, and I'm so grateful that you (almost) always are!

To my therapist, Patti, without whose gentle nudge I never would've gotten started. Thank you for listening to me read and reread the first paragraphs that went on to become this book. I was barely breathing at times with tears and snot running down my face, but you still pushed me to face the trauma and helped me overcome it.

To my editors Evelyn M. Duffy and Adrian Rivera of Open Boat Editing (www.openboatediting.com). This book would be considerably shorter and less interesting without you. Thank you for the constructive criticism and validation that what I had created was indeed worth pursuing.

To AOS Publishing, Michael, Julia, and the whole team, thank you for making my dream a reality.

To my beta readers (family, friends, and strangers) who read various drafts and gave me the confidence to believe in the words I had written, I am forever grateful.

And lastly, though certainly not least, to the people who rescued us and cared for us in the aftermath, my family and I will never be able to thank you enough.

Disclaimer

The events and conversations in this book have been set down to the best of the author's recollection. However, some details and dialogue have been fictionalized or recreated for creative effect. In some cases, names and identifying details have been changed to protect the privacy of individuals.

CONTENTS

PROLOGUE

A shot of adrenaline coursed through me unlike anything I had ever felt. It was pure, unadulterated fear. I'm pretty sure all the blood completely drained out of my face. I grabbed a flashlight and rushed to the front of the house. By pressing the light directly against the window glass, I could see through the early morning darkness. The road and front yard had disappeared under at least three feet of ocean. I raced to the kitchen to see the water travelling up our elevated driveway. My heart pounded, and I could hear the blood pumping in my ears. My mind raced with options. Ideas for survival and safety appeared behind my eyes. I sorted through each idea as possible and impossible, reviewing the consequences of each. I must have gone through a hundred scenarios in the time it took me to blink twice.

The chemical reactions in my body brought on by the fight or flight response reached my muscles, and it was time to act. I remembered the sandbags we had filled and strategically placed around the outside of our three exterior doors. I'd never used sandbags before, but I had watched countless clips and stories, mainly from when Hurricane Katrina slammed into New Orleans in 2005. I explained my plan in a quick conversation with my wife, Catherine, and we opened the three exterior doors to haul the sandbags inside. Two of the doors were reasonably easy to open and move through since they had the benefit of being under the covered porches and not in the direct wind. The third door led to our elevated driveway and was not sheltered at all. We had to hold the door steady to prevent the wind from damaging it as I rushed to haul sandbags inside.

With the speed of the rising water, the ocean would reach above the two or three sandbags at each door soon, but if those bags were inside, they might keep the water out or at least slow it down. Initially, we were protecting property and attempting to prevent interior water damage. In my mind, we would be fine walking around in a few inches of water for several hours. It was going to be annoying but okay, I told myself. Catherine and I managed to move twenty-five or so sandbags in a matter of fifteen minutes. Throughout the process, I never felt the back pain that had plagued me over the last few days of carrying loads of heavy things. The sandbags suddenly were as light as pillows. I moved full steam ahead. By the time the sandbags and tarps were secured inside each of the three doors, the water had reached our back door and hurried up the elevated driveway ramp to the car tires. The water was rising fast.

I heard Catherine shout from the living room, "The water's coming in!"

Anxiety reached yet another monumental high. The sandbags did little to stop the water's progress to the interior of our house. The ocean water advanced quickly through our back door and across our tiled living room floor. Not long after the water started through our back door, it was seeping in quickly through our other two doors as well. In a matter of minutes, we had an inch of water throughout our house.

BEFORE

OCEAN PEOPLE

When we tell people that we are from the Bahamas, we inevitably get looks of amazement. Most people have never met someone from our tiny island home. Many others have visited on a cruise, usually stopping by for just a day. Some assume, incorrectly, that the Bahamas is a part of the United States. It is, in fact, an independent Commonwealth nation. There are almost always comments about how lucky we are. "It must be a dream to live in the islands!" people often say.

They are right. My wife and I were fortunate to both have been born and raised on the islands of the Bahamas. The beaches are simply indescribable. White sands stretch for miles and miles. Turquoise waters spread out from the beaches as clear as any swimming pool. Our reefs are teeming with colourful fish. Turtles, rays, and many species of sharks call our waters home. Our country's natural beauty is an innate part of who we are, and the ocean is a big piece of our souls.

Our parents were all Bahamian, born and raised here too. Most of our ancestors, going back eight generations, were all born and raised in the Bahamas as well. Following the American Revolutionary War in 1783, groups of people wanting to remain loyal to the British crown left America, some headed north toward Canada and others headed south. Our ancestors crossed the oceans and found themselves shipwrecked, in some cases, on the islands, and left to build communities from nothing. All those communities were built near the sea. It didn't matter that some islands were wide enough to build homes away from the ocean, almost all communities throughout the country are built around a central harbour: a haven of community, food, and a need for the ocean.

These Loyalists populated the islands, bringing slaves with them to work their cotton plantations as they were established. As the cotton industry grew, so too did the population of slaves horrifically kidnapped in Africa and brought across the ocean to our shores. By the time slavery was rightfully abolished in the Bahamas in 1834, the population of people of African descent greatly outnumbered those of Loyalist descent in the Bahamas.

As a Bahamian though, being of African or Loyalist descent mattered little. We all grew up with the ocean, having memories and experiences that made us who we are because of our community's proximity and symbiotic relationship with the islands.

Our grandparents, great-grandparents, and great-great-grandparents were fishermen and sailors. They lived their whole lives by the sea. And, of course, so did the wives and children of fishermen and sailors, all waiting for them to return home from long weeks at sea.

Bahamians are all ocean folks by nature and genetics. Harvesting from the sea was a way of life for centuries. A thriving sponge industry took hold of the Bahamas in the nineteenth century. Catherine's grandfather was one of the fishermen who made their living diving, trimming, and preparing sponges harvested from the ocean floor to be exported to places as far away as Europe. That industry folded in the 1930s under the pressure of synthetic replacements.

By the time sponging was over, the Bahamas had gained its primary industry: tourism. Today, showing off our natural beauty to tourists worldwide is the predominant source of income. In 2022 alone, the Bahamas received over seven million visitors by air and sea, with a large portion of that number being cruise ship passengers.[i] There are few places in the world as accessible as our islands with such untouched natural beauty, and for anyone who feels the romantic pull of the ocean, it is one of the premier vacation spots.

Of the seven hundred islands that make up the Bahamas, only about thirty are inhabited. The larger islands function much like states or provinces. The chain stretches from Florida to Cuba in the Atlantic Ocean, with most of the country's population living in the northernmost islands of Grand Bahama, Abaco, New Providence, and Eleuthera. As you island-hop further south, the islands become more and more rural. By the time you reach the southernmost island of Great Inagua, you have travelled back in time, at least one hundred years, as services and access to modern conveniences are almost non-existent.

None of our ancestors ever ventured far from the places of their birth. Both Catherine and I each have relatives from different parts of the country; the "out islands" as they are referred to. Some were born on the island of Long Island (the one in the Bahamas, not the one in New York) or Abaco and moved to the "big city" of Nassau for work or love.

I was born in the capital city of Nassau on the island of New Providence. Anyone who has ever cruised to the Bahamas has visited Nassau. Two-thirds of our country's small population live on the island of New Providence. That's around two hundred and seventy-five thousand people living on an island that's only twenty-one miles long by seven miles wide.

For many people, the flashes of turquoise and teal that marketers use in commercials seem computer-generated. They lure the eye and entice the heart to want a vacation at a Sandals resort in the Bahamas. Those colours are very real and never taken for granted by people like me, whose earliest memories have those colours as their backdrop. The ocean was my childhood.

I could only have been about five when my father worked as a tour boat captain in Nassau. He would pilot the booze cruise that left Nassau Harbour to ferry loads of sunburned tourists to sit and drink tropical cocktails on a beach shack on Rose Island, located only three miles from Nassau. There were odd occasions when my mother, sister, and I would join him for a Saturday trip. I recall one such Saturday, standing on the wooden deck under the shade of a coconut palm thatch roof and looking out at the brilliant blue of the ocean covering the sandbanks at the shoreline. Of course, being a child, the beauty of the scene was not impressed on me until much later in life, as I now recall the memory. My younger sister and I were enjoying the freedom of running amuck, barefoot, with only little girl bikini bottoms on. We both loved to play with the steel drums set up in the corner, usually played by musicians as the day wore on to entertain the guests. With no real rhythm, we beat on the concave aluminum to create tin-sounding melodies with a set of drumsticks.

Being little kids, we did not notice the commotion coming from the beach until our mother raced across the deck, a look of panic on her face. We dropped our sticks on the musical instrument and turned to see our father helping a large man up onto the deck before falling in a heap to the floor. Red-faced and huffing for air, both my father and the guest were soaked from the ocean. Our Dad had saved the large man from drowning after he ventured too far from the shore. Dad was not a lifeguard. In fact, there were no lifeguards on the beach, since the entire operation was grassroots at best, and regulations around such things in the Bahamas at that time were non-existent.

The emotional takeaway from one of my earliest ocean memories isn't a fear of drowning, nor even pride that my dad had saved a man's life. In my childlike memory of that event, the emotional response associated with what could otherwise be traumatic is simple. Beauty. I see the ocean in my memory. The beach, the turquoise colours, the thatch roof, and my dad in the ocean saving a man's life are all just everyday memories of my island life. Normal. The backdrop of a beautiful life, if you will. The ocean, to me, was just the curtain on an otherwise busy stage. It was rarely ever a threat. Something to be respected, yes. I understood that care always had to be taken with the ocean, but I was never frightened of it or by it.

Nassau is a prime cruise stop-over location, but with the population congestion, it is plagued with crime, corruption, and poverty. My family left Nassau and moved to the island of Abaco, with a population of roughly fifteen thousand people, when I was very young.

Abaco and its tiny, isolated group of islands were protected by a coral reef a mile offshore. After that reef, there was nothing but a deep blue ocean for some four thousand miles until the ocean reached the western side of the African Continent. Surrounded by turquoise waters and powdery white sand beaches, this tropical paradise is not even a single pencil dot on a world map. As one might expect, given its remoteness and sparse population, Abaco is a rural place. In many ways, it is still stuck in the 1950s.

I grew up on the even tinier "out island" of Man-O-War Cay, which is only three miles long. The island of Man-O-War Cay had a population of only three hundred people and was only accessible by boat from the mainland and the small town of Marsh Harbour.

While many kids ride a school bus, I rode a small ferry every day to get to high school. The weather didn't matter for the most part. Occasionally, rain squalls were so torrential that riders could not see landmarks from leaving one dock to arriving at the other side. There were crossings through wind-driven waves crashing over the bow in the middle of a storm that tested even the captain's ability to keep their breakfast down. If the ferry crossed the water from my tiny island home to the mainland just three and a half miles away, I was on it.

Of course, as island people, we understood the ocean's power. In my childhood, years before my first hurricane, there was an incident that was often referred to for years after as "the rage." A series of freak ocean swells, rolling into the Bahamas from the depth of the Atlantic Ocean, inundated the western islands in the chain. With nothing between the islands and the coast of Africa, the rage waves had been an odd creation of weather, current, and tide. We watched in awe as the massive waves slammed into the barrier reef. When the broken swells reached the land, they carried the tide far higher than normal, causing the beaches and dunes to disappear completely. Many beachfront properties were flooded. There was no risk to life from these freak waves, but the awesome power they thrust on our island became a vivid memory.

My wife, Catherine, was also born and raised in Nassau, moving as an adult to Abaco in the mid-nineties. Her father started the largest insurance company in the country, and with that success came a bit of luxury. Her childhood is full of magical stories of visits to uninhabited islands by boat with her family. For weeks at a time, they would explore and fish while seeing the landscape of the Bahamas up close and personal. Her childhood home was on the ocean, and her backyard playground was on the beach.

In her early teenage years, Catherine had a very distinct encounter that particularly resonates with what the ocean means to us. One of the family trips was taken during April to coincide with the long Easter holiday weekend. Cath, her mom and dad, one of her older sisters Charlotte, and a crew member cruised through the Berry Islands on their fifty-foot yacht. The Berry Islands are a series of tiny cays, almost completely untouched by man. They fished, explored, and swam, not seeing another boat or person for days at a time. Exploring such an untouched part of planet Earth was not uncommon for them. They'd been doing it as a family for years. In their excursions, they encountered many of the creatures that called the waters of the Bahamas home. But this excursion was a moment clear out of a National Geographic documentary.

The family anchored their larger vessel in the deeper waters off one of the remote cays in the chain. Everyone climbed into their smaller twenty-three-foot Mako to head into the pristine white sand beach that lined the entire shoreline of the island. As they set off from the larger boat, they watched the ocean colour change from deep blue to turquoise as the depth grew shallower. As the ocean bottom grew closer to the water's surface and the shoals and seagrass gave way to a white sandy bottom, the family began noticing a series of small, dark-coloured fish darting away from the boat as they sped forward.

Before long, the boat was surrounded by a crystal-clear ocean so translucent they could make out the ripple design easily on the sandy bottom of the ocean floor. As they continued toward the beach, the handful of dark fish seemed to multiply. They wondered out loud what kind of fish would behave like this. For a moment, they were all dumbfounded at what they were seeing.

They slowed the boat, and as the fish became less spooked by their presence, the shape of the creatures gave away exactly what species they had encountered.

Surrounding their twenty-three-foot boat were thousands of baby hammerhead sharks, each about a foot in length.

Hammerhead sharks are distinct-looking and impossible to mistake for any other creature on Earth. They are also common in the waters of the Bahamas. Another little-known fact about these elusive creatures is that the Great Hammerhead retains fertilized eggs within her body and gives birth to as many as forty live young at a time.

Cath and her family stopped their boat and turned off the engine entirely. They sat marvelling at the massive hammerhead nursery they had stumbled across. With the ocean's surface like a sheet of glass, only rippled slightly as the boat bobbed that beautiful spring day, the group sat awe-struck by the sheer numbers of a creature rarely seen as a single adult. It was a once-in-a-lifetime event accidentally experienced on the way to a family beach day.

The experience has been told and retold in their family over the years. The story is most often recounted with a reverence akin to witnessing a miraculous experience, even though the reproduction of ocean creatures is an everyday occurrence. Being privy to such an intimate offering of the ocean's wonder and innate mystery is another example of just how deeply the ocean is ingrained in us. Such experiences have shaped us in spiritual ways that are difficult to recount precisely. As ocean people, expressing this soul connection and fundamental part of our being is almost elusive.

The ocean that surrounded our home was a part of our identity. The ocean was in the background of almost every story. It was, by definition, what made us island people. Catherine and I each spent time away from the Bahamas before our paths crossed and love intertwined our lives, Catherine, more so than me, during her high school and university years. By the time Catherine was an adult, she had lived in the central part of New England and visited other countries like England and Egypt. When one lives on some of the most beautiful beaches in the world, one vacations far from the beach. My childhood vacations were in central Florida or as far north as the Appalachian Mountains.

No matter how far we travelled, returning home always meant returning to the ocean. Travelling back home from any trip away, the airplane would take off from South Florida and head directly out over the Gulf Stream. My sister and I would always sit with our faces pressed against the small oval window, staring down at the dark blue ocean. Before very long, the ocean's colour would change to teal and turquoise as the depths would grow shallower. We always knew that colour change meant home.

Image courtesy of Catherine Pyfrom

KISMET

The word "kismet" originates from Arabic and Turkish. It means "destiny, or divinely ordained by fate." I was never a huge believer in fate before I met Catherine. And yet, through all our challenges over the years, I come back to think of how we met and why I now believe fate played such a huge role in our lives.

At some point in their relationship, every couple will get the age-old question, "How did you two meet?" Catherine will say that it was love at first sight for her, to which I usually smile, blush, and say, "It just took me two years to notice!" That's the cute version of our story. We typically follow those lines with the much more complicated version: I was dating my now-wife's then-sister-in-law. That is usually harder to follow and generally met with perplexed looks as a new acquaintance tries to work out the semantics.

I began dating a woman in 2005, my first girlfriend. Same-sex couples were virtually non-existent in our tiny town and generally stayed hidden from the public eye to avoid vicious gossip. Many left the country entirely. My first girlfriend and I were not those people. Our first date was at the most popular bar in town on a Friday night. It was the sort of situation where the two of us walked in, and suddenly the room went silent as everyone turned to watch us enter.

My date groaned slightly and explained that her brother and his extended family were sitting at a nearby table. It would have been rude to avoid them entirely in such a cramped space, so my date insisted we go over and say hello. The brother greeted us first, and I was introduced as a friend, though everyone at the table was aware that these introductions were interrupting what was clearly a date. I was then introduced to the brother's wife. Her name was Catherine. The conversation was brief, and my date and I left and returned to the bar.

On the other hand, Catherine's story of that night is very different. She will tell a tale about being out for a meal with her family, bored with her husband's company. She saw her sister-in-law walk in with a mysterious woman with short, dark hair wearing a red top, blue jeans, and a black leather jacket. Catherine watched us as we went to the bar, wondering who the gorgeous woman was with her sister-in-law. After the introductions, Catherine couldn't take her eyes off me from across the room for the remainder of the evening.

I don't remember a great deal about that night. It was pleasant in my memory, nice enough that my first girlfriend and I would eventually move in together and have a two-year-long relationship. We saw the brother and his wife at the odd family function. I always enjoyed those gatherings far more than my girlfriend, usually because I spent most of the time chatting with Catherine. I was utterly oblivious that she was secretly in love with me.

Two years later, as the relationship between my girlfriend and I was coming to an end, we attended her brother's birthday party. That night while dancing together in a larger group, I felt the first spark of attraction and found myself drawn to Cath, wanting to dance closer to her than would have been appropriate. Her smile and laugh lit up the dance floor, and there were moments of cartoon-like tunnel vision where the periphery went fuzzy.

It was another six months between that night of awakening and the time when all the obstacles preventing us from being together were finally removed.

Our first date was a trip to the beach. One would think that living on an island, the beach might become tiresome, but it never did for us. That first date had far less to do with the beach itself, though, and everything to do with privacy. With the island being sparsely populated, once the roads left the few square miles of the town behind, there were miles and miles of empty, pristine beaches. Most of those places were accessible by narrow dirt roads with no signage whatsoever. If an explorer knew where they were going, they could count the number of electrical poles past the bend in the road and look for the tiny piece of pink tape hanging in the tree opposite the turn into the pine forest. If they weren't careful or didn't know the markers, they could easily speed past the turn. I often did!

At the beach, a thirty-minute drive from the nearest settlement and several miles from the paved road, we were met with a tropical paradise beyond our wildest dreams. The powdery white sand, considerably wider than many beaches on the island, was only dotted here and there with seaweed that had washed in with the last high tide. After removing our shoes, the sand under our bare feet was warm but not hot. It swallowed our toes in its softness as though we were walking on Care Bear clouds instead of a real-life place. There were no houses or people for miles. From the beach, our eyes met turquoise waters, calm except for a slight wave as the springtime breeze blew across the ocean.

We set off heading south down the beach, away from the trail we had used to gain access to this hidden place. A seagull flew overhead, casting a shadow that swept over us as it headed out to sea in search of its lunch. Walking along the water's edge as the gentle waves washed over our feet, we held hands and giggled like silly, drunk teenagers. The ocean was warm but still cool enough to send a quick prickle of goosebumps on our skin when a larger wave sent drops of water up our legs as we walked.

We hiked for a quarter of a mile to the far end of the beach and stopped when the sand abruptly met a natural limestone rock wall that was about fifteen feet high. We knew no one would come to the beach from the craggy rocks that hugged the coastline past the cliff. From our spot at the end of the beach, we would see someone walking down the beach long before they arrived.

It was not as though there was logically any chance of that anyway. It was the middle of a normal workday, and few people on the island would make such a hike for an empty beach when there were many more that were easily accessible. It was exactly the privacy we wanted out in the natural world, surrounded by immaculate beauty.

We were beginning a life together where everything was new, and we still had so much to learn about each other. We picnicked on the beach with blue and white towels laid out. We placed our cooler with drinks and sandwiches on the edge of the towel to weigh it down, hoping to prevent the breeze from trying to steal it away. We talked about life, our families, our hopes, and our dreams for the future. We lay on the beach for a while until the sun baked us and sweat started to bead on our foreheads. Then we swam, splashed, and played in the ocean like children, before returning to the beach and enjoying the warm sun drying the salt water from our bodies.

The day was right out of that iconic beach scene in the 1953 movie *From Here to Eternity*. Romantic. Sensual. Memorable. To this day, whenever I recall that day on the beach, the lyrics of a 1997 pop song *Truly Madly Deeply* by Savage Garden come to mind. The song talks about experiencing the world together, forever. That is the soundtrack now looped on repeat in my mind with the memory of that incredible day.

I was already falling head over heels for Catherine, but that day, surrounded by the beauty of the ocean, was a baptism of sorts. That day I saw the ocean and beach through Catherine's eyes with her hand in mine. I felt what the world could be with a soulmate. Someone with whom to always share in the beauty. To never feel alone or lost again. To gain strength and comfort during hard times. To have and to hold for the rest of our lives.

Of course, our lives were not a fairy tale from that moment on, but we joked often that our relationship was as much a fantasy as anyone could imagine. Being together and building our lives as one was never difficult. Eventually, we moved in together in true "U-Haul Lesbian" style. We rarely disagreed, and when we did, we communicated our way through it. We complimented each other's personalities and accepted one another's quirks and eccentricities. To us, it really did seem like fate.

Our story swept across the tiny island, almost constantly on the tongues of gossipmongers with little else to do. Our life in Abaco, outside the bubble with which we surrounded our home, was not ideal. We often walked into a restaurant to have the conversation completely stop. We heard through family and close friends that we were the talk of the town, and often with those rumours came outright lies. However, we stuck it out and held our heads high, due mainly to the euphoria of being in love.

Despite riding on cloud nine, life has a way of bringing the love-struck back to Earth eventually, no matter how high in the sky they manage to float. Before the second anniversary of our relationship, we navigated the death of Catherine's mother and Catherine's prolonged, messy divorce simultaneously. It was an overwhelmingly emotional time, and lesser relationships rarely stand such tumultuous blows. But we did. We simply loved each other through it.

After two years of living in Abaco as a couple, we had had enough of feeling ostracized. We decided to move to Grand Bahama and the city of Freeport in search of a home more open to a same-sex family. We also wanted to be closer to Catherine's older sister, Charlotte, who was living in Freeport then.

The Island of Grand Bahama was only eighty miles east of Fort Lauderdale, Florida. Initially developed in the fifties and sixties, it had the makings of a proper city with infrastructure planned to support a population of one hundred thousand. Sadly, the developer's plans never came to fruition, and the island's population barely broke fifty thousand at its peak in the seventies before tapering off to the forty thousand people who lived there when we moved in 2009. This left tens of thousands of acres of land entirely unoccupied by people and covered either in low-lying pine forests or swamps. Most of the population lives near the coast on the south shore, close to the endless stretches of white sand beaches.

The island's north end is just mangrove swamps for miles and miles, almost entirely inaccessible except by the airboats seen on TV in the bayou. At the bottom of that swamp, under the few feet of ocean water that ebbed and flowed with the tides daily, was thick silty sand that made up the ocean floor. It is not white and sandy like the beautiful beaches of our country. It's thick, brown mud. If stepped in, one would sink at least a foot in. Hundreds of years of mangrove growth in this silted seabed would eventually yield new land in places: the evolution of our islands.

Unlike most of the other islands of the Bahamas, Grand Bahama was never intended to be a tourism hub. Instead, it houses one of the largest container ports on the eastern seaboard, rivalled only by Norfolk, Virginia. Many of the jobs on the island are industrial, and the hotels that cater to tourists are boutique-style and constantly changing ownership. The island is about one hundred miles long by fifteen miles at its widest point, with most of the population living in the middle of the island in the city of Freeport. The proximity to the US, together with the industrial nature of the available jobs, led to a population that was heavily weighted with expats from around the world.

The Bahamas, by self-proclamation, is a Christian nation, and the conservative constitution is based on this fact. While countries like the United States of America have made a concerted effort to maintain a separation of church and state, the Bahamas leaned into its religious background. Prayer and Bible study are regular parts of the public school curriculum. There is a Christian church on every corner, be it Baptist, Catholic, Anglican, Methodist, Pentecostal, or otherwise. Homosexuality is not illegal, but discrimination based on sex and sexual preference is not unlawful, either.

Being a "good" Christian is a hallmark of being a "good" Bahamian for many people. Sadly, much of the Christianity in the Bahamas is filled with hate and damnation instead of its original premise of love. Throughout our lives since "coming out," both Catherine and I have experienced negative comments from family, acquaintances, and strangers alike. I've been called "sissy" on the street corner. While we've never feared for our safety as LGBTQ+ people in the Bahamas, there are regular news stories of gay men being attacked in Nassau or editorials in the newspaper on how homosexuality is a sin.

With the expats influencing the general community culture of Freeport, however, the tolerance for same-sex couples was far more open and welcoming; or at the very least, filled with people more likely to say things out of our earshot. The expat community of people from around the world lent a sense of worldliness to the island that was not present in other Bahamian communities.

Many of the rural areas in the Bahamas struggle against progress and progressive thinking, choosing to believe marriage is ordained by a Christian god who does not accept same-sex relationships. However, in Freeport, surrounded by the influence of more open people, we were able to feel more comfortable. We settled well in Freeport, making friends and feeling like a part of the overall community with far less bigotry to contend with. We created a new home and a new bubble and lived an open life.

In Freeport, we found all new beaches to explore with even more partially hidden dirt trails to secret places it seemed were meant for us alone. We spent countless hours together exploring. Catherine taught me the beautiful art of beachcombing, something I knew nothing about before we met. Gradually she turned me into an amateur conchologist like herself. Having inherited the hobby and knowledge from her mother and older sister, Catherine took her interest in seashells and made it a lifelong pursuit. Our weekends were spent walking miles and miles of empty beaches, hoping to find ocean treasures. I learned that a stingray's egg case, often found on our beaches, is called a mermaid's purse. With more lessons, I could eventually name mollusk species lying on the white sand from a hundred feet away.

After three years of being each other's constant companion, we felt it was important to make our relationship permanent. Sadly, several members of our immediate families were less than comfortable with our decision to get married. We didn't want anyone who wasn't one hundred percent supportive joining us for our special day, but inviting only the accepting family members didn't feel like the right decision for us either.

Ultimately, we eloped and honeymooned in the Green Mountains of Vermont. A far cry from the vast, overwhelming beauty of the Bahamas, Vermont was one of only five states that allowed same-sex marriage in 2010. It didn't matter to us that our legal marriage certificate in Vermont would never be recognised in the Bahamas. We were committed to one another, and we wanted the document that solidified our union. We needed to show the world, and several naysayers closer to home, that our love was real. Part of that need was promising to love, honour, and cherish each other for the rest of our lives. Starting a family was also something we discussed that we might one day want to do, and so the commitment of marriage was important for us.

We travelled extensively in the early years of our relationship. Travelling gave us new experiences to share and beautiful places to explore and create memories. If I'm being honest, though, my desire to travel was also born out of a desire to escape to places where it mattered little if we held hands as we walked or kissed each other on a street corner. Even though we felt more acceptance in Freeport and our close-knit community than we ever did in Abaco, my dream to build our life elsewhere often bounced around at the back of my mind. But it was a dream, meant to be pondered on and placated, and so travelling was my band-aid for an itch I refused to scratch.

Two years after our marriage, we began the process of turning our family of two into a family of three. Some young married couples are lucky enough to decide to have a baby and nine months later, the new family member arrives. That path was not an option for us. Having a child required endless hours of researching options and legal ramifications, in different countries in addition to our home. Since we had each had fertility issues in the past, and given the continued ignorance from some family members, we decided that adoption was best for us.

Of course, since same-sex marriage is not legal in the Bahamas, same-sex adoption was out of the question entirely. Thankfully, several states in the United States were progressive enough to offer private adoption to non-resident, same-sex families. If having a kid is a big deal, adopting a child from another country as a same-sex family is no easy task. There were times when our communication skills were pushed to their limit. But we loved each other through it.

When our daughter, Hazel, came to us just one day after her birth in 2013, it never occurred to us to raise her any differently than we had been raised. Island people need the ocean. Thus, Hazel was raised to let the ocean fill her very soul from birth. At barely twelve weeks old we dressed her in a tiny baby-size bikini, given to us as a gift, and took our daughter to the ocean for a kind of baptism. On a quiet Sunday afternoon, at a deserted beach on a calm summer day, we sat with our infant, only just able to hold her head up on her own. We splashed her feet in the ocean waters of our ancestors and laid her gently on the sand to feel the warmth of the sun. She would never remember her first encounter with the ocean, just as I do not remember my own, having been only an infant myself. However, that connection, that part of our soul, was placed there by the ocean regardless.

In our families, once a child could walk and run, it was time to learn to swim. Believe it or not, that is not a common assumption with all folks from the Bahamas. Many Bahamians wade in the ocean and fish from boats but never learn to swim. By the time Hazel was three, we made swimming lessons a priority. For two hours every Saturday for three months, we sat at the YMCA pool deck and listened to our daughter rage against the learning process. It was exhausting but necessary. We were living with the ocean in our backyard. The ability to swim was as much a necessity out of safety as it was out of family tradition.

Four months after her third birthday, as we sat in pool floats in our backyard saltwater canal, toddler Hazel insisted she could swim. With both of us in the water with her to grab her when she faltered, we let go, in water too deep for her to stand. And she swam. She swam further on her first attempt, completely unaided by armbands or water wings than she had managed to walk in her first few weeks of learning that skill. From then on, Hazel was a fish. She loved the ocean, as we did, from birth.

With the risk of hurricanes aside, one can imagine that living in the Bahamas had not been easy for us as a same-sex family. While we had chosen to surround ourselves with a small group of open-minded friends, most people in the Bahamas have an adverse reaction to our lifestyle. Hazel had already begun to experience the horrors of bullying for being "different" because she had two moms in kindergarten. Our marriage and our adoption of our daughter in the United States would never be recognized back home in the Bahamas. Legally, we would not be a family in the country of our birth. We were even hit with legal difficulties surrounding Hazel's ability to live in the Bahamas, where she was considered a "foreigner." Even though she was the child of Bahamian parents, the government's refusal to acknowledge our legal documents meant toddler Hazel was living in our home country as a tourist.

For us, though, the pull of the ocean and our island upbringing were powerful motivators. Over the years, we had ideas of leaving the Bahamas and moving to another country. Ireland, England, and Canada were among the places we had researched, but various logistical and emotional reasons had kept us in the Bahamas. We desperately wanted to give Hazel the island childhood we had grown up with, so we decided to stay in the Bahamas and continued making it our home despite the legal hurdles.

As part of the original development plans, a series of artificial waterways were constructed at great expense on Grand Bahama in the sixties. The central canal system situated some ten miles east of the city center cuts the island entirely in half. It allowed boats to travel from the north side of the island to the south quickly and easily. For fifty-plus years, the only way to access the two halves of the island was by a single two-lane roadway: Casuarina Bridge. In 2017, a second bridge, Sir Jack Hayward Bridge, was constructed on the north end of the island to improve traffic flow ahead of several planned development projects on the island's east end.

The waterway systems in Freeport are extensive and beautiful. They offer reasonably priced properties in quiet neighbourhoods for homes by the sea and the opportunity to have a boat at your back door. We chose to purchase an acre lot in Pine Bay in 2012 with plans to build our dream home, with the salt-water canal system in our backyard to serve as our closest connection to the ocean.

I often ponder those two years of waiting before Catherine and I began our life together. Any circumstance could have been different, and the two years it took us to clear our paths may not have been possible. I imagine that had Catherine not fallen for me then and there, in that crowded bar on a Friday night, we would never have managed to survive as we have. Despite the universe doing its best to separate us, those two years of waiting for the right time, and mental capacity, to love one another led us to have the incredible life we share today. Perhaps it was destiny, and we were meant to meet as we did on that tiny place on planet Earth. If that's not kismet, I don't know what is.

IT'S COMING

For all the beauty and majesty of living on the islands and having the ocean colours imprinted on our hearts, the ocean is a powerful and dangerous beast. Catherine can fill a book of stories of being caught out on the ocean in horrific lightning storms. There have been times in my life when I have earned a healthy respect for the ocean as well.

Hurricanes have always been a way of life for us. The Atlantic Hurricane Season runs from June first to November thirtieth. For six months out of every year, we watch the weather predictions religiously. Many people like us have gained considerable knowledge of meteorology throughout our lives. How hurricanes form and how they move was just common knowledge to anyone who had just a slight bit of interest. We knew that hurricanes, the big ones at least, weren't likely to come calling until August,

September, and October. Those months always had the hottest ocean temperature: the fuel for hurricanes. Knowing this, we traditionally paid the closest attention during those months.

Hurricanes are measured according to their maximum sustained wind. The wind is measured by weather buoys strategically placed throughout the oceans and by Hurricane Hunter aircraft. Hurricane Hunters are specially designed airplanes with highly trained crews that fly directly into these storms and use advanced meteorological equipment to measure things like barometric pressure, water temperature, and wind speed. The information gathered is then returned to the National Hurricane Center in the United States where computers and experts interpret the data.

Tropical Storms and Hurricanes are rated using something called the Saffir-Simpson Hurricane Wind Scale. A Tropical Storm has winds of thirty-five mph up to seventy-four mph. A Category 1 hurricane has winds of seventy-five to ninety-five mph, and a Category 2 has sustained winds of ninety-six to one hundred and ten mph. Category 3 and 4 storms have one hundred and eleven to one hundred and twenty-nine mph and one hundred and thirty to one hundred and fifty-six mph, respectively. The designation for the strongest hurricanes, Category 5, is reserved for storms with winds of one hundred and fifty-seven mph or higher.

Everyone who lives on the islands knows the threat of a hurricane is ever-present. Even as we splash at the beach on a calm day, we can look out at the vast ocean knowing that with the right temperatures and currents, tides and weather, a monster can be born in what we usually see as breathtakingly beautiful.

Each generation in the Bahamas has a hurricane story. It's always about The Big One, the storm that everyone remembers. Our parents' storm was called Betsy. Hurricane Betsy was a Category 3 storm that directly hit the islands of Abaco and New Providence in 1965, leading to significant flooding and hundreds of thousands of dollars in damages in the Bahamas alone. My mother was very young when Betsy hit, and her memories became stories told over the years.

Her memory is an image in my mind of a much younger version of my grandmother, an apron around her waist, sweeping water out of their garage as the torrents of rain and wind beat more in. My mother and her two siblings huddled in the doorway as the wind whipped their clothes. They had been scolded for playing in the water that was turning their garage into a splash pad. My grandmother tried to keep them out of the way and indoors where it was safe but also attempted to make light of the storm so as not to frighten the kids further.

I don't remember any hurricanes at all until I was ten. That year, there was Hurricane Andrew. It did not impact the island I was living on, nor did it affect Catherine in Nassau. However, the stories of the tornadoes that were birthed from that storm were infamous. The island of Spanish Wells was all but flattened by twisters, born as "waterspouts" over the ocean. They became tornadoes when they crossed onto the tiny island that is less than two thousand feet wide by only a mile and a half long. Hurricane Andrew is better known for leaving horrible scars on the city of Homestead in South Florida. My memory of Hurricane Andrew exists mostly as conversations overheard by my parents discussing the South Florida news.

I was in my teens when I remember experiencing my first hurricane. Some trees went down, we lost electricity, and school was out for a few days. Minor inconveniences. Then Hurricane Floyd hit the island of Abaco in 1999: a Category 4 hurricane.

Still living at home with my parents at the time, I remember standing at the front door of our house to peer out the window. It was the only window in the house that had a gap in the shutter that allowed me to see what was going on outside. All the windows in the house had been shuttered days earlier. As I stood watching the coconut trees wave around wildly, I found myself holding my breath and waiting for them to snap off at any moment. My limited view through the gap in the shutter faced almost due east. I couldn't see the ocean, but I knew that the beach was only four hundred feet away, marked by the end of the line of coconut trees. I wondered briefly if the waves could reach our house, but I brushed it aside as an overreaction. As the long day of the hurricane wore on, I repeatedly returned to the front door window to squint and try to see through the opening.

At the peak of the storm, I pressed my cheek directly against the cold glass and jumped back in shock. Thinking I had imagined the sensation, I placed my palm flat on the glass where my face had been. As I paused, I could feel the glass moving slightly. It was breathing as though it was an organic lifeform. Fear washed over me, and my skin prickled with goosebumps. The wind outside was so powerful that it warped the glass in the window. With each gust, I could easily feel the advance and withdrawal of each of the storm's monstrous breaths.

In the end, Hurricane Floyd left a lot of property damage and scarred the land. It left us without electricity for weeks and sunk or wrecked many boats in the harbour. But we were safe. The house had no major damage and no one we knew was injured.

In my lifetime though, the frequency and strength of these storms has increased remarkably. Since Hurricane Floyd, there have been Michelle, Erika, and Irene. Hurricanes Frances (a Category 3) and Jeanne (a Category 4) hit in 2004, just weeks apart. Hurricane Wilma flooded Grand Bahama in 2005.

The storms I named are just the ones that left visible marks on property and psyches throughout my life. There were many other tropical storms and hurricanes over the years that impacted my home whose names and details I can't recall. The repetition of hurricane season after hurricane season and preparation after preparation have created an abyss in my memory that makes them mundane and not worth remembering. By contrast, I have significant emotional responses to storms like Floyd, Frances, and Jeanne. I, like countless others, could fill a book of just those "big" storms. But this story isn't about those storms or those scars. This story is about the last hurricane I hope to ever experience: Hurricane Dorian.

Scientists and climate change experts tell us that the earth is warming. It's all over the news every day. More fossil fuels are burned by machines using oil. The gases they produce are released into the air that in turn break down the ozone layer surrounding the earth that protects us from the sun's worst heat. As the earth's surface is exposed to higher and higher temperatures, the oceans warm. The Bahamas' mean daily maximum temperature has risen by point-five degrees Celsius since the 1960s.[ii] Warmer oceans mean more fuel for hurricanes that feed on those things.

A warmer planet means the polar ice caps are melting, raising ocean tides and water levels. Our islands are low-lying, with eighty percent of the country less than one to one and a half metres above the current sea level.[iii]

Continued levels of greenhouse emissions released into our atmosphere could raise ocean levels enough to one day send the Bahama Islands back to the bottom of the ocean. As it stands now, higher-than-normal tides, combined with heavy seasonal rains, often flood the main tourist strip of Bay Street in Nassau.

The first time I heard the phrase climate change was after Al Gore's *An Inconvenient Truth* burst onto the pop culture scene in 2006, and suddenly, it was a worldwide debate. Was the idea of climate change real? In all honesty, I didn't take very much notice. It was years later before I even saw the movie. I was twenty-five when it was released, and while I had heard older folks in our community talk about how every year it seemed to be hotter, or the hurricanes' frequency was increasing, I didn't pay nearly enough attention. It didn't feel like it had a direct impact on me, maybe because I was naïve or self-centred at twenty-five. Climate change and its impact on my family, and my life, didn't occur to me until 2013, with the birth of our daughter.

In May 2014, we broke ground on our new home. I had an interest in and a knack for amateur architectural drawing, even though my career had always been in administration and bookkeeping. Catherine was an artist and painter by trade, so her eye for interior design and knowledge of home construction, together with my limited drawing ability, was a perfect match. We spent years designing and drawing the floor plan of our dream home.

When we met with an architect for the first time, we had a complete floor plan ready for him. We planned the rooms around the gorgeous canal view, angling the house just right to maximize the indoor-outdoor feel. We incorporated large windows and an open floor plan.

From our front door, a guest could see through our foyer and massive great room at the center of our home, out our large French doors, and onto our covered deck. Our stone pool deck with an inground pool was two steps down. The pool deck was elevated from the ground level by two feet. From the French door and deck, the fully landscaped yard was visible and inviting. Along the property's perimeter at the edge of the saltwater canal, we constructed a thigh-high concrete wall. It framed the property and created a barrier between the yard and the walkway along the six-foot drop to the water below. For young Hazel and our five dogs, the canal wall was a safety addition and a no-go zone, unless we accompanied them.

Moving from our living room, the kitchen and dining were in the front corner of the house, overlooking the driveway and entry gate. The master bedroom and Hazel's bedroom each entered from the living room, one in each back corner of the home, overlooking the pool, backyard, and canal.

When planning our construction, we used all materials that were known to handle humidity and the possibility of hurricane damage very well. Our exterior walls were constructed with concrete blocks with a poured concrete foundation, while the interior walls were constructed of wood. Ceramic floor tiles, solid wood kitchen cabinets and quartz countertops were expensive, but if they ever got wet, they would dry out and would not need to be completely replaced.

When we designed and built our dream home, Catherine insisted on a pull-down ladder with access to the attic. It wasn't an area we ever intended to use regularly, but it was convenient for additional storage and repairs.

We planned for eventual hurricanes with pricey hurricane-impact windows and an elevated foundation. None of our parents or grandparents had ever had the luxury of hurricane-impact windows. The technology was relatively new and still not cost-effective for many. Though the windows and doors were not one hundred percent water-tight, that fact was never discussed or considered, since our foundation was elevated enough to protect the house and us.

Our neighbourhood, Pine Bay, was known to flood in storms. The year before we bought our property, a tropical storm pushed a foot of water over the roads, and years before, Hurricane Wilma drove a couple of feet through the neighbourhood. Building a two-storey home wasn't ever in our plans—all of that up and down when one of us forgot something from upstairs that was needed downstairs. We weren't into fitness and exercise, and the extra steps sounded unnecessary.

Instead, knowing the flood history, we built an elevated foundation for our home. By our estimations, the ground level of our property was six feet above the high tide mark of our canal wall. We built our foundation another four feet up. We believed that would be more than sufficient. Our contractor agreed, as did numerous other "experts" in the field. We even went so far as to elevate a portion of our driveway to keep our car safe from floodwater. We planned for the eventual possibility of ocean water on our property. We prepared for hurricanes.

When designing our house, we wanted a simple, single roofline without gables. We built a substantial hip roof where all four sides sloped gently down to the walls. The roof was so large that the trusses, the main support structure, had to be built on-site, as they were too large to make off-site and truck in. This design created a vast space in our attic. At the center, the attic was some ten feet high and tapered down to only a foot or two at the eaves on each side of the house. Inside this massive space were beams and criss-cross lumber, all braced to hold up the roof with an enormous number of metal hurricane straps, far exceeding the building codes of South Florida, an area known for stringent building requirements. The roof was built specifically to withstand a hurricane.

The construction, however, made the attic space virtually unusable. With long crisscrossed beams every two or three feet extending from the ceiling of the house to the peak of the roof, there was no open space at all. The attic floor was lined with insulation to keep the hot temperatures of the attic from penetrating the living spaces of the house. Air-conditioning ductwork snaked back and forth, and electrical wiring and PVC plumbing pipes wound their way through the beams.

When the house was completed, and we moved in a month before Christmas in 2014, we decorated it with beiges and blues to compliment the nautical themes in Catherine's massive collection of seashells. Vases lined the shelves, filled with sea glass, all hand-picked from the shore near our home. The tiny pieces of glass, easily considered garbage to many, were a precious treasure to us. Old glass bottles, tossed into the sea, spent years being broken by the waves and tumbled in the rocks and sand on the ocean floor. Eventually, these treasures came to rest on the white sand beaches as much as a hundred years later. Often called mermaid's tears or mermaid's treasure, enthusiasts around the world would have envied our collection. Such colours, as we found in the Bahamas, are almost unheard of in other places. We found even the rarest purple or red occasionally on our expeditions.

Special shelving, display units, and fixtures furnished the house to allow years of antique and nostalgic items to add to the beach décor. Glass floats were a particularly unique part of the nautical style. Sometimes called glass balls, they are netted glass buoys originally used in Norway and Japan in the nineteenth and early twentieth centuries to float fishing nets before plastic and Styrofoam replaced them. Catherine had quite a collection of glass balls, which hung from the ceiling and accented tables and filled vacant corners throughout the house.

The house we had so painstakingly built and decorated with its authentic marine theme quickly became our forever home. Our place of refuge. Our happy place.

Our family was made all the more complete with our beloved pets. Having both grown up with dogs, it was automatic that we would have them as a part of our family. They slept in their dog beds, never stayed outside overnight, and cuddled with us on the couch every evening. When we travelled, we had someone come and stay at our home to look after them rather than boarding them at a shelter.

Pearl was the oldest, at almost thirteen years old. She was a miniature dachshund with dappled grey, black and brown markings, small even for her breed at barely nine pounds. In her younger years, Pearl was our hunter. Whether it was digging crabs on the beach or digging lizards in our garden, she was always catching something in her youth. She spent most of her time those days sleeping, sometimes on the couch but often in the sun on the porch.

Copper was our rescue boy, a golden-coloured long-haired dachshund whom we guessed to be around nine years old. He had been found roaming the streets malnourished with a broken front leg that would never heal correctly. He had a very pronounced limp as a result and had many medical conditions, from arthritis to a damaged heart, requiring daily medication. But he was a love and never stopped wagging his tail. We had been fighting a losing battle with his health for several months. Copper was on heart medication, arthritis medication, diuretics, steroids, and antibiotics by 2019. Five different medications were keeping him alive.

Sky, who was only five, was our odd one out. She was our mixed breed, larger dog, named for her pale blue eyes. She came to us as a beautiful puppy born at the neighbours' house, whose eyes and husky-like appearance made saying no to yet another dog impossible. She had been a terrible handful as a puppy, even occasionally aggressive. As an adult, she was the pack alpha and instigator for everything.

The last two dogs were our "spice girls." Nutmeg, four, and Ginger, three, were miniature dachshunds, both around ten pounds and inseparable unless there was water involved. Nutmeg and Sky loved to swim. Ginger adamantly refused to get anywhere near the water. Nutmeg had longer brown and golden fur. Ginger had short brown hair and was gray spotted, also a dapple. They were our lap dogs and constantly barking at something or another.

Almost two years after moving into our dream home, Hurricane Matthew made a direct hit on our island, just west of the city of Freeport. As with other storms, we prepared. We bought supplies and secured our property. We even had our neighbours stay with us during the storm. At its peak strength, Hurricane Matthew was a Category 5, but it weakened as it moved across various mountainous islands of the Caribbean. When Matthew hit Freeport, it had maximum sustained winds of one hundred and thirty mph.

We had been nervous about Matthew as it approached. We had only been in our home for two years at the time and had not yet tested the validity of the expensive hurricane-impact windows we had installed. It was also our first experience of not shuttering our home. Our windows were supposed to be able to withstand a direct hit from a solid piece of wood travelling at one hundred and fifty mph. On top of that, our elevated foundation would keep us dry from storm surges. We believed we would be safe, and we were. In the end, Matthew blew through our island in just under twenty-four hours.

The aftermath was chaotic. Our gardens were a mess. We lost many of the mature trees we had spent considerable time, effort, and expense cultivating. Luckily, the gardens were the extent of our damage. Our home was just as perfect after the storm as it had been before. No broken windows. No flood waters. No leaks. The rest of the island had not been as lucky.

Hurricane Matthew wrecked the entire city's electrical grid by taking out ninety percent of the poles carrying the electric lines. After the storm, we were without running water for several days and without electricity for weeks. As part of the pre-hurricane prep, we purchased ice and stored it in our freezer, along with several gallon bottles of water. To keep the perishable food cold after the storm, we transferred the food, ice, and frozen bottles into two hard coolers. After two days, all the ice and frozen bottles had melted in the heat. Our friend Kent gave us dry ice from his CO_2 business to keep our food cold for several more days.

After a week of no electricity, our friend Jamie got us a small and very loud gasoline generator. He and his father even came with chainsaws to help us clear out fallen trees. As was our custom, our friends were "Aunt" and "Uncle" to Hazel instead of the formal "Mr." or "Mrs." So to Hazel, instead of Mr. Rose, he was Uncle Jamie. Our kids all attended the same school together. We had been at each other's homes for meals and socialized several times. Ours was a small island, and thus a small community where everyone knew everyone, but we knew Jamie a bit better than many others.

We ran the generator in six-hour increments daily, hauling jugs of gasoline back and forth between the gas station and our porch. We had just enough electricity to maintain food in our refrigerator, a fan, and a few evening lights, but the noise and heat were oppressive. Utility crews from as far away as Canada were brought in by cargo ship with tools and large bucket trucks to help repair the grid. The repairs were painstaking. Electricity wasn't restored in our neighbourhood for three weeks.

In the end, it was eighteen months after Hurricane Matthew before most of the island recovered. However, the scars of Matthew remained for many as hurricane anxiety that few people had experienced before. As with other storms, over our lifetimes and the generations before us, life just continued. We picked up the pieces and got on with loving each other and raising our daughter.

By the summer of 2019, Catherine and I had been married for nine years and together for twelve. As we looked at our little family and our home, we knew life was about as perfect as it could get. Hazel was six, and we loved spending our days playing in our newly completed swimming pool. We were introverts by nature and spent a great deal of our time at home. We enjoyed each other's company and the oasis we had created. We chose to let only a handful of people into our inner circle and entertained friends infrequently. We spent many evenings by the pool watching the sunset, swimming after dark, and having a cocktail while watching the stars.

We took a vacation early that summer for two weeks. It was a lovely trip, a summer ritual for our little family, strategically planned in July to allow us to be at home during the worst of hurricane season.

Hurricane prep could be extensive, hard work that was often time-consuming, even when repeated yearly. Every family had their list of hurricane preparation exercises, and those that owned a business had an even longer list. Shuttering houses and shops, hauling boats out of the water (where possible), storm shopping, and projectile securing, just to name a few. For us, it was better to be at home during this time of year rather than entrust friends with the care of the dogs and hurricane prep responsibilities. No one would look after our home and pets as we would, even if their responsibilities were limited.

That August in Freeport was the picture of a tropical paradise: blue skies, hot days, sunburned noses, and refreshing swims.

By late August, however, news of a developing storm came across our Facebook newsfeed some twelve days before it arrived on our doorstep. As with other storms, this first report of a disturbance was met with mild concern and a mental note to keep track of its progress. There were a few thunderstorms that could turn into a hurricane several hundred miles out into the middle of the Atlantic Ocean. Most Bahamians would brush this off as typical summer weather. We watched the Tropical Update on the Weather Channel once a day to see the progress and the changes as the storm grew from infancy to toddlerhood.

In the beginning, the storm was so far out that Hurricane Hunters couldn't reach it. The National Hurricane Center made predictions based on satellite images and databases filled with over one hundred years of historical weather data. No actual data on this storm could be taken until it got closer to land and within reach of the planes. But predicting the weather is what they do. We trusted that the National Hurricane Center and the Weather Channel experts knew their stuff.

By the time Dorian arrived at the Leeward Islands in the Caribbean and within reach of the Hurricane Hunter aircraft, we watched the update morning and evening. Facebook began offering us news from various friends and acquaintances who were beginning to plan for a storm. Nerves were sensitive in town, and some people were already preparing for the worst.

As Dorian approached and its strength became more apparent, there was a sense of an entire community with Post Traumatic Stress Disorder setting in. Post Traumatic Stress Disorder, or PTSD, is a mental health condition that often presents itself as flashbacks, nightmares, extreme anxiety, and sometimes even panic attacks after experiencing or witnessing a frightening event or situation. PTSD is particularly characterized by overpowering thoughts about that terrifying event.

In Freeport, the only thing on anyone's mind was Dorian. At the grocery store, hardware store, or school pick-up line, there were lots of sombre faces and anxious conversations. Hurricane prep and predictions were the only topics being discussed. Folks were reliving the gruelling weeks and months following Matthew without electricity, conducting repairs in intense heat, all knowing that the repairs would have to be made yet again whenever the next storm arrived. With Matthew having been only three years prior, everyone's memories were still vivid.

Often women will say that they forget the pain of childbirth after a time because the joy of the child overshadows it, allowing for another pregnancy in the future. It is much the same with island people. We have endured a lot, many more storms in the last twenty to thirty years than previous generations. But the length of time in between those storms tended to overshadow the memory. The joy of memories made on the ocean helps us to recover our fortitude in many cases, so we can power through the experience again. With the approach of Dorian so soon after Matthew, there was a good deal of fortitude missing from the community's morale.

With the shadow of Matthew's aftermath hovering over us, more so than the storm itself, we watched Hurricane Dorian begin to organize. We viewed Dorian more through the lens of what the aftermath would look like. Anxiety rose as we remembered the hell of living without electricity and running water. Watching Dorian transition from a Tropical Storm to a Hurricane east of the Leeward Islands was painstaking. The storm was so far away that predicting if it would even have an impact on us specifically was difficult. This fact caused my anxiety to flip-flop between reasonable fear and unreasonable overreaction hour by hour.

Then Dorian grew. And grew. The strength bombed, and the infrared images that splashed across the news were an almost constant angry red. The five-day projected path wobbled east of us, then west. We waited to see if the mountains of Cuba would disturb the storm enough to turn it away from us or weaken it considerably. Meteorologists spoke of frontal systems that might stir the monster away from us in one breath, and we would breathe a tiny hopeful sigh. Then the following speech would begin with how the very same frontal system could turn and push the beast right on top of us.

People with boats began the process of securing them. Trucks towing trailers carrying every size boat, from tiny, inflatable dinghies to large, luxury speedboats, could be seen zipping up and down the town. As we headed into town, we noticed that a larger fishing boat, too large to haul out of the water on a trailer, was being secured near the bridge. A couple of guys were throwing ropes, tied to the boat's cleats, and being tethered to larger trees on either side of a narrow canal inlet.

We didn't own a boat for many reasons. The adage that "a boat is a hole in the water you pour money into" is very true. Boats, even smaller ones, are expensive to purchase and even more expensive to maintain. There wasn't access to mechanics for service and repairs in our immediate area.

We would have had to haul the boat out onto a trailer to get it to a mechanic regularly. Also, the island of Grand Bahama is unique geographically. Many areas of the Bahamas consist of the "main" island, surrounded by many other small islands or cays. Grand Bahama does not. Having a boat in Grand Bahama would mean using it to cruise the canal system or go to a beach we could much more easily reach by car. Crime was also an issue, as there had been a rash of boat thefts throughout the islands over the years.

As hurricane preparations continued, some businesses began boarding up their windows, leaving only their front door open to allow continued customer patronage. A handful of residences began putting up shutters. Hazel's school sent out an email setting an anticipated date for hurricane closure: the Bahamas equivalent of snow days, only with a lot more to lose. Friends discussed how long they would wait to begin their preparation, just in case the storm turned at the last minute and missed us entirely. At five days out, a complete turn was still a possibility. It had happened before.

As the weather predictions became more consistent, Cath and I began our checklist. We went to the grocery store early and stocked up before the cashier lines became insane and pointless. We bought a couple of gallons of water, a few cans of beans, some cereal, and snacks. Our refrigerator, freezer, and pantry were already full, since we had done our monthly stock-up the week before. We filled three gas cans for our portable generator to be used after the storm, and we filled our car's gas tank. Years of preparation and many hurricanes later, we knew that most people would wait until the last minute to prepare. This meant long lines at grocery stores and gas stations in the twenty-four hours before the storm's anticipated arrival. Completing any shopping ahead of the forty-eight-hour mark was a priority for us. Then we started talking about the when, where, and how of our property preparations.

By three days out, most of the spaghetti models were pretty much in agreement that we would get a direct hit. I was nervous. I'm not an idiot. There was a Category 4, soon-to-be Category 5, perfect storm headed straight for us. Catherine was already bordering on freaking out, and it would do neither of us any good for me to freak out, too. She was frightened that this storm would be stronger, bigger, and more destructive than Matthew had been. She worried about things like a tree falling on the house and damaging the roof or a window blowing out and exposing the inside of the house, and us, to the elements. She worried we might not be safe enough in our home.

I kept reassuring her, and in turn, myself that we would be fine. Our house was substantial. And it was still very new, at fewer than five years old. Our hurricane-impact windows had already been tested with one hundred and eighty mph gusts and had come away without a scratch. We knew our garden would be trashed but that it would grow back in the years to come. We knew exactly where to put our patio furniture and how to tie down our propane gas cylinder. We would be fine.

Image courtesy of Catherine Pyfrom

Image courtesy of Catherine Pyfrom

THE CALM BEFORE
THE STORM

We were completely convinced that Hurricane Dorian was just another storm to be weathered. So convinced that two days before its arrival, we had a beach day. It was something we'd been doing together for a few years. Make a trip to the beach before the storm to see the waves, find seashells if possible, and take "before" photos to post online alongside the "after" photos days later. Oftentimes, the waves that a storm creates hundreds of miles away make their way to our shores days before the storm's arrival. Not as large, menacing waves, but as smaller ones, just inconvenient enough to be avoided. The increase in wave action traditionally yielded more treasures tossed onto the beach, and so we walked hoping to find an Atlantic cowrie shell or even a tulip shell.

The beach we chose that Saturday was familiar but remote, accessible only by a dirt road that was a thirty-minute drive from our house. I don't believe the beach had an official name since it was just untouched nature, but the names I had heard it called over the years included Ol' Freetown Beach, Airplane Beach, and Nudey Beach, for various reasons. The western end of the island of Grand Bahama boasts miles and miles of remote stretches of powder-white sand beaches, largely uninhabited. On any given day, one can walk for miles and miles and never see another person.

We had a lovely day, just the three of us. We walked, hunted for seashells, and wet our feet in the ocean. The waves had already become too rough for swimming, in our opinion, so we took photos of the beach and us on it. The air was heavy, made even hotter as the storm to our southeast produced skyrocketing humidity. Breathing was difficult and the humidity caused the slight breeze to push even hotter air onto our sunburned faces. Without the benefit of an ocean swim to cool us off, we only stayed at the beach for a couple of hours before the refreshing call of the swimming pool lured us home for the evening.

The Sunday morning before Dorian's arrival was different in every sense of the word. I didn't know that it was different at the time, though. It felt familiar. It felt like numerous other "calm before the storm" scenarios I've experienced. Like the peace before the arrival of house guests or the day before a major home renovation begins. It's the quiet that comes in knowing that peace will be elusive for a while.

I'd felt this same physical calm quite literally three years before, as Hurricane Matthew arrived. The air becomes still, with the sky bright blue and almost cloudless. The humidity reaches over ninety percent, making the high temperatures feel even higher. All are the literal calm before the storm in meteorology before the hurricane's impending arrival.

Sunday morning, September first, 2019, I woke up as the sun was rising just after six a.m., and my mind raced through the last preparations before yet another hurricane's arrival. I mentally listed the outdoor items that needed to be secured and brought in. I debated the weight of our BBQ grill and if it was heavy enough not to blow around in two hundred and twenty mph wind, as those were the gust estimates being reported by the Weather Channel. As I lay in bed listening to our dogs begin to stir, I wondered whether the winds had risen even higher since we watched the two a.m. update. All these thoughts were very ordinary, matter-of-fact plans. This early morning mental checklist could seem surreal and unbelievable to anyone who has never weathered a hurricane, let alone a Category 5 hurricane. To the four hundred thousand people who called the Bahamas home, this was just another summer day before the arrival of yet another hurricane.

There may have been a sense of futility, but then again, with preparations all but complete, there was still a beautiful day to be enjoyed.

Realizing that my mind would not allow any more sleep that Sunday, or probably for several weeks to come, I decided to get up. I let our five dogs out our front door to do their business in our fenced yard. I glanced briefly at the slight pink hue in the sky as the sun peaked over the horizon. "Pink sky at night sailors' delight. Pink sky in the morning sailors take warning". I've been repeating that poem my whole life. I learned it as a child, and we had already taught Hazel the adage. She quite liked the science behind the weather after learning about it in school the year before.

Tropical cyclones, mostly called Tropical Storms or Hurricanes, form when the ocean temperatures heat up, causing the water on the surface to rise. As the moist air rises, it also cools and then condenses to make storm clouds. This is how your average thundercloud is formed. Over the Atlantic Ocean, however, the sequence is multiplied by the vast amount of warm ocean water feeding into this cycle. The massive amount of water condensing into the atmosphere creates energy that further charges and fuels the development of these clusters of storms. As the wind pushes more warm air across the ocean, the clusters become more intense and compressed. This fast-moving air creates a low-pressure system over the open ocean, often near the Cape Verde Islands, off the coast of Africa in late summer. This is when the ocean is at its warmest. The earth's spin causes these clusters of rapidly intensifying storms to spin counterclockwise. With nothing standing in their way and lots of hot ocean water to feed them, the ocean currents and wind steer these well-organized storms west across the ocean in the direction of the Bahamas and the Caribbean.

I crossed our living room quietly and went to check on Hazel. Generally, she would be up and watching cartoons on her iPad by this time of day, but I didn't hear her. It was so unusual that I briefly worried she might be coming down with something: the only possible reason she could still be asleep after six a.m. I gently opened her bedroom door and stuck my head in her room to find her still fast asleep in her princess pajamas. I closed her door and wondered what to do with myself. Deciding it was too early to begin final hurricane prep work, I glanced out the back window at our backyard and marvelled at how green everything was. I decided the back deck would be an excellent way to start this day.

For two years before beginning construction, we planned and tended the gardens of what would become our home. Catherine's father had been an amateur horticulturist, something he passed on to all his children. For me, the love of gardening came with my love for

Catherine. My grandmother had tended her gardens and loved her roses, but I never picked up the interest until Catherine and I began landscaping our first home together. From then on, I was hooked. Because Catherine had back injuries from youthful follies, I tended to do the heavy lifting with her expertise guiding me. More than once over the years, in the heat of the summer, when gardening midday was impossible, we would garden late in the evening or even after dark. I once planted a rather large key lime tree by the light of a full moon. Perhaps the lunar energy and spirit of Mother Nature blessed the tree. Years later we dug it back up and replanted it in our current oasis, though it never fully recovered after being trashed by Matthew.

When designing and creating our garden, we planted seeds and transplanted full-grown trees from the island's surrounding forests onto our property. We hired heavy machines to carefully dig up massive tropical trees like frangipanis and African tulips, then replanted them on our property. We moved a hundred cut stone blocks that were being used as garden retaining walls from our old house and created new ones on the new property by the canal. We had a huge fence installed and specially secured to allow the dogs on the property with us as we worked tirelessly. We spent hours every day watering, pruning, and babying the massive number of plants, shrubs, and trees we planted long before we ever broke ground for the new house. Our landscaped yard with the saltwater canal in our backyard became our pride and joy and felt like our own private botanical garden. All of it was built with our blood, sweat, and tears to create our dream home.

I took great care when I opened our very noisy back door, trying not to wake Hazel or alert the dogs and miss out on the five minutes of peace I was hoping to steal into my day. Mission accomplished. No one heard the door close. I had nowhere to sit since we had secured most of the patio furniture the day before. Two concrete benches had been left at the end of our pool deck. We decided that they would be safe from the wind: far too heavy to be moved by the storm. The benches were more decorative and far less comfortable, so I chose to sit on the top step of our deck.

The covered porch shaded my seat on the deck. It was warm, bordering on hot at just after six in the morning. I took a deep breath and listened. It was tranquil; no breeze to blow the trees and no barking dogs. I wondered why our dogs were not demanding their breakfast yet. I could hear tiny birds chirping, and I watched them flit around the yard. Everything was exceptionally green: the grass, the trees, and the canal water were all varying shades. *After tomorrow, nothing will be green for a very long time*, I thought to myself.

I sat there on our back deck looking at our beautifully landscaped yard and the crystal-clear water of the pool that hadn't yet seen the second anniversary of its completion. I thought about taking a swim later if the weather held long enough. I knew that after tomorrow the pristine pool water would be brown with debris. I worried about whether saltwater from the canal, just twenty feet from the pool deck, would rise high enough to fill the chlorine pool.

We had enough experience with hurricanes to know what data to look for to help in our own version of weather forecasting. Such amateur estimations had been reasonably accurate in the past, again, mostly during Hurricane Matthew. If I had brought my phone out onto the porch with me, I could have looked up what time the tide would be high and checked that against the anticipated time of arrival of the worst of Dorian's wind. That would tell me whether the storm would arrive at high tide or low tide. If the storm was expected to arrive at high tide, we might see a higher storm surge with the wind-driven waves. I tried to calculate the anticipated tide at the hurricane's expected arrival based on days-old data stuck in the back of my mind. The effort got too complicated without the aid of my iPhone. I gave up trying. Weather and water calculations would only serve to stress me out. I was trying to achieve calm, not more anxiety.

Our backyard had a spectacular view by all accounts. The porch, the deck, and the gardens were magnificent. All of it was orchestrated at just the right angle to maximize the view of the canal and the sunset each night. We spent so much of our free time enjoying the very view I sat looking at. I knew the approaching storm would wreck it, but I didn't really know what was coming. My mind lingered on what the aftermath of this storm would look like.

Matthew had sustained winds of one hundred and fifty mph. Sitting in the sunshine, I tried again to mathematically calculate how much longer we would be without electricity after a storm with wind gusts of up to two hundred and twenty mph. I realized again that my attempt at enjoying the calm before the storm was going nowhere at all.

Now with Dorian approaching, thinking about life after the storm set off a bit of apprehension that I didn't have before Hurricane Matthew. We didn't experience any life-or-death trauma then. There had been anxiety about property damages, but even then, we never feared for our lives during the hours that the storm battered our island. However, the weeks after Matthew were a real struggle, and imagining living through it all yet again was uncomfortable. The anxiety left from having endured Matthew's aftermath was now present in the form of a quickened heartbeat, shallow breathing, and very tense neck muscles. Sitting on the porch in the calm, I thought that perhaps if I could quiet my mind for just a while, I might be better able to cope with the chaos to come.

I closed my eyes and tried to clear my head. I repeated a deep breath several times in a semi-meditative attempt at centering myself. For thirty seconds I sat and felt the sun, felt the warmth of the deck beneath me and the earth beneath that. I let the joy of the mockingbird's song fill me, and I opened my eyes and took one last look at our beautiful, full breadfruit tree and the palms and the frangipanis. The water in the canal looked like a sheet of ocean glass, reflecting the houses and trees along its edges. I stored the image of our Garden of Eden in my mind. I preserved the calm in a special place in my psyche, knowing full well that in a couple of days, when the generator's noise started to drive me insane, I would need to recall the serenity I felt at this moment and use it to push through.

Image courtesy of Catherine Pyfrom

Image courtesy of Catherine Pyfrom

DURING

ABACO:
THE BEGINNING
OF THE END

Sunday continued to be as beautiful as any postcard of the Bahamas ever published. We spent that day before Dorian moving possible projectiles, tying back gates to secure them, and chatting with friends and family about their preparations. The heaviest items like patio furniture and glass balls had been secured days before. We puttered around with garden ornaments and small plant pots, securing them as best we could. We moved a stack of PVC pipe scraps, left over from our irrigation system installation. We forcibly pulled the generator inside to keep it safe for use after the storm. Cath opened the ladder access to the attic. This, in theory, assisted with pressure regulation in the roof. Whether it was an old wives' tale or a scientific tip in hurricane prep, it was something we had both done in the past. In fear of losing communication during the storm, we gave our neighbours across the canal one of a set of walkie-talkies. The units were originally gifted to Hazel as toys, but they had incredible signal strength. By mid-afternoon, we had exhausted all but the last of our chores.

The day before Dorian arrived in Freeport, Grand Bahama, it reached Abaco, about one hundred miles east of Freeport.

That Sunday morning, we started to get news from Abaco about just how much of a monster this storm was. Having grown up on Abaco, some of my close family still lived there. My sister and nephew had evacuated with her pregnant best friend days ahead of Dorian's arrival. My brother-in-law remained in Marsh Harbour, and my mother and stepfather were in South Abaco. We were in contact with them off and on as the storm approached. We heard about their preparations and fears, and discussed our plans leading up to the storm's arrival. Catherine's sister, Rosalie, was in the process of moving away from Abaco in the months before Dorian's arrival. Three weeks before the storm, she was settled in her new home in Eleuthera, out of Dorian's immediate path.

Running from hurricanes was just not something that anyone in our family ever did. That fact is difficult to explain to many. Because hurricanes are a way of life, and for centuries running away was never an option, the idea of leaving the island ahead of a storm was just not considered. Even if we had considered evacuating the island, it would have been quite a task.

Living on a small island meant leaving could only be done one of two ways: either by boat or by airplane. By boat, a small cruise ship made the trip between Freeport and Fort Lauderdale, Florida several times a week. It would have been an eight-hour journey over very rough seas several days before the storm. By airplane, the flight was only thirty minutes. In either case, the decision and reservations for those options had to be made in advance. As the weather became worse and worse, eventually the airport was closed. Evacuating ahead of a hurricane meant leaving three or four days ahead of the storm's anticipated arrival, during a time when the predictions of the storm's path were still unsure.

Even with advances in meteorological science over the last several decades, predicting where and when a storm will arrive, along with how strong the wind, waves, and storm surge will be are nowhere near one hundred percent accurate. In 2004, after taking a pounding by Hurricane Frances, Hurricane Jeanne made its way toward the Bahamas. The track then changed, sending the storm out to sea much to the relief of everyone in the northern Bahamas. A couple of days later, the storm's track did a complete loop in the open ocean and turned to barrel directly over the Bahamas and straight into South Florida. That loop was not predicted by the meteorologists, and while there was a warning of the change in track, anyone planning to leave the island ahead of that storm would've gotten stuck without enough time to plan an evacuation.

The year before Dorian's arrival we had purchased a second home, a condo in Fort Lauderdale. We found ourselves spending more and more time there visiting friends, seeing doctors, and shopping for groceries that were much cheaper and fresher than those available on the island. Our vacation home in Florida had been an investment in our comfort. It was an easy weekend trip for the school holidays and summer vacation. We could have chosen to evacuate Grand Bahama and go to our Florida home four days ahead of Dorian, but the logistics of such a plan were even more complicated than the logistics of remaining in our home. With five dogs we could not stay in our condo, as there was a restriction on the number of pets allowed. We were not prepared to board our four-legged children in a shelter, either in Freeport or in Florida. To add to those challenges, hurricanes that hit the northern Bahamas very often continue on to hit South Florida. This meant that running from the Bahamas to escape a storm could very well mean running from Florida to escape the same storm twenty-four or forty-eight hours later.

And so, we stayed in Freeport in our home, confident that we were safe.

As the worst of the storm began, we stayed in contact with our family in Abaco well enough to know that they were fine. Sadly, we learned that many others were not safe. By midday on Sunday, the stories began filtering out of Abaco. Unlike any previous storm, almost all communications remained open. Because of advances in and access to satellite technology in the upgraded communication systems on the islands, cell phones on one network worked into and through the end of the Category 5 hurricane. It was a first to my knowledge.

The first Facebook video we saw was of a wall of ocean water inundating the downtown area of Marsh Harbour, miles from the waterfront. The person behind the camera panned back to show the view from the second story of an apartment building, whose roof was gone. The videos were like real-life horror films for the world to see. For us specifically, the locations were very familiar, and the devastation was terrifying. A dozen people in the video had no means of escape and could be heard screaming prayers for their lives as the ocean floodwater moved cars, boats, and rooftops through the middle of downtown Marsh Harbour.

My heart broke for those people and tears filled my eyes. A feeling of total helplessness inundated my mind. We were watching people we did not know, almost one hundred miles away, fight for their lives over a Facebook Live post. It was horrific. We couldn't do anything to help them. In floods like these, no one could help.

The saving grace for Abaco was the eye of the storm. It passed directly over Hope Town and Marsh Harbour for a couple of hours, allowing some stranded people to make their way to higher, safer locations. We made more phone calls, through static-ridden lines, to family. We heard from my brother-in-law that he was safe. He was not in a flooded area and their roof had sustained only minor damage during the first half of the storm. My parents were twenty miles farther south, and while the storm did more than its fair share of damage there, it was nothing compared to Marsh Harbour and the cays. While we feared for the lives of the strangers in the videos, we breathed sighs of relief that our loved ones were still safe.

The news from Abaco was terrifying for Catherine. It only served to exacerbate her fears further. It frightened me, too, but I was standing on the Weather Channel's prediction that Dorian would turn just shy of our back door. I needed something rational to cling to, as the fear I had been so good at tempering was rising. For me, science was the most rational thing in which to hold faith at the time. A weak low-pressure system moving slowly down the Florida peninsula was forecast to grab Dorian and shoot it up the eastern seaboard. Since it was a compact storm, this shift could mean we wouldn't get the eye or the worst of the winds. The problem was that the meteorologist could not predict when this weather phenomenon would occur, nor how fast its effects might be felt.

My logical mind held on to the inexact science of weather predicting in an attempt to unconsciously calm, or trick, my emotional mind into submission. The two sides of my brain were at odds as I fought an internal battle to remain in control of an uncontrollable situation. I continued to insist that we would be fine. We had been fine in all the previous hurricanes we had weathered.

Various areas in Grand Bahama were under mandatory evacuation orders. These areas were low-lying and prone to storm surges along with more remote settlements to our east. However, the Government's mandatory evacuation order never listed our neighbourhood, Pine Bay. We kept a close eye on all the announcements coming in but never received word that we were recommended to take shelter elsewhere. No one thought that our area was in any more danger than other coastal areas, also not evacuated. I took this to mean we were safe.

Even still, after the initial videos of the catastrophic flooding in Marsh Harbour, Catherine and I discussed evacuating our house. The only hurricane shelters on the island were makeshift at best. A few of the public schools, already in a severe state of disrepair, had a few dozen cots and bottled water with volunteers. Anyone who chose to wait out the storm in a shelter would do so by sitting on the floor in a disorganized mess clutching their belongings, hoping nothing would be stolen. None of the shelters allowed dogs and none of our friends had the space to house the three of us plus five dogs. If we were going to leave our house, we had only one place we could go.

Catherine's sister, Charlotte, had a home just a half-mile away, also in Pine Bay on the canal. Before her permanent move to Connecticut years before, Charlotte's house had been her full-time home for many years. It housed her valuables, both monetary and sentimental. The difference was that her house had a second storey. The house sat empty as Charlotte and her wife Pattie lived full-time in the northeast and used the house as a vacation home. We debated whether the water would get high enough to need a second storey to be safe. I talked Catherine out of this idea. I truly believed we would be safer and more comfortable in our own home and did not want the hassle of a last-minute strategy change. Ultimately the decision was made by the amount of effort required to pack up just twelve hours before the storm and move to Charlotte's house. It just seemed like too much work for a what-if scenario. We had weathered storms before and had always been safe staying at home.

Even with the decision to remain made with reasonable confidence, we thought of sandbags. Days before during pre-storm shopping, we had purchased thirty bags to be filled with sand to act as a barrier for minor floodwater. My back already screamed at me for the heavy lifting of various things in need of securing during the previous few days. When Cath suggested we fill the bags to be on the safe side, I was not inclined to agree. I was already tired and overwhelmed, but "better safe than sorry" seemed like a good insurance policy. Images of ocean surge from Abaco were motivation enough to add this new job to the "just in case" list. Rather than driving ten minutes to the nearest beach to haul sand, we chose to visit our neighbour's yard.

The neighbours were a European couple who had purchased the house the year before and were in the middle of a complete interior renovation. They visited only occasionally for vacation and the home stood empty as the homeowners watched the storm from news feeds on the other side of the world. In their front yard sat a large pile of sand, left over from a recent upgrade to their concrete driveway. Armed with shovels and my back brace, we filled twenty-five bags with sand and moved them from the neighbour's yard to our house in the back of our SUV in two trips. We strategically placed them against the exterior of our three doors. If by some unforeseen chance the water reached that high, the sandbags should keep at least some of the water out.

Filling and moving the sandbags was draining. Neither of us was particularly physically fit. Joining a gym had always sounded very unappealing. We tried to eat well and take care of ourselves. Occasionally losing weight and diets would be a topic of conversation, but we never got around to it. Most of our strength and fitness came from gardening, beach walking, and chasing Hazel or the dogs around. Hurricane prep is physically demanding, and by the end of our pre-Dorian work, we were exhausted.

With all preparations complete by mid-afternoon and nothing left to do but wait, we all went for a much-needed swim in the pool. The water temperature was cool against our hot skin, even though the actual water temperature hovered at a balmy eighty-five degrees Fahrenheit. Diving under the water and watching the refracted light swirl along the bottom of the pool, I could almost forget the impending doom. Almost. Playing in the pool with Hazel and enjoying the sun baking down on us was a welcome distraction.

By five p.m., the winds began to pick up slightly. It was just like a regular windy, winter day, minus the cool temperatures, of course. We had our dinner as a family, and with it came the million-and-one questions about hurricanes and how they work, and why we prepare the way we do. Hazel was a naturally curious child, and very intuitive.

"Why do some people have wood on their windows, but we don't?" Hazel asked. We explained how hurricane-resistant windows work.

"What if the water comes in the house?" Hazel asked after a few more bites of her dinner. This question was a sore subject, literally and figuratively, as my back screamed at me for hauling sandbags.

"Then we'll have wet feet! But that's what the sandbags are for. To keep the water outside," I responded with a laugh. Sneaking a glance at Catherine, I could see from her face she didn't feel as enthusiastic about this idea as I did. This launched Hazel into a fit of giggles with a pretend scenario of surfing dogs inside the house.

"Are Nana and Poppa safe in Abaco?" was the next even more sombre question.

She was aware that many people in Abaco were having a terrible time with this storm, and she was understandably a bit anxious. How could she not be? Our TV had been set to the Weather Channel constantly for days. We had been tuning in every three hours to check the National Hurricane Center updates and hoping the turn north would happen sooner rather than later. Scientific terms like 'millibars', 'wind sheer,' and 'eyewall' had become regularly used phrases in the last seventy-two hours in our household.

Darkness fell as the sound of the wind became more prominent. By our typical bedtime, it sounded like a tropical storm outside. Growing up with hurricanes, we were both accustomed to going out in them. As crazy as it sounds, we have both been out in seventy-five mph winds more than once. Walking the dogs in that weather is a challenge since they don't like the wind and rain. Dressed in a big yellow slicker with a flashlight in hand, I called the dogs outside with me, trying to get them to do their business. We knew this would be the last opportunity for them to relieve themselves outside for the duration of the storm.

We lost electricity at ten p.m. after watching the lights flicker several times during the hours before. For safety reasons, the electrical company turns off the power once the winds reach enough intensity to bring down wires. We checked the water level in the canal, which wasn't high. We watched the eleven p.m. update on our phones to find that Dorian had barely begun to crawl along the south shore of Grand Bahama.

Impending destruction was on the horizon, but the storm's forward motion had slowed considerably as predicted: inching along toward us at barely three miles per hour. When we laid down after the eleven p.m. update, I studied the projected models. I squinted at the maps, trying to predict precisely when the turn would happen while calculating how far the hurricane-force winds extended from the eye. I was hoping, desperately, that the calculations kept our tiny piece of the earth out of the outer bands of the eyewall. I was still entirely convinced we would be fine, but it was like waiting for the tortoise to cross the finish line. Everything was as ready as it could be. We went to bed to wait out the very long night.

Each of us only slept for an hour or two at a time. I slept more than Catherine, as usual. Each time I would roll over or hear a dog stirring, I would listen briefly to the wind outside. The frequency of the howling noise or the intervals of the roof creaking were gauges I used to estimate the increase in intensity as the hours ticked by. Cath rechecked the storm update at two a.m. There was no change in intensity, speed, or direction. We both got up and used a flashlight, shining out our back door toward the canal to check the water level. We could just barely see through the darkness out to the canal wall. We could make out a few inches of ocean water in our backyard as the water level in the canal crested the six-foot seawall. Through the darkness, we could see that most of the lawn was just underwater at ankle height. Our nerves amped up quickly, but I continued to reassure Catherine that we were okay. Water in the yard was to be expected. We paced around the house for a while before settling back in bed, but there was no more sleep—just us listening to the groaning roof and the storm outside.

Image courtesy of Catherine Pyfrom

Image courtesy of Catherine Pyfrom

THE ONSLAUGHT

J ust before four a.m., we got up to check the water level again. By pressing the flashlight directly against the glass of our back door, we were able to cast light directly onto our back porch and illuminate just a small portion of the inky darkness outside. The slight bit of light that lit the porch showed the beginnings of a horror film. We saw that the ocean water had reached the top step of our back porch. From our canal wall with our higher-than-normal foundation, this was an elevation gain of about ten feet. Two hours before, at our last check, the ocean had still been at the canal's edge. We received an early-morning call from our neighbours, the Butlers, and learned that the water had begun to enter their first floor.

The noise and rushing around to secure sandbags in adrenaline-fueled panic woke Hazel around five a.m. She had luckily been sleeping peacefully throughout the night.

She groggily opened her door to discover her feet were wet from the few steps between her bed and bedroom door. I checked on her, reassured her, and asked her to stay on her bed for a minute. I rushed around Hazel's bedroom, grabbed some clothes and her rain boots, and helped her into them. She had three of her stuffed toys tucked under her arms, her eyes wide as she watched us race around. After getting her dressed, we put Hazel on the couch, out of the water's reach. I lifted our older dogs, Pearl and Copper, onto the couch to avoid the water too. The other three dogs splashed through the water as it streamed in through every crack it could find. Before long it reached a few inches throughout the inside of our house, splashing above our ankles.

We made several early-morning calls to family and friends. On one of those frantic calls, someone mentioned packing food and medications to keep with us. We had never packed an emergency bug-out bag before. It had never crossed either of our minds to do so. Emergency bags were for tornadoes or floods in the central part of the US, like those we'd seen on TV. It had never occurred to us that we would be in a position of needing to abandon our house in an emergency, even in a hurricane. We had always been safe within the four walls of whatever house we rode out a storm in before.

With another mission at hand, we moved Hazel onto the top of the kitchen island as the water continued to rush in. As Catherine and I trudged through the saltwater, moving quickly became impossible. We pushed floating couch cushions, glass balls, and giant plastic toys out of our path to get to our bedroom. We could hear glass break from the living room as the water upended furniture and shelves with bottles and vases. I grabbed a soft-sided beach cooler bag from our bedroom and trudged back to the kitchen.

Catherine began packing a few shirts and bottoms, stuffing them into an old blue backpack. She remembered to shove our medications in there too. As she packed in the bedrooms, I opened the doors of our pantry. In my mind, I was packing food for use at the neighbour's house during the rest of the storm—food for us to contribute to a household for the next day or two. I was packing for rescue. I wasn't thinking clearly as the terror clouded my thought process into tunnel vision. I packed a bag of brown rice, cans of food, crackers, peanut butter, and granola bars. Food packing complete, I grabbed two gallons of water off the kitchen countertop and put them up on the top shelf near the refrigerator, along with some dog food. I thought at least they wouldn't float away in this location.

Moving those items up higher gave me another idea. I called out to Catherine across the house that I was going to move our photo albums up to high shelves. The day before, during hurricane prep, we had already moved the albums out of the low cabinets where they were usually stored to put them on tabletops in the event of interior water. These photo albums contained thousands of photos from Catherine's childhood, all only in physical form, with no digital backups. Catherine's father had been an amateur photographer, and her childhood was well documented. Now I lifted a dozen albums, wrapped in garbage bags, up onto the highest shelves in the foyer, just a foot from the ceiling.

While moving the irreplaceable albums, I remembered our passports and important documents in our fire safe, fastened to our master closet floor. We used the safe to store our important papers, but in it was also thousands of dollars worth of Catherine's mother's jewelry, handed down to Catherine after her mother's passing. The fire safe also housed two external hard drives with all our digital photographs stored on them. Those hard drives were my prized possession. They held twelve years of amateur photography by both of us of local flora and fauna, family photos and Hazel's babyhood, and countless trips all over the world. Having never assigned much importance to cloud back-ups, those hard drives were the only copy of over fifteen thousand digital photographs, and so they too were stored in the place we deemed the most secure in our home.

Water had already penetrated the door as I opened the safe and grabbed the documents, already saturated. I pushed the passports inside Ziploc bags, along with our cell phones. The remaining folder of documents went into the blue backpack with the clothes. We put our packed clothes, documents, and food up on the kitchen counter to stay dry. In the kitchen again, Catherine shoved her wallet into the blue backpack as my attention went to Hazel.

Catherine and I had been frantically racing from one room to another. We shouted brief conversations back and forth to one another as we monitored the water levels throughout the house. Several times we stopped, looking at each other, completely at a loss on how to react and what to do. After our packing was completed, Catherine and I paused again in our kitchen command center to catch our breath and re-assess, but our circumstances seemed even more dire than before.

As we sat perched on our kitchen countertop, we sent more messages to family and friends, telling them that we had water inside the house. We quickly scrolled through Facebook posts to learn that the absolute onslaught of the storm had begun to hit Freeport. Facebook was our only light to the outside world as we began to feel more and more isolated in the early morning darkness and constant roaring of the Category 5 hurricane raging outside.

Within an hour, when the water reached almost to our knees, more furniture began to float, and all hell broke loose. We were no longer fighting to maintain the property. We were full-on fighting to figure out how to stay safe. Fear was building in Hazel as the water rose. We reassured

Hazel that everything would be okay. We reminded her that she was a strong swimmer, and this seemed to help her anxiety marginally. Being a strong swimmer was of little consequence, as we watched the water level continue to rise rapidly, but it seemed the best way to reassure Hazel at the time.

The dogs were frantic. They all wanted to be near us, as they could feel our fear and anxiety. Only two of our five dogs liked water, but it was clear that swimming inside the house was not their idea of fun. We tried to keep our four dachshunds on the furniture, but their separation anxiety made it impossible. The chaos of preparing and problem-solving was punctuated by retrieving swimming dogs and returning them to the couch and then the dining room table, which soon began to float as well. When we finally got a few of them settled on the blanket with Hazel nested on the kitchen counter, the dogs felt safe enough to stay still for a longer time. Our larger dog, Sky, continued to follow us and hop from furniture island to furniture island as she couch-surfed her way around the room. No amount of yelling or comforting got the dogs to sit still for long.

The smell inside of our house was absolutely wretched. The now thigh-high water had backed up our sewage through our toilets and drains. Our septic tank was ground level and already under over four feet of ocean. The house smelled like feces. The water we were wading through was gray and thick. One of Hazel's My Little Pony toys floated by as I gagged. I heaved when I breathed too deeply, trying to calm my pounding heart. There was no escaping the heavy sulphuric smell in the air.

Image courtesy of Catherine Pyfrom

THE ISLAND OF CHAOS

The sun began to peek through the heavy rain and storm clouds later than usual. With the light came the realization that we had become an island separated from the entire rest of the universe. We were surrounded by the water as our entire neighbourhood had sunk below the surface of the ocean. It seemed the storm had come to swallow us all. I imagine something of this nature must have happened to the people who once called Atlantis home. As I stared out over the ocean, very rapidly turning our home into an underwater kingdom in the early morning dawn, I had the fleeting thought of those doomed souls of Atlantis flash briefly in my subconscious.

We built our home to take advantage of the view, but now, looking out through our extra-large, hurricane-impact windows and doors, we were struck by the severity of our situation. Looking out our kitchen window toward our closest neighbours, Cath and I debated our ability to swim to them. The worst of the wind and rain had not yet arrived. We judged the wind at one hundred and twenty mph with four-foot waves. The ocean that separated us from the Butler's house was six to seven feet deep. Hazel was a strong swimmer but not strong enough to be swimming several hundred feet in one hundred and twenty mph wind.

I never took swimming lessons like the ones we insisted Hazel have. I grew up on a tiny island, surrounded by the ocean, and yet I learned to swim in my grandparents' swimming pool. I could cannonball into the blue water, surface, and swim to the side of the pool to haul myself out long before I could actually swim the length of that very same pool. I never had formal instructions on swimming strokes. In elementary school, there was a yearly swim meet held in the harbour with the lanes set up between dock pilings. No instruction on competitive swimming, just racing your peers while doing your best impression of freestyle or the like. I always had an excuse not to participate. Competitive anything was not for me. That didn't mean I wasn't a good swimmer. It just meant that as an adult, I never found myself in the situation of needing to swim a distance longer than a swimming pool, and even then, just for pleasure. Never to save my life or the lives of my family.

Though Catherine never swam competitively, her sister Charlotte was a swim coach for most of her career. Catherine was a strong swimmer. She grew up with a swimming pool in their backyard and endless vacations on the ocean. She may very well have been able to swim to the Butlers' house in the middle of a hurricane, but it was a gamble, and she certainly wouldn't consider doing it without us.

We discussed what we could use as a boat to move the five dogs, and us, to take shelter in the Butlers' second storey. As we talked, it seemed far more dangerous to try to move than to stay where we were. All the survival stories dictate that shelter is one of the most critical things. But our shelter was rapidly filling with water like a damn fishbowl.

During the onslaught, Catherine had been taking photos with her phone and our digital camera: photos of the water height throughout our house, photos of the dogs and Hazel sitting haphazardly trying to stay dry, and photos of the water level outside as the morning dawn broke. The Nikon underwater camera was purchased the year before for fun action shots in our swimming pool. Now it was documenting our worst nightmare. At one point, she spotted an area in our living room where bubbles were fizzing up from our foundation through the tiles like seltzer water. She took photos of that, too. At various times the camera, equipped with a floatation hand strap, was left to float around as we used our hands for one project or another before one of us retrieved it again and took more photos.

Documenting our lives in photographs was just what we did. For Catherine, this situation was no different. She photographed to show our family members what the ordeal had been like in the aftermath. She documented knowing full well, with her family business background, that insurance claims were far more successful when photographs could accompany them. She took pictures as memories for us and for Hazel of what this moment in our history looked like.

Catherine, as an artist, was a very visual person. Seeing the situation through the lens of a camera made the scene easier to interpret in her mind. For me, the urgency and the fear that I had been keeping tempered for days was spilling out in a maddening rush. Photographs were not important to me at that moment. I was in overwhelmed, problem-solving mode in a situation that had zero solutions.

We heard from various neighbours, all of whom seemed continents away despite our ability to see their homes. As the storm intensified, we used the walkie-talkies to talk to the Mackey MacLeay family about the flood levels. Water had invaded everyone's home in the neighbourhood. Two sets of neighbours had already retreated to the dry safety of their second floors. Another set had moved to higher ground before the storm began.

We spoke again to family and friends farther away by Facetime and issued our formal cry for help. Catherine took a couple more photos and posted an SOS on Facebook. We had reached the point of total helplessness. We knew we needed rescue. However, we also knew that no one could come out in the middle of a storm of this magnitude to rescue us. We knew we were on our own for hours to come, with no way of predicting exactly how fast the water would continue to rise, when it would plateau, or how long the winds would last. Our last weather update terrified us as it confirmed that Dorian had stopped forward motion with its eye just ten miles or so to our east. The eyewall was going to just sit on top of our neighbourhood for God knows how long.

"I need to go to the bathroom," came the inevitable cry from a tiny voice. Hazel needed a toilet, but the toilets were already underwater. I lifted Hazel from the kitchen counter and carried her to the opposite end of the living room. I helped her stand on a floating table and told her that this was the best we could do. I removed her wet clothes and maneuvered around our makeshift toilet, trying to hold my emotions together as the uncomfortable reality set in of just how bad things had gotten.

When Cath and I paused again to reassure the dogs and child, I looked down onto our kitchen countertop and my eyes fell onto a tiny, hand-painted dish I had gotten from Italy years before. Inside the dish were our wedding and engagement rings. I thought of our jewelry boxes sitting on our dresser in the bedroom. I quickly pushed all four rings onto my fingers and set off on yet another trek across our living room with garbage bags in hand. I wrapped each box in plastic and hauled them back to put them in a high cabinet in the kitchen. The tall cabinets were the highest, safest place I could think of. Along the way, I pushed a floating end table out of my way and dodged floating sewage. I purposefully dragged my feet in a shuffle instead of lifting them to avoid falling over the debris in the now thigh-high sewage saltwater.

Not long after I returned to the kitchen, the water reached the engine of the car outside on the elevated driveway. The car lights flashed, and the alarm began to scream as if to announce a wake-up call. The electrical system meant to keep the vehicle safe from thieves now died a rapid and corrosive death. It was just after seven a.m. The noise startled Hazel, and she threw her hands up over her ears, dropping one of her stuffed toys in the water. I grabbed the toy, shaking the water off, and returned it to the comfort of her arms. For ten minutes, we sat silently as the car wailed, its rhythm matching the pounding of our hearts.

When the car alarm stopped, we listened silently to the storm. The wind pushed against the house, sending vibrations of the heavy raindrops scattering across our kitchen windows in an erratic motion. The sound of the rain wasn't steady like a normal summer shower. It roared and then hummed loudly for just a second before the next gust of wind would rattle the impact glass. The roof continued to whine and creak and groan as the pressure of the monumental wind gusts tried desperately to rip it from the concrete walls of our house. The dogs panted in fear. Now and then, Ginger would moan with a high-pitched squeak, sounding more like a dog toy than an actual dog. Occasionally, there would be a sudden thud, a tree ripped from the forest and sent scattering across the roof before disappearing into oblivion. There was no rhythm to any of the storm sounds. Each noise was as unpredictable as the last.

Catherine and I sat on our kitchen countertops at opposite ends of the kitchen. Hazel continued to sit on the island wrapped in a wet blanket, clutching her stuffed toys with three of the five dogs snuggled around her. Copper and Sky sat on our floating dining room table not far away. Hazel spoke first. "I'm hungry." With that, we were up again. Catherine grabbed a honeybun and offered it to Hazel. Half of our pantry was already underwater, and things like cereal or Pop-Tarts were already swimming. Cath and I each had a piece of dry bread. It was tough to chew and swallow. As tapped out of energy as we were from the last four hours of anxiety and adrenaline-fueled action, the process of eating was painstaking and necessary. I only managed to eat two-thirds of a slice of bread while gagging from fear and exhaustion and the overwhelming smell of feces before giving up. Our breakfast that morning was something akin to the last meal for a death row inmate. The ever-pressing realization surrounded us that the dire situation was getting worse. Our next meal was utterly unknown.

As the water reached above the kitchen countertops, desperation set in. What if the water reached the ceiling? What could we use as a raft? Could we swim to the neighbours if the eye of the storm arrived soon and gave us a few calm hours? Should we go outside to avoid drowning inside our house? Should we go into our attic and risk drowning up there? Can we get on the roof of our garden shed? Should we strap ourselves to the roof of our car? How do we survive?

All those questions raced through our minds. In all honesty, I'm unclear how many conversations were out loud and how many were sorted into the "not-feasible category" without bothering with a wasted discussion. I am quite sure that Hazel heard every fear-induced, psychotic plan that we discussed out loud and discarded as foolhardy. We had no way of sheltering her from the trauma we were living.

The car in the driveway was just about to start floating. There was no longer anywhere to stay even a little dry for Hazel or the dogs. As the water rose an inch above our kitchen countertops, we both started scrambling for things inside our house that could float. We needed a boat, a really big boat, but we didn't have one. We didn't have a small one or even a kayak. We had pool floats. Then Catherine remembered we had a single cot mattress with a waterproof cover which amounted to a semi-buoyant pillow.

I watched as the inside water level reached the bottom of most of our windows. Outside, the water level was a good foot higher, with wind-driven waves crashing into the sides of our house. The water was brown outside. Inside it was gray. Despite the large windows and daylight, the inside of our home was beginning to feel claustrophobic as the not-flooded part became smaller than the flooded part. It was time for a bigger plan.

Image courtesy of Catherine Pyfrom

Image courtesy of Catherine Pyfrom

Image courtesy of Catherine Pyfrom

DESPERATE TIMES CALL FOR DESPERATE MEASURES

Survival was all that mattered. How do we survive? My instinct was to get out of the house. If we stayed in the house and the water reached the ceiling, we would drown, and the floatation devices we were searching for would be pointless. As I watched the water level at the windows, I realized that if the pressure became too great, we would be unable to open a window, let alone a door, to get out. Images of car crashes that end with the vehicle in a lake, river, or ocean came to mind. In those circumstances, I knew that opening the car door to get out became impossible, and often a window had to be broken to escape. In our current situation, breaking a window to get out would not be possible. Hurricane-impact windows installed to protect us now became the reason we could be trapped inside the house. Outside seemed the only option for survival.

I immediately began the logistical checklist of how we could survive outside of the house until the eye arrived and we could swim to the nearest house. I looked out at our neighbours' house again. It was at least three hundred feet away. We could just make out the roofline through the torrents of rain and wind. In my fear-clouded mind, I believed we could swim to it if the storm calmed during the eye. I plotted using the buoyant mattress to carry the dogs with Hazel swimming along with the pool float around her waist. Catherine and I could swim and push the mattress and Hazel ahead. I imagined we might be able to accomplish the impossible. However, we had no idea how long it would be before the eye arrived. Nor did we know just how calm or not calm it might get.

The inside of a hurricane's eye is eerie and much like an episode of *The Twilight Zone*: unreal and yet genuine. I have been inside the eye of a major hurricane once. In Hurricane Floyd in 1999, the eye of the storm passed directly over my family home. I was able to go outside for over an hour and assess the damages. I went as far as to drive to check on the harbour a mile away from home and see many boats wrecked on the shore. I felt the sun on my face and saw the bluest sky as humidity made the air thick with impending doom. From firsthand experience, I knew what a proper hurricane eye looked like and acted like from the inside. If we got the eye of the storm, we might be able to make it to the neighbours, but we still didn't know if the eye would even make it to our doorstep. There was no way to predict it, as our last hurricane update said the storm had stopped moving forward altogether. I tried to calculate in my mind how long we could last, waiting for that wishful reprieve.

"We need to go outside," I said firmly. They were insane words to say out loud. They made no sense at all, even to my logical mind. "We need to get out of the house while we still can." I looked again at the windows and could see the height increase in the water level during my internalized problem-solving.

Of course, Catherine resisted.

"If we stay inside and the water reaches the ceiling, we'll drown," I insisted fervently, my eyes flashing with fear. "We won't have any air to breathe."

"If we go outside, we'll drown!" Catherine retorted sharply, "Or the wind will take us away. We don't have a boat or anything to put us all in."

I had an answer for that. I had a plan. I pointed at the bright orange extension cords lying on top of a floating end table. They had been put there to be used after the storm to connect our refrigerator to the generator. Now instead of electrical cords, I saw a rope.

"We can use the cords and tie them around our waists and then tie them together so we can't get separated. And if the water gets high enough outside under the porch roof, we can tie the end of the cord to the porch post so the waves can't take us away from the house."

Cath looked at me blankly, trying to picture how the whole process was going to work. "I think we should go to the attic," she concluded.

"We can't go to the attic!" I cried, "If we go to the attic and the water keeps rising, we won't have enough space to breathe and we won't have any way to get out!"

Text conversations with family and friends only an hour before had yielded a mixed bag of advice. Some said the attic was the safest place. Others insisted, like me, that going to the attic increased the risk of drowning. The water was continuing to rise quickly and visibly inside the house. All I could think of was being trapped. Trapped inside the house or trapped inside the attic with water so high we had no more room to breathe. In the attic, there would be no escape from the rising water. There was no trap door or a powerful tool to break a hole in our sheet metal-covered roof to escape.

"We don't have any tools inside the house to cut a hole in the roof to get out of the attic if the water gets that high." I turned and motioned toward the garden shed, with just its roof visible through the window. "And I can't go out there to find any tools or I'll be washed away." The garden shed sat on the other side of the rapidly disappearing car. That side of the house was bearing the brunt of the wind, rain, and waves. Trying to make it to the shed to hunt for submerged tools would've been disastrous.

The more we talked, the more adamant and frantic I became. Fear had created tunnel vision, and I was entirely convinced that going outside was the only option for our survival. My imagination was playing wildly fanatic tricks on my thought process. Flashing behind my eyes was every disaster movie I'd ever seen, in full colour and stereo. In the scene, the protagonist is trapped inside a small space as the water rises visibly higher. They dive frantically through often murky water trying to open a door or break a window to let the water out. Ultimately the hero is forced to return to the ever-shrinking air bubble gasping for air and choking on water. If a cohort accompanies the hero, they look at each other to say their last goodbyes or confess some long-held secret in the final minutes before their watery grave consumes them.

The familiar, often anti-climactic movie scene never frightened me before. In fact, I have garnered great entertainment in the past from those movies. Now, my very worst fear was living through a recreation of that scene. It was a fear so intense that going outside in a Category 5 hurricane was preferable to the catastrophe I pictured in my mind. I imagined holding on to Catherine and Hazel, the dogs long since drowned, saying our last goodbyes.

"How are we even going to get outside?" Cath asked. "The doors probably won't open."

"The windows still will. Our bedroom window is high enough out of the water that we can still get it opened. We can all fit through the window and it's under cover." I had an answer for every one of her concerns.

I pushed my survival plan. It wasn't a pros-versus-cons kind of conversation a married couple usually has before a major decision like installing a pool. It was a desperate conversation, punctuated by imminent death if we didn't make the right choices. I frantically reiterated my concern about losing breathing room and insisted that our only option was to get out of the house. It was almost ten a.m., six hours since the water first invaded our home.

Our large, covered porch faced south and was on the side of the house which was sheltered from the worst of the wind and torrential rain. Through our giant glass French door, we could see the single piece of patio furniture we had not moved to our garden shed bobbing in the corner. It was light enough to float but heavy enough to fight the storm's current. The surrounding ocean had not yet pulled it out and carried it away. In my plan, we needed floatation devices and a way to make sure we all stayed together. If we got outside under our porch roof, we could use the pool floats and the mattress as rafts. Hazel and the dogs could lie on the bed. Cath and I could stand or hold onto the floating furniture to avoid having to tread water. We had a neon pink flamingo pool tube for Hazel to use as a life jacket. As I said the logistics out loud, I was fully aware that they sounded completely insane.

The imaginary movie scene continued to stir my decision-making ability. The fight or flight response within my body insisted we needed to avoid that scene at all costs. We HAD to get out of the house! With that, the decision was made. It wasn't a joint decision. I was leading, entirely blinded by fear, with Catherine following, not wanting to be separated and trusting that my decision wasn't pure insanity.

As we prepared to move from the inside of the house out into the elements, we assessed the necessities that needed to stay with us. The blue backpack filled with clothes and documents and the food cooler were left sitting on the kitchen countertop. The backpack was already waterlogged and heavy and offered nothing to help with survival at that point. The food cooler seemed of no consequence either, as drowning was our greatest fear, not starvation. Somehow our cell phones and the walkie-talkie were still our lifelines to the outside world. In an unspoken decision, Catherine grabbed a small white plastic garbage can that had floated from Hazel's bathroom into the living room and used it as a makeshift basket for housing our Ziploc-packaged electronics.

We made our way from the kitchen into our living room in the stinking water, and I tried desperately to push open our back door. I shoved and kicked, bruising my skin as I hurled my body against the door, sending water splashing in every direction. No amount of pushing would make it budge. The pressure from the competing water levels had already made opening the door impossible. The dogs floated on furniture pieces as we trudged through the chest-high water, Hazel clinging tightly to Cath. I only spent sixty seconds trying the door before I moved into the master bedroom. Luckily our bedroom window opened onto our back porch, and the water level had not yet created suction to make opening it impossible.

As I pushed the window up, a rush of water came into the house, pushing me back. I grabbed a piece of furniture to brace myself, then set about shoving the screen out of the way. Next, I twisted and shoved the waterproof single-cot mattress out of a standard-size window as the current pushed against me. The adrenaline pulsing through my muscles gave me more strength than I knew possible.

Once the bed was out, we tied the bright orange electrical cord around each of our waists and tied another cord around Hazel to attach her to us. I fumbled several times as my fingers slipped and refused to grip. My skin was long since saturated, leaving my fingers wrinkled and slippery. At best, the knotwork was flimsy: tied underwater with shaky hands, as I prepared to drag my family outside in a Category 5 hurricane.

When I pushed myself through the opening, the water level was higher than the bottom of the window. Once I was out, Catherine helped guide Hazel out the window and into my arms. Next out the window was the flamingo pool tube. Taking care to hold onto the very lightweight inflatable, I pushed it over Hazel's head and arms. I grabbed Hazel and tried to hoist her onto the mattress. My toes barely brushed the deck beneath my feet, and I held onto the window frame with one hand to steady myself. The bed slipped and sank a bit under Hazel's weight as she climbed onto it, but it remained upright enough to keep her from having to swim. I turned back to Cath inside the house and grabbed a small dog through the window opening, then another, and then a third. Each dog was tossed like a stuffed animal onto Hazel's back to scramble for a section of the mattress as the added weight pushed it lower in the water. I could feel the electrical cord pull around my waist as the waves tried to pull the mattress and Hazel away from me.

I looked inside, prepared to grab the next dog, but there was no dog to catch. The rush of water and floating furniture inside our bedroom had closed our bedroom door behind us. Catherine untied herself and moved to the door, trying to open it. The current and suction of the competing water levels made opening the door impossible. Copper and Sky were stuck in the living room, separated from the rest of us.

I yelled at Cath through the window, "Just leave them!"

"I can't leave them!" Cath hollered back, panic in her voice.

"They'll be okay!" I insisted, "You have to get out of the house while you still can. We can't get separated!" I pressed my face against the window and pleaded with Catherine. Finally, Cath left the bedroom door and slipped through the window to join us.

Once outside, we tried to get our bearings as we bobbed near the window. Outside the house, the wind and rain and waves were thunderous, amplified by the covered porch. We had to shout to hear each other's voices. The wind whipped through on a mission to move everything and anything daring to be in its path.

Before we could make much of a plan, Catherine insisted, "We can't leave the dogs trapped inside the house to drown!"

Without waiting for me to agree, she moved back to the exit window. I followed with the floating mattress and precious cargo in tow. Catherine took a deep breath, braced her hands under the window frame, pushed her body below the water, and wiggled back inside. As she moved through the window, she collided with a piece of wooden furniture, floating below the opaque surface. She saw stars as her head came back above the water, now inside the house again. She was so determined in her mission to save the dogs that she didn't falter. From my view outside the rain-spotted window, I never even knew she had hit her head.

Catherine moved toward the bedroom door in search of a way to rescue the other two dogs. I yelled and then screamed at her to get out of the house. She refused. She would not leave the last two dogs now floating on the couch in the living room. I turned to check on Hazel, still tethered to me, and grabbed Nutmeg, who had fallen from the mattress and was struggling to swim. I tossed the dog back onto the makeshift raft and turned my attention back to Catherine.

I could see her struggling with the bedroom door through the clear glass windowpane, spotted with ocean and seaweed and tree debris, trying desperately to force the bedroom door open. The water was rising. I screamed again, begging Catherine to leave the dogs and get out of the house. I was terrified that we would be separated, and Catherine would be trapped inside the house while trying to get to the other two dogs.

I braced myself against the window, and waves crashed over my head again and again. I watched as Catherine beat against the saturated, hollow-core door. She kicked and shoved, and I saw the door start to buckle. It was a ray of hope. Catherine grabbed a wooden shelf from a nearby floating cabinet, and she beat again and again at the buckled door until it gave way. Then I watched in horror as I lost sight of her when she moved toward the living room, calling the dogs' names, hoping they would swim toward her. Her voice was muffled against Hazel's screams of fear and the water filling my ears as the waves pounded.

Hazel cried out for me as she slipped off the mattress, and the three dogs fell with her. I felt the extension cord around my waist go tight. I turned and grabbed Hazel as one of the dogs crawled its way onto my head, pushing me down into the water. I gulped saltwater instead of air. Fear pushed me up, and a new round of adrenaline brought on by the inevitability of drowning surged through my body. I secured Hazel and the dogs again on the mattress and turned back to see Catherine's face at the window and with her the two dogs. I didn't have time to feel relieved. She pushed Copper under the water-filled window and into my arms. He, too, was tossed in the direction of the mattress.

Getting a terrified fifty-pound dog out of the house with the current pushing water in through the window was, in and of itself, an incredible undertaking. Catherine pushed from the inside. I pulled from the outside. Sky fought against us. Instinct told her that outside was a terrible place to go. Finally, I reached inside, grabbed her collar and the scruff of her neck, and pulled with all my might. How I didn't break her legs on the way out, I have no idea. Once out, I simply let her go, hoping her already strong swimming ability would be enough to keep her above water as I tried to guide Catherine out the window. When Catherine slipped out of the bedroom window and onto our back porch area, the ocean water had almost entirely submerged the window opening, and she dove out of our house.

Catherine and I swam toward the inner section of the porch toward our back door, pushing the mattress with the dogs and Hazel ahead of us. We called to Sky, encouraging her to swim toward us. In my mind, while planning from inside the house, I hoped that the three-sided, concrete, covered porch would provide enough coverage from the wind and waves to keep us together. We maneuvered various pieces of floating furniture, as we tiptoed in chin-high water, hoping to use something as a raft for the dogs or ourselves. Everything we tried failed.

We turned to realize that the mattress had tipped once again, and all its precious cargo was swimming frantically. Catherine grabbed the dogs, and I grabbed the bed, hoisting Hazel up once again. The dogs were frantic, wanting only to be on us, near us, wanting reassurance. Their continuous movement meant constantly retrieving one or several of them from swimming in the wrong direction: the direction out into the open water. If any of us ended up outside the no-longer-visible porch railing, the noticeable current would have separated us permanently.

Debris filled the water. Leaves and tree branches were ripped to shreds by the storm's wind and then left to float on the surface of the ocean as it rose around us. In the debris was a mixture of seaweed, blossoms, berries, and fruit from various trees. Many were from our garden, even more from the bushes and trees surrounding our oasis. The organic debris clung to everything: our hair, the dogs' fur, the mattress, Hazel's pink floatie. As we moved, bits and pieces found their way inside our clothing, into the raincoats and sneakers we still wore. Before venturing outside, we had no time to consider the weight these things added when swimming instead of trying to stay dry.

At one point, when all the dogs and Hazel were still, there was an ebb in the almost constant brigade of waves. I turned to Cath and tried to hand her the end of the electrical cord still tied around my and Hazel's waists. Finding the end of the cord was proving impossible. As I tried to express my concern about how important it was to get tied together for safety, a wave barreled through, causing me to lose my tiptoe balance and sink under the water. I immediately and automatically held my breath to avoid inhaling more saltwater. Catherine grabbed the back of my neck and the rain jacket I was wearing and pulled me up as my feet pushed off from the deck below. I breathed in sharply and coughed more from fear than from actual water in my airway.

Together we tried once again to push our fibreglass marine storage box, and then our wicker couch, below the water level. We wanted to climb on it or stand on it or use it somehow to make ourselves more stable. For a few minutes, I was able to stop treading water.

Another wave came and ripped away the stuffed toys that Hazel had continued to cling to through it all. I grabbed Hazel as she reached for the toys, almost toppling the mattress once again. Catherine reached for the toys and only managed to grab one of the three. The current quickly stole one of her favourites, a stuffed purple dachshund named Ellie. Cath swam away from our tiny congregation in the corner of our porch toward the no-go zone marked by the wooden porch posts. She managed to grab Ellie the stuffed dachshund before she was taken away by the storm, and she returned two of the lost toys to Hazel's arms.

Hazel screamed and cried as we bobbed in the ocean. She was terrified. The mattress was not stable and rocked as it floated just below the surface of the waves. It was loud, and the dogs were constantly crawling over her. Through her tears and fear, she cried, "I want to go back in."

In the shuffle of toy rescue, the plastic garbage can had also come loose from our huddle. Catherine grabbed the garbage can, full of water and sinking. She tossed the Ziplocked cell phones on the mattress and secured the camera around her wrist with its flotation strap. She allowed the ocean to take the walkie-talkie as she prioritized the necessities.

The fact that the camera had remained with Catherine all this time was for a very decisive reason. Initially, the camera was documenting memories. Somewhere around the time we issued our SOS and realized that we were in real trouble, the camera began documenting what Catherine saw as our last moments on Earth. If we drowned or were carried away by the storm, perhaps one day the waterproof camera might be found and give some answers or even solace to our loved ones left behind. The thought was morbid at best and downright horrible at worst. Even when faced with the possibility of her mortality, Catherine was thinking of the loss and impact on our families.

Once again, after the chaos of another mini disaster averted, we paused. But it wasn't a calm, quiet, catch-your-breath moment by any means. We watched the waves and the sheets of heavy rain. I saw Hazel's toy motorized *Frozen* car, floating just below the surface, move swiftly by, with only a single wheel and light blue fender visible briefly. We watched the water level, marked by the six-by-six porch posts and the French door at our backs. I turned to Cath and saw that she had another desperate soul trying to survive, clinging to her hair near her face.

"There's a lizard in your hair," I told her. It was small and almost translucent. Exhausted from swimming, it had taken refuge there.

"We've all got to survive somehow," she responded dryly.

It would have been comical under almost any other circumstance.

I rested my chin on the mattress as I danced on tiptoes, trying to keep the mattress stable. Two of the smaller dogs saw my face and immediately came to me for comfort, crawling over Hazel and onto my head and shoulders.

Our dogs wanted us to save them. I wanted to save everyone: Hazel, Cath, the dogs, and myself, in that order.

The figurative and literal weight was more than I could bear. With a ten-pound dog on each shoulder, my head went under again. This time I couldn't hold my breath. Water filled my nose and mouth. I wasn't under long enough to struggle or have a "life flashing before my eyes" moment. However, it was long enough to feel death and my overwhelming inability to save us all. Catherine saved me. She grabbed me by the back of the neck again, and I kicked my feet, pushing against the extra dog weight on my body. My feet no longer touched the deck below. I coughed, spat, and tossed dogs off my shoulders in the general direction of our makeshift raft. And I breathed: deeply, panicked, in gulps.

Despite living on the ocean my entire life, I had never found myself in the position to experience the fear of drowning. I'd never fallen into the ocean and been unable to get back out. I had never been hurt and unable to swim. I can count on one hand the number of times I've ever even had on a lifejacket. Even with weeks, or as much as months, of time accumulated being on the water, Catherine had never been anywhere near close to the situation we found ourselves in, either. The ocean, even at its most violent in my memory, had never spoken to me in death's fatal whisper.

In our desperate attempts to keep our heads above the rising water, there was something of a pause yet again, only not really. I breathed and held on to the mattress, kicking my feet, trying to find something beneath them to support me. I could see Catherine with the camera in her hands, held out in front of her. She was speaking, though not to Hazel or me or the dogs. She was recording our situation and a message. I couldn't hear her or comprehend her words, but I understood what she was doing. It was a goodbye video. This realization punched me in the gut so hard that I suddenly felt actual physical pain there. I could hear her voice shake through her unscripted words. The waterproof camera in her hand would float. A storm like this could take it anywhere. It was the epitome of a message in a bottle.

When she finished speaking, she turned to me, and for one-tenth of a second, we looked into each other's souls. We weren't close enough to reach out a hand to hold. Our hands were busy holding on to the thread of a lifeline in the floating objects around us. Hazel screamed and cried over and over and over again: "I want to go back inside. I want to go back inside. I don't want to die. I want to go back inside." And as she screamed and waves crashed into us, I looked into my wife's eyes. I saw the life we had built and the connection we had shared. There I saw our undying love, and it ripped through my insides. I said, "I love you," and Cath repeated those exact words. It was a goodbye. A goodbye no one should ever have to say, at the beginning of what we both saw as inevitable, horrific death. And then the one-tenth of a second moment was broken by yet another dog losing her battle with the waves.

A moment passed and then Catherine said to me, "We have to go back in." It wasn't a question or an exclamation. It wasn't forced, and it wasn't adrenaline-fueled. It just was. I think I said, "Yes," but I'm not sure if I said anything at all. With Catherine's statement came the factory line process of inverting our re-entry into temporary safety. We swam toward the window to get back in. There were brief questions of how and who once we reached the window opening, now eighteen inches below the water level.

Catherine went in first, holding her breath to dive back into the submerged open window. When she surfaced, she immediately turned and reached through the window, ready to receive our precious cargo of dogs one at a time and our Ziploc-packaged cell phones. We felt the dogs and telecommunication connection to the world were at greater risk without any buoyancy or support, so they went in first. Hazel, at least, was still tethered to me by the extension cord with her pink, inflatable flamingo float wrapped around her waist.

Finally, it was Hazel's turn. As I pulled Hazel off the mattress and into my arms at the window, the storm immediately took the bed that was our lifeline. There was no way for me to push the pool float back into the house. I pulled it over Hazel's head and tossed it to Dorian's abyss as well. In my arms, our faces close together at the window,

I told Hazel to take a deep breath. Then I pushed her under the water in the direction of Catherine's arms on the other side of the window. As she made it inside to safety, the electrical cord pulled tightly on her waist. Cath and I each took a moment on both sides of the window, trying to untangle the makeshift rope. Once loose, I braced my hands on the window frame, closed my eyes, and pushed my body through the window.

Image courtesy of Catherine Pyfrom

Image courtesy of Catherine Pyfrom

Image courtesy of Catherine Pyfrom

NOW WHAT?

As I broke the surface on the other side, the calm, the quiet, and the relief struck me. Outside had been loud and a constant fight against current and waves. Inside, sheltered by the concrete walls, there were no waves save for the ones we created as we moved around. Despite the roar of the storm outside echoing in my ears, the muffled noise inside struck me as peaceful. For a moment, we felt safe.

Finding ourselves back inside the protection of the four walls of our home, now filled with close to six feet of saltwater, was not a moment to recover. The water was still rising, and we still had to get to a place, both physically and mentally, where we could settle for a longer and still indeterminate period of time. Much of the chaos was quieted for now but the fear and desperation remained.

Maneuvering around our master bedroom, filling with water, was hard. Heavy wooden furniture was floating, and it turned the room into an obstacle course. First, we had to get Hazel and the dogs to a place of stability for the short term to figure out our next move. Our king-size solid wood bed frame, mattress, and box springs were floating like an island in the middle of the room, braced against the ceiling fan and light. Our ceiling height was nine feet.

Catherine and I hoisted Hazel up onto the bed as she helped pull herself up by clinging to the fitted sheet saturated by the ocean. Once Hazel was secure, one by one, we tossed dog after dog up onto the bed as well, with Hazel's help. We hoisted Sky up last, a much easier process than forcing her out of the window just thirty minutes before. Once our most precious cargo was stable and not swimming, we turned our attention to our other priorities.

Exhaustion was rapidly setting in, and our attempts at wading, swimming, and tiptoeing to stay above the water were becoming more and more difficult. Catherine noticed one of our dining room chairs floating near the crushed bedroom door and grabbed at it. She offered it to me to attempt to force it below the water level. The lightweight chair was easy to maneuver, and I could stand on it with its legs planted firmly on the floor below. However, I had to take care to keep my weight balanced and steady, or its buoyancy took over. Settling for a moment was possible inside when it was not possible outside, partly because of the cover from the wind and waves provided by the house walls.

We had a brief conversation about retrieving the blue backpack and cooler bag filled with food, clothes, and essential documents. We had packed in haste only two hours before and had last seen them sitting on the kitchen counter. The master bedroom would become the new command center as we plotted our next steps. This was due mainly to the stability of the bed housing Hazel and the dogs, but also because the only attic access was in our extra-large master closet.

Having the ladder already in place to take us to the safety of the attic was yet another miracle. If the ladder had not already been opened, getting to it with the house filling with water would've been even more challenging.

Catherine left the bedroom, attempting to swim to the kitchen through the debris. In the living room, she found Hazel's large plastic toy horse floating, and she grabbed onto it, pushing it under her arm to help her float along. I lost sight of Cath as she moved toward the kitchen to retrieve our bags. I spoke to Hazel and asked if she was all right.

The bedroom smelled no less putrid than the kitchen had. The water on the interior of the house was still a mix of ocean, rain, and sewage. More and more ocean water inundating the inside of the house did nothing to taper the heavy swamp smell that hung in the air.

In the scuffle of our dive back into our house, Hazel's glasses had fallen off her face. Her glasses were new; she had only just learned a few months before that she had an astigmatism when she complained that the school board was a bit blurry to see. She was very proud of her "cheetah" frames, and their loss upset her considerably. I tried looking around the room, filled with random, floating pieces of our lives mixed with muck.

Toys, pillows, figurines, and even a flashlight all floated around me. Our curio cabinet usually held some collectibles and a small urn with our previous dogs' ashes in it. Now the cabinet floated near the window we had just swum back into. In all likelihood, her glasses had fallen to the bedroom floor during the dive. Finding a needle in a haystack would've been easier. Hazel insisted she wanted to find her glasses. She could see just fine without them, but the overwhelming emotions of all that had already transpired for her young brain turned lost glasses into a tear-filled plea for an end that was nowhere in sight.

Cath returned from her swim to the kitchen with two bags dragging behind her. One was the waterproof cooler bag filled with food, and the other was the backpack with clothes, medication, and important documents like birth certificates and our marriage license. The backpack was not watertight and was saturated with the ocean, making it incredibly heavy to lift though it still floated. Once Cath made it into the bedroom with our waterlogged luggage, she retrieved a second dining room chair for her to stand on as well.

In that moment of pause, a red can of Coke caught my eye as it floated around the room. I reached for it and turned to Cath to show her my discovery. At first, I was concerned about drinking it, covered in sewage-filled saltwater. A brief reality check reminded me that I had already had sewage in my eyes, nose, and mouth from swimming through the contaminated water. If bacteria were going to invade my body, it was already too late to be worrying about it.

I cracked the top and took a quick sip before passing it to Cath, and then she passed it to Hazel up on the bed, floating next to us. The hot soda burned as I swallowed and caused a brief spasm in my throat as the dark liquid and carbonation went down. The soda was such a moment of normalcy, and it partially filled the hole in my stomach from a lack of food. The extended presence of adrenaline in my body, without adding any sort of fuel, would cause me to crash soon. The soda, at least, added a quick zip of sugar and caffeine my mind and body needed to continue the seemingly endless hamster wheel of survival. Once the soda was gone, we tossed the empty can back into the floodwater and started to plot our next move.

I was still terrified of going into the attic, but other options were exhausted. The attic was now our only course of action to get away from the ever-rising water. Catherine suggested we try again to contact her sister, Charlotte, at her home in Connecticut before making any more moves.

Our decision to go outside could have gone even more horribly wrong than it had. Speaking to someone outside of the chaos to confirm the next plan of action seemed wise. Not to mention, having had death breathing so closely on the backs of our necks, we wanted reassurance and encouragement from our loved ones.

And so, while perched on dining room chairs in our bedroom in the middle of Hurricane Dorian, we retrieved the cell phones from the safety of their Ziploc packaging. We had somehow managed to keep these small but essential items through the chaos of packing and our near-death excursion outside. I took great care when removing the phone from the plastic, terrified of dropping the tiny piece of miracle communication into the dark water surrounding us and losing it forever. I gripped the plastic casing with extra conscious pressure. When I pressed the button on my phone, I expected it to be dead from the beating it had taken. Miraculously, yet again, it turned on. Missed phone calls, voicemail messages, text messages, and Facebook alerts all appeared as banners across the phone. I swiped quickly past the tons of notifications that appeared in a flash on the screen. On my home screen, I saw a photo of the three of us, all smiles. It was already a memory from another life, staring back at me.

I pressed the Facetime app on my phone, and to my astonishment, I was connected instantly with Charlotte, a thousand miles away. Seeing Charlotte and Pattie's concerned faces appear on the screen was both relief and torture. My hand shook as I held the phone outstretched so that they could see all our faces for a moment. All that had already happened, and the ever-pressing need to get to a place of calm and safety, was vibrating through my body, making my hand shake. I tried to steady my hand, unsuccessfully, as we spoke.

Through the screen, we saw them dry and sitting in their very normal-looking living room. It was as if we were watching them from inside a horror movie and they, in turn, were watching our own real-life horror through their screen. Now and then, we could hear the familiar voice of members of their extended family, having all congregated in their tiny house following our SOS. The family gathering, in any other situation, would have been a joyous occasion. Now the cell phone in my hand held our only connection to our loved ones and the hopes for our survival.

Throughout the early morning hours leading up to eleven a.m., our cell service and data access had remained reliable. We had spoken to neighbours near and far, friends and family on other islands and in another country. A stable cell signal was something that had never happened in my memory of previous storms. Once the winds reached hurricane force, most lines and towers went offline, making communication utterly impossible. This was not the case during Dorian. This time the signal remained so strong that it was as if we were speaking to Charlotte from another room in the same house.

The conversation was brief, rushed, and punctuated by fear, chaos, and confusion. There was no time for detailed storytelling of all that had already transpired. We discussed the attic and its pros and cons. I was still terrified we would drown there in a watery grave above our home. Charlotte, Pattie, and Catherine insisted that moving us all to the attic was the only way to survive. With that, we pledged our love to each other through the video call and hung up. We turned the cell phones off to conserve battery life and again placed them into the safety of their Ziploc bags.

With a deep breath, we started the process of getting into the attic. Somehow the floating bed had not blocked the doorway to the closet and the only access to the attic ladder. I went first, maneuvering around the debris to climb into the attic and assess logistics. I carried the heavier of the two bags with me on my first trip. I tried putting the backpack on my back to haul it up the ladder, but its weight pulled me back, and I almost lost my footing as I tried to climb. Forcing the extremely weighted backpack up the ladder ahead of me instead, one step at a time, took more strength, willpower, and adrenaline. The ladder was semi-vertical, with metal ribbed steps; it was very strong and sturdy, but the angle was challenging without the full use of both my hands. When I finally reached the top, I was heaving for air.

I didn't pause to feel much relief at the sight of an area still dry and secure from the storm. There was no respite in the new plan. With the decision to go to the attic made, I pushed my fears deep within my subconscious. With my arrival in the attic alone, I replaced my tunnel vision of escaping the house with a new goal: to get above the water. I knew within my heart that we had no other choice in our bid for survival. And I knew the water was still rising.

The attic floor was lined with individual two-by-four beams every two feet, with only drywall and insulation in between. If any amount of weight was put on the drywall instead of the wooden beams, the drywall would cave in. A cave-in would cause whatever was standing on it to fall through. We would have to be extremely careful each time we moved that we stepped only on the beams while taking care not to run into cross-bracing or hit our heads anywhere, all in the dark. The tiny holes in the soffits along the roof eaves were the primary source of light. A bit more light from the closet illuminated the area immediately around the ladder access. I squinted through the dimly lit space, trying to plan, before turning on the flashlight that I grabbed in haste from the flooded bedroom. A quick scan of the attic showed that the roof remained intact with no holes and no apparent leaks. There was brief reassurance at that moment.

In the attic, the sound of the wind pounding on the roof and echoing in the rafters was frightening. The rain boomed as it poured down onto the sheet metal-covered roof. The need to move everyone resonated in my mind urgently. The space between the water level and the ceiling in the bedroom below me was shrinking. Adrenaline hit me once again. Fear certainly does produce superpowers.

My eyes caught sight of the pile of empty Rubbermaid packing containers stored near the attic access, along with a box that previously held a free-standing fan and some reindeer that lived in our front yard during Christmas. I shoved the reindeer away and turned the Rubbermaid containers over to act as seats. I braced each end of the rectangular-shaped container on the edges of the two-by-four beams. The box was barely long enough to stabilize each end this way.

With initial prep work completed, I ascended the ladder back into the ocean in our closet. I called out to Catherine with instructions on what to do next. She would need to go up into the attic next to receive the dogs and Hazel as I pushed them up. As I treaded water at the bottom of the ladder, Catherine slowly made her way up into the darkness with the food bag slung over one shoulder.

Some of our couch cushions and pillows from our bed floated around me in the closet. When Catherine reached the top, she hollered down for me to throw some of the pillows up. Soggy pillows, however, do not toss easily. Getting four of them into the attic along with a floating dog bed meant climbing the ladder halfway a few more times and handing them up. Catherine noticed four small plastic containers on the top shelf of our closet. Inside were more old photographs. These prized possessions were passed up into the attic darkness for safety as well. As I worked, I called out to reassure Hazel, who was out of sight, waiting impatiently, on the floating bed with the five dogs.

"Mom!" Hazel called out from the bedroom.

"It's okay, sweetie," I comforted, though I did not believe the words at all. I tried desperately to keep my voice steady to offer Hazel the confidence that she needed. "I'm just getting this stuff up into the attic. I'll be right back."

"I want to come with you!" she cried again, a high-pitched sob accompanying her words.

"Two seconds, sweetie," I called down from the top of the attic ladder as I worked, heaving for air. "I'm coming back down right now."

"It's okay, Hazel!" Catherine called from inside the attic.

I descended the ladder and swam from the closet and back to Hazel.

"Come to me, babe," I said as I motioned with one hand out of the water, while the other held on to the side of the floating bed. She slid off the bed and into my arms, and we made our way to the ladder. Hazel made it up the ladder quickly, and I returned to the bedroom, calling the dogs. I grabbed Pearl and Ginger from the bed and made a trip up the ladder with a dog under each arm, then made another trip for Nutmeg. With only Copper left on the bed, I called to Sky, and she slid down, scrambling toward me. I guided her toward the closet as she swam. I coaxed the fifty-pound dog onto the ladder and shoved her halfway up as I ascended with her. She seemed reasonably happy with the idea of climbing the ladder to the attic. Perhaps she sensed safety, the same way she felt disaster when we tried hauling her outside less than an hour before.

With Hazel and four of the five dogs settled in the attic, I paused for a minute to catch my breath and help better assemble seating options. Then, I made one last trip to the bedroom. There was only about two feet of breathing room between the water level and the ceiling on my final trip below. The bed was firmly wedged under the ceiling fan.

"Copper!" I called out, but I could not see the little dog on top of the bed. I tried to pull myself up onto the mattress several times, but I could not haul my body weight up by grasping the bedsheets as Hazel had done. I looked around, hunting for something to stand on to elevate myself. The now cramped space became increasingly tricky as the room came closer to reaching its water capacity.

"Coppie Boy. Little man," I called again with a forced sing-song voice hoping to encourage him through the fear but got no response.

"Fuck," I cursed out loud and splashed my hand in frustration on the top of the water. I turned back to look at the doorway to the closet.

"What's wrong?" Cath yelled down from the attic, her voice muffled by the storm and disappearing doorway.

"I can't get Copper!" I hollered back, unsure whether she could even hear me.

The water level had consumed the door frame almost entirely. I turned again to the bed that floated above my line of vision. For a minute or two as I trod water, I considered leaving the dog there, hoping he would be safe. Then I thought of how Catherine had refused to leave him behind. I made one last effort, kicking my feet in the water as hard as I could and propelled myself as high out of the water as possible with my arm and hand reaching out. When my hand came down on the bed, I caught the very end of the dog's tail, and grabbing it, I pulled. Copper came tumbling into my arms in the water, looking very surprised.

I turned and paddled toward the closet doorway. I paused, took a breath, and then dived myself and Copper under the top of the door frame and into the now darkened closet. As my eyes adjusted to the darkness, I moved to the ladder and climbed it for the last time with Copper under one arm. At the top of the ladder, I dumped him into the soggy dog bed already housing the three other little dogs. As I turned to locate a place to sit, Catherine motioned to a floating Rubbermaid container in the water below, in the stairwell. Completely exhausted, I leaned down to grab it and heaved it into the attic with the last bit of strength I had. We discovered that inside the container were adult winter clothes, all dry, stored for the snow vacations we were all so fond of.

I sat on a plastic container within view of the rising water at the ladder access. I breathed in and out. My muscles screamed at me. My mind raced. I listened to the howling wind, and I could hear the waves outside breaking under the eaves of the house. It was so incredibly loud in the attic with just the roof between us and the monster raging outside, trying to get in. Every gust sent a series of cracks and groans through the wooden rafters that echoed in the wide-open space. I looked around the attic, and through the darkness, I could just make out HVAC ducting and electrical wires. I could see Hazel's face just a few feet away as she clung to her two toys. We were once again "safe," but we didn't know for how long.

Image courtesy of Catherine Pyfrom

Image courtesy of Catherine Pyfrom

THE NEXT DILEMMA

None of us could sit with one another because of the criss-cross bracing in the attic and the need to secure inverted plastic bins for seats. Between the darkness and the insulation, air-conditioning ducting, cable, and electric wires, finding stable seating was challenging. We had to try multiple times and places to get secure. Thankfully the dogs were not heavy enough to cause them to fall through the drywall ceiling, but we took care to explain the precarious footing situation to Hazel and encouraged her to stay put whenever possible. We watched the water level in the stairwell almost constantly.

"I'm hungry," Hazel whimpered.

We scrambled to dig through the pile of items we brought into the attic for survival. The dim light made finding anything complicated. The flashlight that had been retrieved from the water in the bedroom continued to work, but with its exposure to saltwater, it was sure to die soon. We took great care to have it on for as little time as necessary. I fished a granola bar out of the food bag, completely dry amid the water soaking us all, and handed it to Hazel.

"I don't want a granola bar. Can I have cookies?" she inquired, softly.

"We don't have any, sweetie. This is all we have for now," Catherine insisted, and Hazel reluctantly and quietly ate the granola bar.

With the beginnings of lunch underway, the realization came that we had no drinking water with us at all. My stomach bottomed out. In our rush to pack and survive, drinking water had been left behind in the kitchen. I paused and searched my mind for the last time I had seen the gallon bottles of water. The memory resurfaced, and I recalled having stuck each of them into a cabinet high in the kitchen near the refrigerator as the water level had reached the countertop height.

I glanced down at the water in our closet, instantly knowing that there was no feasible way to make my way back to the kitchen through the water below. The water level had reached just a foot below the ceiling in the closet and was still rising. I briefly considered descending back into my nightmare to retrieve water for us. I knew that water was very important. It might take a considerable time for either of us to become dehydrated, but with shock rapidly setting in from the ordeal, drinking water would certainly make us all more comfortable.

I hung over the edge of the stairwell but couldn't see anything except the inside of our dark closet. If I tried swimming back under the doorway toward the kitchen, I would do so without any knowledge of how much breathing space there was in the other rooms of the house. The water was still visibly rising in the closet. I couldn't guess how long it would be before there was no breathing room left at all. There was also the possibility of heavy furniture blocking, or at the very least impeding, my path. I decided the mission was completely impossible. There were too many very dangerous scenarios that could happen below. Attempting to swim back to the kitchen would no doubt result in drowning long before I ever made it back with drinking water.

There were so very many unknowns. We had no idea how long we might be trapped in the attic. No idea how long the storm would last. No clue if the water level would get even higher and reach inside the attic. We were now trapped in this dark but dry space and could only wait to know how, when, and if the water would advance or recede. The wind blew and howled as it forced its way inside the attic through the grooved eave soffits. A chill hit me as shock finally began to set in, after hours of trauma. We were all still in cold, wet clothes.

"I'm cold," Hazel mumbled. With that, we were both up again, trying to maneuver around the awkward space. I opened the backpack. None of the clothes packed there would help at all, as they were all soaked. Catherine opened the dry plastic bin of winter clothes to find an almost brand-new winter coat we had purchased for Hazel on our last vacation. She handed the jacket to Hazel to put on in hopes of warming her. As we sifted haphazardly through the clothes, we found sweatpants, socks, and long-sleeved shirts, all dry. The hurricane wind finding its way in small bursts into the attic met our wet clothes and shock-filled bodies. As we prepared to change into dry clothes, we shivered. I thought again of the water bottles in the kitchen.

At the current water level I could see in the stairwell, the cupboard where the water was sitting would still be out of water. Quite quickly, a plan formed in my mind. We needed water, but shock and sheer exhaustion were setting in fast, and the water was still rising. My mouth felt tacky and dry as I contemplated logistics once again on how to accomplish the impossible. In my mind, if I could calculate the location of the cabinet by studying the light fixture hardware in the attic, I could estimate the bottle location. Then I could stomp a hole in the drywall and lean down to reach the water bottle in the high cupboard.

I paused in my clothes changing and explained to Cath that I was going to try to retrieve the water.

"How are you going to get into the kitchen, though?" Catherine asked with a look more of concern than skepticism on her face.

"I'll punch a hole through the drywall with my foot," I replied quite matter-of-factly.

"Okay, but we're coming with you," Cath insisted. She wanted to come with me to help, but the new project meant walking through and around beams in very little light to the other side of the house, at least fifty feet away. Hazel, understandably, refused to be left sitting in the dark by herself after all the trauma thus far. I insisted that Cath stay with Hazel and the dogs.

"What if you need help?" Cath asked.

"I think I'll be fine. I've only got to lean in through the hole to reach the water, and I only need to grab one bottle." As always, I had an answer for everything. "I'll holler if I need anything," I called over my shoulder as we separated.

In theory, I should have been able to manage the job myself. An entirely new adrenaline rush burst through me as I made my way on my new mission. Two of the five dogs insisted on accompanying me. Having already begun to recover from their ordeal, Sky and Nutmeg thought that an exploration of their new surroundings was in order. I tried sending them back to Cath, but to no avail, so I pushed on, banging my shin on a two-by-four when I misjudged a step.

When I reached the area above our kitchen, I paused and began counting light fixture hardware. The canister for a recessed or pot light is large and easy to recognise. Judging the location of the cabinet I was trying to locate; I found a scrap piece of wood and used it to try to punch holes in the drywall. My first attempt barely made a dent. I stabbed harder at the drywall, managing to punch a small hole, but soon realized that the stick would not work for the job. I dropped the wood, braced myself on a crossbeam, and stomped my foot through the drywall with ease. A few swift blows to the hole opened it up enough for me to see into the space below.

The water level in the kitchen was the same as the closet, with only a foot of space between the water and the ceiling. As I stooped down and peered through the hole I had created, I realized quickly that I had misjudged my location by about three feet. The discrepancy was too much for me to overcome by reaching, so I moved closer to my intended location. I stomped again, this time aware of just how much pressure I needed to create the hole. As I finished my access hole, Sky and Nutmeg arrived, snooping in curiosity. I called out to Catherine and asked her to call the dogs back. She tried, but they refused to leave me. Catherine called out through the darkness to ask if I needed help, but I declined, knowing that her support meant leaving Hazel alone.

I stooped down again, bracing my left hand on one side of the two-foot by three-foot hole I had created. Using my dominant hand, I tried to reach through the hole to grab the cabinet door, which held the water. My arm wasn't quite long enough, so I leaned a bit further into the hole. I lost my balance as more of my body weight was hovering over the hole than my legs could support. My foot slipped and I fell, in somewhat slow motion, into the access hole. I tried to save myself and banged my arm quite hard on the wooden beam in the process. The bruise stung, but thankfully the sudden fall was short, and there was nothing but water below me to break my fall.

I suddenly found myself in the exact position I had been trying all this time to avoid. My heart pounded in fear, and I could hear my pulse in my ears. There was very little breathing space, and only a tiny amount of light made it through the submerged kitchen windows. I was hit again with the overwhelming smell of sewage. As I kicked my feet to keep my head above the water, various items knocked my arms and legs. Old glass bottles from our massive collection floated around me, together with various kitchen items that had floated out of now-open kitchen cabinets. Next to me, I could see the refrigerator, having floated with the rising water. It had shifted and wedged, face up, against the kitchen island.

I pushed my rising fear down deep within me and tried to orient myself. I did a quick scan for anything that might be useful. As I searched, not moving from my access hole as I tread water, I heard the dogs above my head before I saw them. As I looked up, I saw Nutmeg fall into the hole with me. Before I could even begin to assess how to solve this new dilemma, Sky too took a misstep, and the front portion of her body caved in more of my access hole. I hollered, "NO!" but it was no use. Now I had one small dog swimming with me in the submerged kitchen and a second struggling and hanging precariously over my head. As I scrambled to push Sky back into the attic to regain her footing, Nutmeg crawled up my shoulders, obviously regretting her curiosity. Sky scrambled back into the attic with my shove from below without a complete fall into the water. Once Sky was out of the way, I grabbed Nutmeg and hurled her back up into the attic as well.

I breathed a brief sigh of relief and got to work. I knew I had to get out of the situation I was in, and fast. I opened the cabinet in front of me and various plastic plates floated out. On the top shelf, exactly where I remembered putting it, was the gallon bottle of water. I grabbed it and pushed it into the attic. One of the dog's stainless steel food bowls floated in the water to my right. I grabbed it and tossed it easily through the hole. Then I noticed a Tupperware container of dog food in the same cabinet and grabbed it to shove into the attic as well. The container hit the edge of the ceiling in the rushed process, sending the dog food floating in the ocean around me. "Fuck," I cursed out loud again, my frustration and fear bubbling out.

As I peered up at the access hole to begin to figure out how to get back up, I saw a Ziploc bag floating by my face. I recognised it immediately. It was a spare set of Hazel's school uniform, completely dry inside. It usually lived inside her school backpack, which was left sitting on the kitchen counter. Hazel had no dry clothes in the plastic bin rescued from the closet. This incredible find meant that Hazel could get dry and warm. I grabbed the bag and threw it easily into the attic.

Having retrieved all I had come for, I reached up over my head with a hand on the wooden beam on each side of my drywall hole. I pulled with all my strength and managed to get one elbow up and onto the wood above me. I tried insisting that my muscles continue to haul my one hundred and ninety pounds up and out of the kitchen, but I did not have the upper body strength to pull my body weight. Losing strength, I slipped back into the water, scraping the inside of my arm on the jagged drywall as I splashed back down.

Back in the sewage water, the waves I had created caused the floating objects to bump into me. I started to panic and worried that I would be stuck in this space until the water level got high enough to float me to the attic or worse. Images of being stuck in the kitchen floating until the end of the hurricane flashed before my eyes.

I looked toward the windows, submerged below the surface of the water, hoping to see a break in the rain or onslaught of the wind, but I couldn't see outside at all. I studied the distance between the water level and the ceiling. I couldn't see any noticeable rise in the water during my mission. The water level seemed to have stabilized a bit.

I moved closer to the cabinet and was able to stand on the countertop with water up to my shoulders. I thought of calling out to Catherine but was unsure if my voice would travel up and through the roar of the storm in the attic. Calling for help was slotted in my head as a Plan B. Then I noticed our living room ottoman floating on the kitchen island opposite me. I thought perhaps I could force it below the water's surface onto the countertop at my feet and climb on it to give me the extra height I needed to get back into the attic. I tried twice to push it down but never managed to push it nearly deep enough to climb on. I was running out of options once again and rapidly running out of steam. Fear and shock sent a shiver through my body as I desperately tried to come up with a new plan.

I tried again to grab the wooden beam in the attic, this time with both hands on the same side of the access hole. I managed to get both elbows up into the attic this time and held firm with the beam under my armpits. Sky was there, licking my face. "Move!" I roared at her. I kicked my feet in the water below, trying to propel myself upward, kicking debris as I did. I got a bit higher out of the water and braced the beam roughly under my rib cage. That gained me even more stability, and I was able to haul myself out of the hole, scraping my back as I wiggled up and out of the submerged kitchen.

Finally back in the attic, I didn't sit or pause to catch my breath. With my new bruises still stinging, I grabbed the water bottle and hunted around for the Ziploc of dry clothes and dog bowl I had tossed. Somehow finding them in the dark, I began to make my way back to the other side of the house, calling Sky and Nutmeg behind me. I remained cautious of my footing. Even though it had taken an effort to punch through the drywall, I worried about a fall or any major injury if I took a misstep.

I paused near an open section of the soffit allowing some light to filter into the darkness. Two of the soffit panels had been pulled out by the waves, and through the hole, I could make out the brown, rough water on the outside of the house. I stood for thirty seconds and contemplated this as an escape route. I was still terrified of the water reaching the attic space. As I stood studying the hole, images of the three of us diving out of the attic through that tiny space and out into the raging waters began to materialize in my mind. I was plotting the next move in the horrible list of what-if scenarios still to come.

If we were to escape the rising ocean levels inside the attic, struggling against the open ocean seemed futile. I did not believe in our ability to fight the monster anymore. Our brief trip outside with the aid of floats showed me just how mismatched we were against this opponent. Without the stability and presumed strength of our house, we would be fighting the beast full-on with no weapons or support. There was no hope that we could win the battle. As I stood studying our only exit strategy, my mind flashed briefly with memories of times when the ocean was a cherished friend, even a confidante to tell my innermost secrets. Now, the brown rush of the brute's waves clawed at the opening. This was no longer a friend; the ocean was now a foe, hell-bent on my death.

"Are you okay?" Catherine called out to me through the darkness, breaking the escape plan in the making.

"Yes! I'm coming back now," I shouted in response.

When I reached Catherine and Hazel, I passed the water bottle to Catherine, flopped onto the makeshift Rubbermaid seat, and took several deep breaths. We passed the water around, all having some and pouring a tiny bit into the dog bowl. I began shivering again, my adrenaline having been completely spent. I needed to get dry. We helped each other as we dug out some winter clothes and peeled off the wet rain jackets, t-shirts, pants, socks, and underclothes. Once we were out of the cold clothes, Hazel put on the school uniform I'd found along with the winter coat as Catherine and I pulled on our dry winter gear.

Every other hurricane I can recall was humid and sticky and uncomfortable. We usually suffered through them with no electricity and sweat dripping from our faces. This time, stranded in the attic with no way out, the air was cold on our skin. Between the air temperature and the shock, it took a long time for the shivering of our tense muscles to ease.

TWENTY-FOUR HOURS
OF DARKNESS

~~~

A brief inspection of our food yielded an unfortunate discovery. The food I packed in haste was not the type of food for our current situation. In the mad rush of fear packing, I packed things like cans of soup and brown rice. It was not food we could eat uncooked, and I hadn't packed a can opener. And so peanut butter and crackers were all we had, along with one more granola bar. After the shivering subsided and we were all warmer, we shared a tiny lunch. We only had a single roll of Ritz crackers and knew they needed to be conserved. Hazel ate more than we did.

We used the flashlight as little as possible to preserve the battery. Every time we needed something, we would turn it on, and shine it in the direction we needed to see. Once we got a good mental picture, we would turn it off
~~~

again. Then we would fumble our way along in the dark. We were trying to save what we had. We still had no idea how long we would be there or how much worse things could get.

Every few minutes, I would lean over or stand to stretch, my feet balancing on the wooden beams, and I would check the water level. The rising water had slowed considerably, and we used the ladder rungs to keep tabs on the increase. We had lost another step to the ocean since entering the attic two hours before.

Outside, the storm continued to rage on. With no visual cues, we had only sound to assess the severity of Dorian from our attic prison. The wind continued to howl with unreasonable abandon. Every minute or so, the sharp whistle of Dorian's claws trying to penetrate our fortress zipped through the air. He was trying desperately to breach our stronghold. Each time the wind tried to pull on the roof from the outside, the inside structure would hold tight, insisting with monumental strength that it would not be moved. The cracks and groans of the roof's determination to win the battle with the wind echoed. Each noise, no matter how repetitious, sent a shiver of fear down my back. I didn't have faith that the wooden structure could possibly stand up to this kind of single-minded destruction.

Seating was an incredibly uncomfortable issue. The two plastic Rubbermaid bins in the attic were flimsy and cracked from years of storage in the heat and humidity.

Their length allowed us to brace them on the wooden beams under our feet at each end but only just barely. The space between the wooden beams was about thirty-six inches with only pink insulation and drywall separating each beam. The bins were about thirty-six inches long but rounded at the sides. If we moved too much or too suddenly, one end of the bin would slip into the unsupported area between the wooden beams. This would cause the flat surface of the plastic we were using as a seat to lean at a forty-five-degree angle suddenly. This was especially difficult for Hazel. Sitting still is not something most six-year-olds do well. Add to that itchy skin from the ocean, sewage water, tree debris, and contact with the bright pink insulation in the attic, and we had a very wiggly kid.

It also didn't help that it was dark, loud, and scary. Hazel wanted to be close to us and sit on our laps for comfort. There was no reasonable way to do this without cutting off the circulation of one of our arms or legs or overstretching some body part. As a result, we were almost constantly adjusting and moving, trying to locate a solution to the discomfort. Most often, comforting Hazel meant Catherine leaning with her arm outstretched to rest on Hazel's leg or back.

The roof of our home capped both the interior rooms and the exterior covered porches of the house. The exterior wall of our house, the place in the attic where we could discern the change from interior space to exterior space below, was very distinguishable. It was visible as a concrete strip in the attic floor some twelve feet long by eight inches wide. The wall then turned at a ninety-degree angle to continue to the outer section of the roof near the eaves. This strip, as it appeared in the attic, was the top portion of our exterior concrete block wall. Unlike the space between the wooden beams filled with pink insulation, the concrete slab was the only space in the attic that we were sure we couldn't fall through. We stacked pillows along the narrow space and tried taking turns laying on it. The soggy pillows from our couch that we had retrieved helped a little. This was the only way either of us could briefly put our exhausted leg muscles at ease and stretch out. However, laying on concrete on top of stinking, wet pillows is uncomfortable in other ways, so we continued the rotation.

Three of the five dogs remained curled up in the wet dog bed near the attic access. That was where we had dropped the heavy bed in the scramble to get to the attic. Moving it would not have been easy to manage, and so it remained there. Pearl, Ginger, and Copper had not moved from the bed since our arrival in the attic. I worried about Pearl and Copper, the two elderly dogs. Surely if we were exhausted, with overworked muscles and joints screaming at us, they were, too. We had been forced to handle them all far more roughly than ever before and I suddenly felt badly for how I had pulled Copper from the floating bed. I wondered if I had accidentally aggravated his old injuries.

We checked on the dogs regularly. Hazel would rub their heads every now and then. When Catherine leaned over to pet them, Copper wagged his tail in greeting, though he made no attempt to get up. Ginger, usually eager for attention, barely lifted her head when we spoke to the dogs in a sing-song voice, comforting them as much as ourselves. They were not injured as far as we could tell in the darkness, just too traumatized to be bothered moving around or too exhausted to care. We offered them each water from the bowl I had retrieved from the kitchen.

Nutmeg and Sky took turns wandering around the attic. In the darkness, we kept losing sight of them and would call them back every few minutes. Eventually, they settled in a pile of insulation near us. They begged for the crackers from us, but we couldn't share them. We were too worried we would run out as it was.

After another hour or two, we retrieved the cell phones from the safety of their Ziploc bags and again held our breath as we tried to turn them on. Once again, the technology cooperated without a problem, but we no longer had a cellular signal. We had no way of knowing whether the loss of signal resulted from the storm or the closed-in space we found ourselves in. We had hoped to check the storm's progress on the Internet, but with no data signal or ability to call anyone to say that we were safe, we found ourselves completely alone.

Then came the inevitable bodily needs. In the darkness of the attic, where moving around was hard, we had nowhere to use a bathroom. We didn't have a spare bucket, and if we chose a corner away from the attic access light, the dogs would likely find the spot quickly and roll in urine or feces and bring the mess back to our laps.

The only option was to use the water in our closet below as our bathroom. Despite having very little to eat or drink in the previous twelve hours, the stress of the situation had turned all our stomachs, and our bowels were reacting accordingly. We would hang over the stairs one at a time, squatting as best we could to avoid soiling our now-dry clothes. This bathroom process was particularly challenging for Hazel, since we had to remove the clothes from her lower half with each "bathroom visit" to keep her dry and clean. Toilet paper was also a luxury we did not have. We grabbed stacks of dry winter socks from the plastic bin to use in its place, making the most of what we had. As a sock reached the extent of its usability, it was discarded into the water below. The water swirling in the closet was already foul-smelling. Using it as a toilet did nothing to improve the air quality.

The whole process was like using your front door as a toilet. The ladder area was our only way out and our only light source, but we had no choice in the matter. We knew that the closet and the house below were already covered in sewage. What was the point in worrying about adding to the mess, we thought.

We waited for the water to reach us throughout those first few hours in the attic and saturate us once more. We checked the water level at the ladder every few minutes. We listened to waves splash up through the soffits. In the dim light, we could just barely see the little bit of water coming up through the grooves there. The wind howled incessantly. Every few minutes, we would get a bigger gust, and the roof would creak and groan and crack with deafening volume. Each time the gusts increased, we held our breath, waiting for a panel to be ripped off the roof, exposing us to the outside elements.

Before long, the tiny amount of light we had been relying on started to wean. The sun was beginning to set. With the heavy cloud cover, torrential rain, and windows in the house below us underwater, nighttime came very early. Knowing that moving at all would be impossible once we lost all light, we set about having a bit of dinner: a few more crackers, peanut butter, and the granola bar shared between us. We passed the water around again. We didn't want to drink too much, knowing that using the bathroom would be even more challenging by flashlight or without light at all.

Once we had eaten and had another round of bathroom attention, we tried to figure out how to set up sleeping arrangements. The makeshift seat was long enough for Hazel to lie on with knees and feet hanging off, but she would fall off if she moved at all. More so than most kids,

Hazel did not hold still when sleeping, so we decided quickly that this would not work. Instead, we turned the plastic bin right-side-up and dropped a soggy pillow in the bottom. She climbed inside, curling her knees up to her chest to fit. With her winter jacket still wrapped around her, she tried to settle. It wasn't easy. After an hour in the pitch blackness, listening to her mumble and hum to herself, she went quiet. She had fallen asleep on her back with her knees bent and her lower legs hanging outside of the bin. As she slept, Hazel clung to her stuffed toys, Ellie the purple dachshund and Moxie the pink Ugly Doll, for comfort.

Our beds for the night were even more makeshift. Catherine stayed on the exterior wall and the concrete strip with pillows lined up. Eight inches is an extremely narrow area to balance the length of your body while in significant discomfort. It was necessary to shift constantly to ease pinched nerves and bruised limbs. I sat on the silver air-conditioning ducting. Usually a long rectangular box, my weight had flattened it out with the wooden beams underneath supporting it. I used a long plastic lid from the bin to add support and had a soggy pillow under my upper back and head. It felt precarious, and I had to take a great deal of care to shift and move. I often waited until the pain was screaming at me from one position before moving to another for fear the whole mess would cave in.

Every muscle in my body was exhausted from all that I had physically demanded of it. My legs felt heavy and weary from swimming, climbing up and down the ladder, and the extra careful maneuvering in the attic. Without the comfort of a stable seat, I sat perched, with back and leg muscles tensed. The lifting, shoving, and moving of the pre-hurricane preparation and survival of the current situation had knotted my lower back muscles to an agonizing level. It hurt to breathe. It hurt more to move. All I wanted was to elevate my feet and lie down to relax my aching body and find some reprieve.

The darkness that night was so all-consuming that it could hardly be explained. Most people know how dark it can be in a closet or basement with no window or light. Nights without a moon in the outdoors can be pretty dark too. The bigger issue was that the darkness was not just physical. I literally could not see a hand an inch from my face, but the night was more than that. It was like a demon consuming us from the outside-in. Fear, isolation, and death hovered in the air, making the blackness so very heavy.

The three of us were separated by the physical circumstances of the attic structure. I couldn't reach out and hold Catherine's hand through the darkness to feel her warmth and find solace in her presence. Each bang we heard from a tree branch hitting the roof above our heads made me jump and look in Cath's direction, desperately wanting to disappear into her arms and make the outside world melt away as I had so often done in the past.

Occasionally, Nutmeg or Sky would come through the blackness for attention. Their presence was both comforting and then frustrating. Nutmeg's warm body curled in my lap, breathing deeply, was sweet and helped calm me, but quickly it became a problem as shifting in the crooked bed was impossible with the extra weight. Eventually, I had to insist she lie in the insulation near me.

Now and then, Cath and I would whisper to each other through the darkness. We wondered about the time, the water level, and the wind speed. And then we would go quiet again. I would shine the flashlight briefly to check the time on my wristwatch and the water level, which had finally stopped rising. Watching the clock became painstaking. What seemed like hours of endless pain and fear and darkness turned out to be mere minutes in between quick checks of the time and flood water.

Sometime around two a.m., Hazel called out in fear from her makeshift bed, obviously dreaming of the real nightmare we were living. We turned on the flashlight and called to her as best we could. "You're all right. You're safe. We are all safe."

Catherine leaned toward Hazel and placed a hand on her leg. She settled again relatively quickly. Cath remained outstretched in physical contact with Hazel for long after she fell asleep again.

As the hours wore on, I listened to the wind and hammering rain. I alternated holding my breath and sighing with relief. We both did. Each time the wind gust would pick up and howl and push against the roof, causing cracks and squeaks and growls, I would hold my breath. I mentally repeated, "Please let the roof hold. Please let the roof hold. Please let the roof hold." again and again.

It was something akin to a prayer, though not spoken to a specific deity. So many people in near-death experiences find spirituality and speak directly to their god, in hopes of redemption before death. They search for sympathy from a higher power to end the suffering. My plea was not directed to a god, Christian or otherwise. It was a wish, a hope, a mantra, really. A seemingly endless prospect that things simply could not get any worse. And yet as I repeated those words for hours and hours, my mind still managed to imagine how much worse our situation could still get.

During those long, dark hours, Catherine called to her deceased parents and prayed to them for our safety. Christianity was a part of her upbringing, as it was mine. Whether she prayed to her parents in Heaven, begging for some unseen force to grant a miracle, or to their spirits in a universal realm unknown to us, mattered little. Her silent pleas were repeated again and again, much like my own. We were both hoping for salvation of any kind.

I studied the sounds outside, wondering about and fearing the freight train noise of a tornado. Tornados or waterspouts are common inside hurricanes. Several of them had pounded parts of Freeport during Hurricane Matthew just three years before. Their path had been obvious in the aftermath and marked by holes in roofs and large trees down in a definitive track of destruction. Having never been through a tornado, I had only stories and TV to go on, but all accounts agreed to the freight train sound that accompanied them.

As I shifted uncomfortably in the inky blackness, eyes open or closed without seeing anything, I listened for the freight train that would rip our roof off and take us all into the abyss of Dorian.

"Please let the roof hold. Please let the roof hold." I waited and kept repeating those five words over and over. I held my breath and felt the beams and wooden bracing shift under the weight of the roof as the wind pushed against it.

Eventually, the exhaustion and shock began to overtake the fear, my eyes would close, and my brain would slip off into oblivion for just a moment or two. Before my brain could properly leave the consciousness of the living hell, the noise of the monster outside would bring me back, and I would begin my silent plea again. Alternating between holding my breath and exhaling in sharp bursts as I listened to the wind, I wondered what we would do when the roof came off.

Each time the wind would seem to slow ever so slightly, and the volume would drop for more than a minute or two, a tiny bit of hope would blossom. Maybe, just maybe, the eye had arrived, indicating that we were at least halfway through the storm. I turned on the cell phone once through the night during a bathroom event to use the light and hope that we had a cellular signal. We never did. I had hoped at least to find out where the storm was and when it would leave or when the tide and ocean would recede, but we had no information except the horrible imaginings of our exhausted minds.

At one point, Cath and I spoke to each other through the darkness and complained of the painful muscles. I offered to switch places with her. We contemplated the move briefly but knew that moving meant flashlight use, disturbing the dogs, and likely waking Hazel, who was still thankfully sleeping most of the night. In the end, we chose to remain as we were.

In complete darkness and shrouded in constant fear, time ceased. We had very few brief conversations that night. "Conversation" is probably the wrong word to use. Catherine and I didn't discuss all that had already transpired. We didn't talk about any next steps post-Dorian. We focused only on necessities and movement in our tiny space surrounded by so much noise and destruction. We focused on staying alive.

When Hazel awoke again, she was very alert and asked if the storm was over. The wind was still obviously strong, and the creaking roof was still groaning, but over the last hour or so before Hazel woke, we could hear a definite decrease in the intensity. Another check of the cell phone with no service showed that it was five-thirty a.m. Seeing the time, a sense of relief washed over me. The time meant the pitch blackness of the night would soon be over. Unfortunately, with the storm continuing, it would still take hours before we would have much light. Hazel was antsy. She tried to entertain herself with her soggy stuffed toys. She kept hassling the dogs to act as playmates, and she insisted we check the water level at the stairs again several times.

Before the sun appeared, the flashlight finally began to die. We had to smack the rubber casing several times to activate the corroded batteries inside. Inspecting the ladder with the flashlight revealed that the top step of the ladder, previously submerged, had reappeared. The water was receding! The brief inspection also showed furniture, debris, and piles of wet clothing surrounding the ladder. We turned off the flashlight and waited for sunrise, still more than an hour away.

DAYLIGHT

W**atching the dawn break and the water recede was painstaking, but with it came the realization that the storm was finally moving away. The wind noises were decreasing, and we could no longer hear the rain pounding on the roof. We had survived!

As the sun rose, the light grew just enough to see the watch on my wrist without the flashlight, a luxury I had not had during the hours of the pitch-black night. We sat unmoving in our attic and simply stared at the water level on the ladder. Ever so slowly, one step reappeared, then another, and finally a third. We ate a bit more peanut butter and crackers and had more water. By that time, the three dogs who had been virtually comatose during the entire night were beginning to move around. They were recovering from their ordeal as well.

With all three dogs out of the bed and a fair amount of light now reaching the attic through the ladder access and the eaves, we were able to see that the drywall under the wet dog bed was saturated and very near caving in. We grabbed the bed and moved it to a new spot not far away. To add light and see a bit more of what was happening below, we gently pushed on the wet drywall to open a hole. Directly below, we could see our bed. Catherine and I discussed how we would get ourselves and the dogs out of the attic once the water receded enough. We contemplated dropping the dogs through the hole, but as the water level dropped, so did the bed. It seemed wiser to use the ladder.

The three of us again sat and waited. Mentally I took note of the speed and distance at which the water was dropping and tried to estimate how long it might be before we could get out of the attic. I noted with a glance at my watch that Hazel had been awake for about four hours, and it was nearly nine-thirty a.m. We were all exhausted and hungry and no longer cold. The standard humidity that accompanies a hurricane had set up residence in the attic, and as the sun rose, though still covered by clouds and storm, the air was getting stickier. We had been holed up in the attic since eleven a.m. the previous day, over twenty-two hours at that point. We knew we were close to escaping the confines of the attic, and we all wanted out as quickly as possible, but we could still hear the storm.

While the ever-pressing intensity of the Category 5 storm was clearly behind us, as indicated by the volume change of the wind in the attic, it was still very stormy. Without visible cues like wave height and tree movement, it was difficult for us to gauge how bad the weather still was outside. Regardless of the current intensity, with the water level dropping, we knew this meant that the storm was leaving, and the worst was behind us. Patience was not something any of us had after our ordeal, and so the almost constant conversation was all about exactly when we would be able to leave the attic. My best guess was noon.

We had no plan for what would happen once we descended the ladder. Our psyches couldn't muster the strength to plot what post-Dorian would look like just yet. The anticipation of that eventuality hung heavy in the air around us. For the first time since the ordeal began, we no longer feared for our lives. If there was relief in that fact, it was overshadowed by our desperate need to see the daylight again. The only thing that mattered to all of us was getting out of that attic.

Those last few hours ticked by just as slowly as the long night had. Perhaps even more slowly as we now had the advantage (or disadvantage) of seeing our watches and knowing that only five or ten minutes passed with each glance at the time and falling water level. Hazel fidgeted. The dogs shuffled around. Cath and I shifted our seats a few more times. Once the water level dropped to the halfway point, about four feet of ocean still swirling through our now-demolished home, I climbed part way down the ladder. The sheer sight of the destruction I saw stunned me.

The wall of the master closet had been ripped off almost entirely, exposing the wooden studs of the interior structure. Through the now-open wall, I could see what was left of our living room, the now-dead heart of our home. Furniture still floated, and ocean water moved everything to and fro in a whirlpool. The French glass doors that I had tried so desperately to open just twenty-four hours before were now blown open and swinging, giving a loud bang every time a wave caused it to hit the wall. I realized now that this was part of the loud noises that we had listened to all night. We had imagined the noise coming from the roof, but part of the volume had come from below us.

I stood perched halfway down the ladder at the water's edge and studied the contents of what was left of our closet. The rods that had held our clothes had fallen under the weight of soaked clothing, leaving soggy piles riddled with bits and pieces of our possessions. Everywhere I looked, I saw grey sludge. A small wooden toy chest with an image of Winnie the Pooh was braced against the bottom of the ladder and in the doorway. The lid of the box was smeared with feces from our bathroom visits. Everything floating in the closet was covered in some form of excrement, whether new from our time in the attic or old from the overflowing septic tank caused by the flood.

Through the open French doors, I could make out the wind and rain still ravaging the outdoors. The storm had not yet made its full exit from our home. Our porch railing, last seen the day before, was just becoming visible again. The trees that I could make out in the distance still swayed with marked abandon. The fact that many were still standing was of little interest at the time. I could not see the pool below the surface of the grey waves of the ocean flood. With the wind still clearly at hurricane force, the waves surrounding us were still capped with angry white foam. The ocean was still furious and wasn't done letting that be known just yet.

I returned to the attic and relayed all I had seen to Catherine and Hazel, but the reality of it did not sink into my brain. We sat and waited for the water to recede even more.

Image courtesy of Catherine Pyfrom

AFTER

THE BOAT

By just after eleven a.m. on Tuesday, September third, almost thirty-six hours after the winds of Hurricane Dorian had first begun, we decided to make our way out of the attic. There was still ankle-deep water in the closet, but everyone's patience had worn thin.

"Can you stay up here with the dogs for just a couple of minutes?" I asked Hazel. "I'm worried that it's very slippery down there and I don't want you to get hurt," I explained further, hoping that my words would be enough to convince her.

"No! I don't want you to leave me!" was her quick response, as she shook her head rapidly to punctuate the statement. She cuddled her soggy toys closer under her chin. It was understandable, after all the trauma she had already endured, that Hazel didn't want to be left alone in the dark attic, even briefly.

I turned to Catherine, my forehead scrunched up as I tried to come up with Plan B.

"It's pretty bad down there but we can get out," I stated. "But I'm worried about her or one of the dogs getting cut." We definitely didn't need a nasty gash after surviving what we had. At least we knew we didn't need to fear injury from electricity. The power lines would not be reenergized until the entire grid was inspected and all areas needing repair isolated. If Hurricane Matthew was any indication, electricity was not something we would have for months.

"Okay, why don't you go down first, Cath," I instructed, taking the lead on our next move. "Once you get down, I'll help Hazel down."

Cath had to take great care and thoughtfulness with each step down the ladder so as not to slip on the mess clinging to the rungs. I followed her part of the way down to act as an extra set of eyes to help decide the best places to put her feet once she left the ladder. The Winnie the Pooh toy box was wedged in the doorway, and Catherine had to stand on it to pass. When her foot slipped, I gasped.

"What? What's wrong?" came Hazel's anxious voice above me in the attic.

"Nothing, babe," Cath reassured her. "It's okay. My foot just slipped."

After a few more precarious steps on the toy box, Cath finally stepped out into our bedroom. From my perch halfway down the ladder, I could see our bed had settled back on the ground almost in the exact location it had been floating, only partially blocking our exit route.

Once Catherine had her feet on solid ground, I returned to the attic and the six beings awaiting release from our elevated dungeon.

"Okay, Hazel, can you move over there, please? I'm going to drop some of our stuff down to Mommy," I instructed, trying to soothe Hazel's nerves by giving her as much information as possible.

Through the hole in the drywall created by the saturated dog bed, I dropped Hazel's toys onto the bed below and then slowly guided her down the ladder. "Stay!" I commanded when I noticed two of the dogs wagging their tails eagerly in the attic above me.

At the bottom, Catherine gave Hazel instructions on where to put her feet, and she slowly made her way once again onto the safety of our saturated bed to avoid slipping down or getting cut. The ground under Catherine's feet crunched as she walked carefully, judging her every movement. At that moment, I was grateful for the soggy sneakers we still wore to keep our feet safe.

I made several more trips to the attic and retrieved the dogs one or two at a time. Passing them to Cath, she would then deposit them onto the bed and the comfort of Hazel's arms. Sky remained in the attic until my last trip. Descending with the fifty-pound dog was no more manageable than the climb into the attic, but leaving her up there was not an option. I worried she would simply jump from the top and injure herself in the process. She half-slid and half-fell down the final few steps. I struggled to maintain my footing on the slippery, muck-covered flooring littered with random items as I guided the dog up and onto the bed. I told her to stay quite firmly, but she refused. Instead of remaining on the bed with Hazel and the others, Sky followed Catherine and me as we moved through the broken bedroom doorway to inspect our surroundings. We worried about her getting injured by the debris, but we pushed the worry aside as being unimportant when faced with all we could now see.

Images of flood-ravaged plains in the central parts of the US or bombed-out homes in Syria come to mind when I try to describe what we saw as we stood in the middle of what was once our dream home. Multiple windows in the house were now open when we had last seen them closed. The pressure and suction of the storm had somehow opened but not broken them. The French door at our backs continued to swing and bang with the wind as it howled through the open house. Some of our furniture was moved to different parts of the open floor plan. Others remained in their rightful places. Some were upended completely. After the storm, the generator, now flooded and unusable, remained exactly as we had left it. Its weight was far too heavy even for Dorian to move.

The glass-front entertainment shelving units which lined our living room wall were all piled one on top of the other, face down. Our flat-screen TV lay face down and smashed. One of our extra-large blue couches was pushed toward our dining room and turned over. The other couch was sitting on top of our kitchen island. Our custom-built open shelving unit was bare of all the photo albums that I had stuck there in a rush to save what I could. The dining room table sat in our foyer near more exposed walls. Drywall had been peeled off various walls like the peel of a banana, and fragments of soggy seaweed clung in its place. Near the top of the walls, only eight to twelve inches from the ceiling, we could see the line of seaweed and water as a tell-tale sign of where Dorian's monster flood had stopped its ascent. Another foot to foot-and-a-half of water rise and the ocean would have met us in the attic.

Hazel's toys were spread out all over. Books and magazines had floated off shelves and now carpeted the floor in places, partially disintegrated and held together only by a solid book spine in some cases. Clothes and pillows and towels were spread out or piled in places, often hiding more of our lives underneath. I noticed our small bar fridge had floated out and into the middle of the living room next to an intact glass ball. More red cans of Coke were scattered around, and a waterlogged cereal box caught my eye. Little trinkets lay broken everywhere.

In the far corner of the living room, I could make out what used to be vases, now surrounded by a mound of turquoise, teal, and emerald-green sea glass. The glass was scattered. Mermaid's tears, indeed. They were tears from the ocean, now lost to the sea once more.

As we stood, barely managing to move around what was left of our living room, obstacles made exploring all but impossible. Furniture blocked every path we thought to try, and the slipperiness of the ground made movement precarious at best. Looking out of the windows, we could see that we were still an island unto our own. The water level still covered our back porch and the surrounding yard, driveway, and road. We couldn't see the car out the window in the place we had last laid eyes on it. It seemed to have disappeared completely. The raging ocean must have taken it as well. Out of our front windows, we could make out our neighbours' homes, intact but still underwater as well.

Just as the overwhelming fear we had spent over twenty-four hours grappling with began to give way to overwhelming grief, Catherine and I heard a noise on our porch. We turned to see a person in a wetsuit, goggles, and fins surface in the water off our back porch. The shock of the image made it seem like a figment of our imaginations. Perhaps, we both thought, it was a mirage brought on by the hysteria of trauma.

As the person stood from the water and planted their finned feet firmly on our porch, they removed their goggles and snorkel to reveal a familiar face. We instantly recognised our friend Jamie. The surrealness of the moment was intense. After all that we had endured together, the appearance of another person, an air of confidence and strength surrounding him, was like something out of a dream.

"Are you guys all okay?" was the first thing he said. With that, I leapt forward and threw my arms around his neck in a hug so fierce that it shattered the grief that had begun only a moment before. When I let go of Jamie, Catherine swooped in quickly with arms outstretched and almost buckled into him with relief.

I called out to Hazel in sheer joy, "Hazel! It's Uncle Jamie!"

"Hi, Hazel," Jamie called to her. Hazel was still seated obediently and safely on our bed. Seeing Jamie pop up out of the hurricane floodwaters in full rescue gear was the lighthouse we needed to see to guide us the rest of the way through the storm.

At first, we had no idea from where Jamie had materialized. Surely, he couldn't have swum from his parents' house some two miles away.

"How did you get here?" Catherine inquired, bewildered.

"The guys are in the boat in the next canal to keep out of the wind. They dropped me in your canal, and I swam in," he explained.

We learned from Jamie that everyone on our Facebook feed had received our SOS. Charlotte and Pattie had pleaded for help from the Bahamas Air and Sea Rescue Association (BASRA) and the United States Coast Guard. Unfortunately, the storm's intensity had made it impossible for any rescue attempts before now. Even still, the weather was not boat-worthy, and it was extremely dangerous for them to be out at all. The rain continued to come down steadily and the wind gusts were still fierce.

"Mom and Dad are fine. They are in their attic with the Campbell family as well. We spoke to them on the phone," Jamie confirmed quickly, "No one's heard from you guys in twenty-four hours, and with Hazel..." he paused to lower his voice. "We were worried. We've only just come out to start moving people. You're our first stop."

Hearing this would have been heartwarming on any other occasion. We were grateful for Jamie and that our SOS had been received, but there was still urgency in the situation, and we didn't have the luxury of time to feel complex emotions just yet.

"Do you guys want to leave?" was Jamie's next question. As simple a question as it might appear to be, it was one that we had to discuss. "We have a rescue command center set up at the Sailing Club. Christian is there with food, water, and dry clothes for you guys." The Grand Bahama Sailing Club was several miles away. Usually easily reached by car, now with the flooding, it would only be reached by boat.

Cath and I turned and looked at each other and asked, "What should we do?"

Jamie interjected, "Do you have water?"

"Maybe a gallon left," I responded, "and no food."

"Listen guys, the storm is still pretty intense and it's moving out very slowly. It's only moving away at two miles per hour. We'll probably still have flooding and wind and rain for another twenty-four hours," Jamie advised without waiting for us to ask his opinion, "No telling how accessible the roads will be when the water is gone."

"Can we take the dogs?" was our next question. Without discussion between us, we knew the dogs were second in priority only to ourselves and Hazel. We would not leave without them. When Jamie, a dog lover himself, replied, "Of course!", we set about getting the hell out of there.

Jamie took Sky first. He grabbed her collar and towed her with him as he swam off our back deck toward the canal. Sky went quite willingly and swam alongside him. She had always loved to swim, and even in the hurricane-force wind over seventy-five mph, she did as she was asked.

As we watched from the porch, the rain poured down on them as they made their way toward the canal. We could make out the top of the aluminum handrail for the pool ladder just above the wave-capped water and used that to gauge where the canal began. The location of the retaining wall at the canal's edge could only be estimated as the yard, pool, and patio were all still underwater. Jamie was familiar with our property and paused near the canal where he knew our wall to be, though it was completely submerged. It marked the point that the rescue boat couldn't cross. As the boat approached, seemingly out of nowhere through the rain, Jamie passed Sky off to the two other men in the boat, who hauled her in and tried to strap a life jacket on her. In fear, she tried to nip at them for their efforts.

When Jamie returned, I moved back to the bedroom to grab our older dog, Pearl, off the bed and dumped her in his arms. As he left on his next trip to the boat, I explained to Hazel what we were doing. When Jamie returned, he tucked a small dog under each arm. Catherine grabbed Copper, and I lifted Hazel off the bed and into my arms. With that, we set off away from our broken home and out into the ocean surrounding us. I do not remember looking back at the house, though I'm sure it was completely broken and barely recognizable. As we stepped down into the ocean water once again, the cold hit me. The wind gusts were still hurricane-force. Later accounts would estimate seventy-five to eighty mph with ninety mph gusts when we were rescued: still a Category 1 hurricane.

We made our way along the pool deck, shuffling through the waist-high water, fearful of unseen debris in the sea that could trip us and allow the current to take us away. We maneuvered around the pool handrail, knowing this was the direction to go to avoid stepping into the depth of the swimming pool. We stepped down into deeper water at the end of the pool deck, bringing the water up to our chests, and made our way to the submerged canal wall. My knees pressed against the wall in the shoulder-high water. The wind, current, and waves tried to drag me away. I held on tightly to Hazel, who was still wrapped around my chest and waist. We waited for the boat to reappear from around the corner of the waterway, where it was sheltering from the worst of the wind and waves.

I was frightened, knowing there was danger in our current situation, but I had put my trust in Jamie and the other rescuers. They wouldn't have us out in the weather with a young child if they weren't completely sure this was the best option to get us to safety. The rain continued to come down in sheets. As we waited, though, I became more and more aware that our physical strength and pure luck were the only things keeping us safe in a chest-high ocean with wind strong enough to blow us over.

As I glanced across our still-submerge garden, the ocean seemed just as formidable as it had throughout our ordeal. However, with my feet planted on the ground, I felt a brief sense of power over Dorian's reckless and destructive tendencies. We had almost beaten the ocean at its own game. We only had to make it to safety now, with the help of our rescuers. Confidence grew in my psyche as I realized in a flash that maybe the bully that terrorized us might be bested simply by us standing up to it.

And so, we waited, and we waited. Hazel cried, wanting to go back to the house. The skiff arrived but never made it close enough. The guys called out to Jamie, but their words were lost in the wind before I could make out what was said. As the boat left again, Jamie shouted to us over the roar of the wind. The bilge pump in the boat was malfunctioning and not removing the ocean and rain fast enough from inside the boat. They would need to maneuver in just such a way to avoid taking on too much water and risk sinking right there and then. We watched as the skiff disappeared around the corner again. My back muscles, exhausted from all that had already been demanded of them, screamed at me as I tried to maintain my balance.

On Jamie's instruction, we all climbed up onto the two-and-a-half-foot high canal wall to raise ourselves out of the water a bit and have a better chance at fighting the current. We waited. I swayed with the wind. I looked at Catherine, with Copper in her arms. At one point, he seemed to have a seizure or stroke. With her arms wrapped tightly around his chest and under his rear, Cath felt his whole body suddenly tense and shake uncontrollably. Looking down at his face, she could see his eyes widen and roll back slightly. The seizure lasted only a few seconds before his body went limp again. He didn't lose consciousness but briefly, he seemed disoriented.

Watching Copper, I lost my concentration and balance. With the house at our backs some forty feet away, I slipped off the wall backwards. Thankfully my feet met the lawn, completely unseen under the ocean that had invaded our home. Had I fallen forward, I might have ended up in the canal, far too deep to stand or regain any footing. If that had been the case, the raging current of ocean tearing at us would have swallowed me quickly and the rescue mission that was underway could have taken an even more dangerous turn. I managed to regain my footing quickly without losing Hazel, still clinging to my chest.

As we waited, I worried that our rescue may have been premature and that we might be stuck for even longer. The monster storm that raged around us was desperate to separate us, to have us succumb to the exhaustion of our bodies and minds. As Hazel cried, Jamie suggested we go back to the shelter of the house to await the boat. We turned to move back in the direction we had come, but the boat arrived again.

The guys on board shouted that we had to move fast during a brief lull in the gusty wind. They grabbed Hazel from my arms first, then the dogs.

When it was Catherine's turn, she tried desperately to haul herself into the bow of the bobbing, center-console boat, but it was difficult. Time was not on our side.

The guys grabbed Cath's arms and pulled her, and she landed in a bit of a heap on the floor of the small boat, scrambling out of the way to make room for me.

On my turn into the boat, we met the same problem. The boat driver yelled that we had to go as the outboard engine dipped under the waves and made a noise that sounded an awful lot like a dying animal.

I, too, was hauled in the boat by my arms, bruising my leg in the process. As the upper part of my body made it into the boat, I felt the driver turn sharply to avoid another wave dangerously close to swamping the boat entirely.

Jamie hauled himself into the boat from the back and yelled for the driver to move out.

They bailed water out of the back of the boat as we moved forward. We were handed life jackets, and we fumbled in the moving boat to get them on. Finally, we were given a bottle of water each. We sat in the bottom of the twenty-five-foot center console boat and felt each wave as we crashed into it, making our way out of our canal. I held onto two of the dogs while Catherine held on to Hazel. From our seats on the bouncing floor, we could just see over the edge of the boat. There was a mountain of debris floating in the canal as the driver swerved, again and again, to miss a floating tree or dock piling. The ocean water was beige and thick, like a milkshake. It did not resemble the translucent saltwater canal we knew and loved at all.

We asked after our neighbours over the roar of the boat engine and raging storm. The Mackey MacLeay household had been confirmed safe, but we heard the guys in the boat speak of having seen bodies floating in the canal on the way to reach us. I shuddered knowing they could easily have been us. During our time outside on our porch, if anything had gone wrong and the current had separated us, I knew I would have lost everything and possibly even my own life. Tears welled in my eyes as I looked at Catherine and Hazel. It was heart-wrenching knowing that people on the island, people we probably knew, had lost their wife or child or parent to this terrible storm.

The rain stung our faces as the boat continued. The fifteen-minute ride seemed so much longer in my mind. Finally, I was able to get my bearings through the sheets of rain and make out the outline of the Sailing Club House as we approached.

Image courtesy of Catherine Pyfrom

Image courtesy of Catherine Pyfrom

WHERE TO?

We scrambled off the boat, though the water was calmer now in the shelter of the harbour. Jamie instructed us to head up to the main building, and we moved that way in a bit of slow motion through the pouring rain, completely dazed and in shock. We called the dogs along with us as best we could. We had no leads for any of them, and the dogs weren't used to being loose without restrictions. Luckily, with lots of calls, they all managed to follow us up the stairs and into the shelter of the Sailing Club community center.

Inside, Christian, the club manager, met us with dry towels, which we wrapped around ourselves as we shivered. He offered us more water, food, and dry clothes. We accepted the water and dry clothes but asked for a moment on the food. We got Hazel out of the wet clothes and into a dry men's t-shirt, tying it at the bottom to take care of some of the extra space as it swallowed her. Cath and I each took some dry sweatpants and t-shirts and took turns excusing ourselves to the bathroom nearby to change.

The club floor was wet with puddles near the doors and windows with soggy towels stacked in the corners. They were a testament to the battle Christian had already run with Dorian. The air was cool but also humid as the hurricane raged on. With all the windows and doors open, the wind whipped through the room often. The Sailing Club was a familiar place to us. It was often the location of fundraisers and parties, but most recently, we had come weekly with Hazel for swimming lessons in the club pool.

Once we were dry, I drank more water and took a few bites of a dry Pop-Tart.

My body settled into the realization that we were now safe, and I began to feel nauseous. The water I had so desperately gulped down started to make its way back up into my throat. I coughed sharply several times and leaned over a nearby garbage can, fearing that I might vomit.

When the initial nausea passed, I crumpled to the ground with my back against the garbage can, and I sobbed briefly. The weight of the experience was heavy. We had all come so close to death. I had almost lost everything in the world that was so precious to me. As I sat sobbing with tears falling down my face, Cath and Hazel joined me, and we held each other for a few moments of tear-filled relief.

I only allowed myself a few moments to feel the weight of the emotions. Before long, the reality of it all set in again and my mind began reeling with new problems to solve.

Hazel needed food, and despite my upset stomach, so did I. When Christian offered food again, we accepted. He graciously made Catherine and Hazel steak sandwiches and a tuna sandwich for me. Slowly I forced the food into my mouth and chewed, often having to chase each bite with water to get it down my throat.

I knew I needed to eat, but the food was not my top priority at that moment. My mind continued to race and try to solve our next dilemma.

We retrieved our cell phones from the Ziploc bags that had kept them safe through the storm, flood, and rescue. Yet again, they came on as usual, but the cellular signal was sketchy at best. Christian offered us his phone, and we immediately called Charlotte and Pattie in Connecticut. There was a chorus of cheers and joyous tears at our rescue and our safety on the other end of the phone. Pattie's entire family had spent the last twenty-four hours with her and Charlotte, making phone calls to the various rescue agencies. They had been monitoring rescue efforts while hoping and praying for our safe return. The phone connection was terrible, but we could hear and express our joy and gratitude at being alive.

With the joy, though, came the inevitable question, "Now what?" If our house and Jamie's parents' home had been underwater, every house on the canal was underwater, including Charlotte's. We knew we couldn't go there. The Sailing Club was a staging area, not a shelter. We couldn't go to any of the actual shelters on the island with five dogs. We needed somewhere to go.

Suddenly, Copper began barking and ran as fast as his limp would allow in the direction of the stage that was set up against the far wall. The other dogs followed suit immediately, their barking amplified in the large, open room despite the wind that howled outside. They seemed to be trying to get under the stage after something.

"Oh, they've probably found my cat," remarked Christian, though he did not seem very concerned about this at all.

Without a word to Christian or each other, Cath and I dashed across the room, yelling over the barking, trying to call them off: "No! Sky! Come! Nutmeg, Ginger!" We had seen our dogs hunt and kill lizards and birds in our yard many times. There was no doubt in our minds that if they managed to catch the cat, it would not live through the experience.

As I reached the huddle of dogs, with their heads buried in the gap under the stage, I grabbed at Sky's collar first, deeming her the most dangerous. She resisted and pulled hard against my attempts to drag her away from the pack. As I stepped back, I almost tripped over Pearl. As I righted myself, I bent and scooped her up easily with my free hand.

I backed away to give Cath room to grab whichever dog she could. "I'm gonna put them in the bathroom," I called to Cath as I moved in that direction. The bathroom was the only place in the building where we could close the door to keep the dogs isolated from the now-terrified cat.

I shoved the two dogs into the women's bathroom and closed the door with a loud bang. As I moved swiftly in the direction of the stage again, I could see Catherine had managed to grab Nutmeg and Ginger under each arm. Copper, ever the hunter despite the near-death experience, was the instigator and continued to bark incessantly. Before I made it back to grab Copper, an orange and white tabby cat made an appearance, trying to escape from under the stage with most of the pack now restrained. "No, Copper!" I yelled as I reached him. There was a rolling ball of dog and cat that slid across the floor as they fought before the cat made a run for it, and I grabbed Copper before he could give chase.

As I walked behind Cath into the bathroom with Copper in my arms, I could feel his heart beating rapidly in my palm and his tail wagging happily. "Fool dog!" I scolded under my breath at him, but he didn't seem bothered.

Once all the dogs were secured, I went to the little kitchen and found a water bowl. I took it to the bathroom for the dogs, but all I saw was blood when I opened the door. There was blood up the wall, on the interior of the door, and along the ground.

"Cath! There's blood everywhere," I called for help.

We inspected each dog and found the source of the blood. The cat attack had left Copper with a hole in his chest the size of my fingernail. Catherine tried to clean up some of the blood in the room as I sat on the floor, with all the dogs crowding me, trying to stop the bleeding with pressure and a hand towel.

With most of the blood cleaned and Hazel calling for us, Catherine left me on the bathroom floor with Copper in my lap to check on Hazel. I continued the pressure for a while until most of the bleeding stopped, then cleaned up what I could. I checked the other dogs for injuries and insisted they each drink water. By then, I could hear more voices and noise in the main room. Someone else had arrived. I left the dogs locked in the bathroom to investigate.

In the main room, I saw Jamie's parents, the Roses, and their friends, the Campbells, who had been sheltering with them during Dorian. Jamie and the other rescuers had dropped us off and immediately gone back out to retrieve these folks. These people were more acquaintances, but we all hugged nonetheless in the relief of everyone's safety.

"We had a bunch of buckets in the attic, so we all sat on those. And we used one for a toilet," I heard Jamie's mother, Chris, explaining. "We went into our attic once the water got as high as our knees. It was rising so fast we didn't want to wait!"

"At least you had buckets," Cath retorted. "We weren't so lucky. Poor Hazel slept inside of a Rubbermaid bin."

"We heard that Dave and Cathy had knee-high water in their second story," another person recalled.

"Yes, that's what Jamie told us," I responded quietly. "If the water had come any higher, it would've been inside our attic." I really did not feel like socializing and exchanging pleasantries. I was exhausted and overwhelmed, and making small talk was not something I felt capable of just then.

"We heard from friends out east that it's even worse past High Rock," Colin, Jamie's father, told us. "People tried to escape their houses by boat, but the storm was too much and took them away. There are a lot of people missing."

This statement made us think of our friends who owned a farm near there. "Has anyone heard from George and Sissel? Did they stay at the farm for the storm?" Cath asked.

"No one has heard yet. The roads aren't passable, and no one has been able to reach them," came the response.

The conversation grew quiet as everyone in the group pondered if our friends were even safe as we stood recounting our own stories. There was a silent moment, and then Colin changed the subject and spoke up: "The sailboat is gone. We didn't see it anywhere on the ride in."

With the shift from fear for the lives lost to more conversations about the damaged property, Cath and I took a slight step back from the group to breathe. Introverts by nature, crowds were not comfortable for us. With the arrival of more people imminent, we started discussing where we could go. The Roses would make their way to Jamie's house when the weather improved.

Chris overheard us and said, "I'm sure you could come with us to Nikki and Jamie's house. It'll be a tight squeeze, but we can make it work."

We thanked her for the offer but knew that would not work. Our five dogs, with their four dogs, plus a dozen people, was not going to be a situation we could recover well in. When asked if we had somewhere else we could go, we were at a loss.

"Should we try to call your cousins?' I asked Cath in a hushed voice.

Catherine used Christian's cell phone and tried to reach her cousins but was unsuccessful. Based on the information coming in, Catherine's cousins' home should have been spared from the floodwater. Assuming their home had not been damaged by the wind, perhaps we might be able to shelter there until the storm was gone and more permanent plans could be made. We couldn't reach any of our other friends on the island to ask for help and a place to stay.

As we talked with the group, more and more stories of the storm emerged. Sections of the island had been under over thirty feet of ocean. The airport was all but gone. Grocery stores and hardware stores were underwater.

Hazel's school was under three feet of water. The hospital was underwater. Roads were still blocked in many places with floodwater, and getting around at that moment still meant a large vehicle, high off the ground, a lot of ingenuity, and a whole lot of luck. The storm outside continued at Tropical Storm force.

Then there were the stories of people. We heard some of our neighbours had left before the storm and were safe with friends in a different section of the island. However, there were stories of those who had not won their battle with Dorian. A man's body had been found clinging high in the trees. The image of this person who met such a horrific death alone, hoping to hold on long enough to survive, made my stomach churn. It sounded like a terrible way to end a life. I have thought of this person, whose name I never learned, often. His death has continued to be an image in my mind of what could have happened to any of us.

Rumours were being retold under hushed breath and out of Hazel's earshot. There were stories of children who had been ripped away from their parents in the floodwaters. The stories were dreadful and there was no way to know how much was hearsay and how much was the truth. The images of people lost to the storm were more than my trauma brain could take. We moved decidedly away from the conversation to a corner on our own.

As Catherine and I pulled away from the group, we tried again to reach her cousins. Hazel sat curled in a blanket on the couch, a soggy stuffed toy tucked under each arm. We knew we needed to find someplace more stable and quieter to settle for her, if not for ourselves. Our ordeal was still far from over. On our third try, we finally reached Catherine's cousins. More acquaintances than friends, they were the only ones we could reach with certainty that their situation was more stable than our own.

The conversation with the cousins was disjointed with bad reception and dropped calls. We tried texting, but a full discussion was virtually impossible. Finally, after a lot of back and forth, we asked for a place to stay. The answer came to us on a delay: "We'll get back to you." Her cousins had room for us in an already full house but nowhere (or no desire) to accommodate the five dogs we had almost died trying to save. This was a kick in the gut when we were at our lowest. We struggled to think of somewhere else we could go but did not come up with an answer. None of the hotels on the island would take dogs, and leaving the dogs behind at the Sailing Club was not an option.

There were more disjointed conversations by text and static-ridden calls. It was suggested that perhaps the cousins could house us and put the dogs in the neighbours' garage. We waited for confirmation. As we waited, a truck arrived with more acquaintances carrying towels and supplies for the club as more evacuees were expected.

There were more hugs and expressions of gratefulness exchanged, and more stories were retold.

The new arrivals, Nathalie and her husband Wayne, had maneuvered their single cab truck around the island to reach the Sailing Club in two feet of water at times. Wayne explained how they had to backtrack several times to get around debris and deeper flood water to find a safe path. Nathalie asked us if we needed a ride somewhere as they prepared to head back home. We did need a ride, but we had nowhere to go. We had not yet heard back from Catherine's cousins with confirmation that we could come. At the same time, the Sailing Club was less than ideal with the dogs still locked in the bathroom and more people expected as the rescuers made their way back from their third trip. We quickly decided to go with Nathalie and Wayne to the cousins' house and figure everything else out once we got there.

Rain was still coming down in torrents with winds of at least sixty mph. I released the dogs from the bathroom, and chaos ensued as we each tried to grab a dog and corral Hazel toward the waiting truck. The single cab truck could hold two adults, maybe three in a pinch. We squeezed four adults, a child, and five dogs in the truck in the middle of tropical storm-force wind. Closing the passenger side door took several attempts. In the end, we were piled high on top of one another, and I found myself curled between the seat and the dashboard, my foot twisted at an abnormal angle underneath me, with legs and dogs everywhere.

Once the doors were closed, Wayne pulled out of the parking lot away from the Sailing Club very slowly. As he drove, he had to avoid water and debris, downed electrical poles and wires, all while trying to maneuver with terrified dogs sitting on the stick shift half the time. Less than five minutes into the ride, my right foot, still curled under me, went completely numb. Each bump in the road or quick stop pinched my tired muscles. I took several deep breaths, forcing my body to remain as calm as possible in the impossible circumstances.

Less than halfway to our intended destination, we came upon another vehicle on the road. Nathalie and Wayne recognised the SUV and its driver. They had already been in touch and knew the driver, yet another acquaintance, was out in the storm intending to help where he could as well. The two vehicles stopped in the middle of the isolated road, and we rolled down the window to talk. Noel, seeing and hearing our predicament, insisted some of us get into the SUV with him, and he would help ferry us to the cousin's house. More quick decisions were made. Cath, Hazel, and I got out of the truck, leaving the dogs with Nathalie and Wayne. As I uncurled my legs, I could not feel my foot, but somehow still managed to hobble into the front seat of the SUV as Cath and Hazel got into the back, once again saturated with rain.

The truck led the way toward town with the SUV following as we told Noel our story of survival. It was a brief version, recounted with little emotion, as the shock continued to press down on our psyches. We told Noel where we were heading and the tentative nature of our plans. Without hesitation, he explained that he, his wife and kids, and another family were staying in a foreigner's vacation home in one of the island's affluent neighbourhoods, Fortune Bay. The house had seven bedrooms and a generator. We were more than welcome to come there if we needed to. I turned briefly to look at Catherine in the back seat. She and I had an entire conversation in the space of five seconds without saying a word. We thanked Noel and accepted gratefully. A quick cell call to the truck in front and our new destination was set.

Noel recounted more stories of storm damage, avoiding floodwater and downed trees, as he spoke. I only listened vaguely and responded with "Oh, okay" or "Wow" every few minutes in a feeble attempt to feign attention. I was too exhausted for small talk, even with someone who was offering a roof over our heads. I knew that I should try to muster more enthusiasm for the conversation. After all, it was pure chance that we had run into Noel. As an acquaintance, we had only ever said a quick hello at the school drop-off line. There was no reason we would ever have reached out to him or his family for help like he was now offering us. I knew people were relying on strangers at that very moment. Somehow good fortune was purely on our side in yet another miracle that we happened to cross Noel's path.

As we drove to the Fortune Bay house, we looked at the devastation of the island. Trees were uprooted or stripped bare of leaves. Power lines were down everywhere. Homes were flooded and cars floated. We passed a couple of other vehicles on the road during our journey, but the storm was still too dangerous for anyone to be outside. Some vehicles were civilian rescuers, like Jamie and crew, out trying to help where they could. Others were gawkers with homes unaffected by the storm. We drove off-road in places to avoid water. At one point, I lost my bearings, unsure what street we were on, then I saw a familiar entry gate sign and recognized we were close to our destination.

When we arrived at the big vacation house, it became apparent that parts of the island had fared far better than others. In this affluent neighbourhood, roofs and windows remained intact, partly due to better, more recent construction, and partly due to the neighbourhood's location away from the worst of the floodwaters. No storm surge flood water inundated the streets and yards. A few fences were down with lots of tree debris, but all in all, the area looked unscathed. The rain began to abate, though the wind continued. There were very few people outside their homes, as most continued to remain indoors, waiting for the storm to pass.

At the Fortune Bay house, we herded the dogs into the two-car garage that Noel and Wayne manually opened for us. We stood for a moment and thanked Nathalie and Wayne profusely for all their help. The conversation was short-lived as Hazel was eager to get inside, and we were all still wet. The garage doors were closed behind us, and we followed Noel through a long hallway toward the living area of the house. Noel's wife, Britton, was surprised to see him back so soon. Noel quickly explained why we were in tow, and more hugs were spread around. Britt welcomed us, as did the other family staying there. Again, we recounted our harrowing ordeal with little emotional reaction on our part. We hadn't yet begun to process our trauma. Our story was met with awe and our new hosts sang praises at our ability to survive. Britt offered us food and water, which we declined initially. Then she offered Hazel some dry clothes from her girls' suitcases. We readily accepted, and we were grateful to be able to get Hazel dry and warm. In clean clothes and with a roof over our heads, Hazel happily joined Britt and Noel's two daughters on the floor in the living room to play.

With Hazel settled, we turned again to check on the dogs and bring them water. The garage was very dark and noisy as the wind whipped through the spaces between the garage doors. The looming storm clouds made it quite dark, and there was only a single window to let a tiny amount of light in. The dogs all but mauled me, having been left alone in a strange place for only five or ten minutes. I loved on them, comforting them as much as I was gathering comfort for myself. I shivered as a blast of wind crossed my still-wet back. I reassured the dogs that I would be back, but I had to physically force them not to follow me into the house as I closed the door.

Back in the living room, a neighbour arrived with more dry clothes. The men's t-shirts, sports shorts, and boxers would fit us well enough to get out of the wet clothes. Someone mentioned the swimming pool in the backyard. Even though the Fortune Bay house was on the canal, like ours, the ocean had not risen high enough there to swamp the pool with salt water. The swimming pool remained fresh, filled with rainwater and floating palm fronds. It was the closest thing to a bath we would get with no running water yet restored. Britt grabbed us soap, shampoo, and some dry towels. Cath and I went outside with Hazel and stripped down to our underwear. The pool was ice cold, and the sharp temperature change cut our breath. Hazel squealed as I dunked her in the pool water and rubbed soap over her, trying to wash off most of the bacteria and saltwater from our last forty hours of existence.

Once Hazel was clean, dry, and redressed, Cath and I each took our turn to get clean. It mattered very little that the pool was completely open, and all the neighbours could see us. Our modesty was completely non-existent as our basic needs took overall thought. The water was cold, but it was clean. The smell and dry, crusted salt were removed. We worked quickly as spits of rain continued off and on. The wind grabbed at our towels, trying to tear them away.

Once we were dry and redressed in strangers' clothes, I checked on the dogs again. This time I was able to feed them with a bag of dry dog food brought to the house by someone else, another neighbour, wanting to help. The dogs picked at the food, too stressed to consider food a priority just yet. They barked and whined at the closed door as I returned to the living room once again. This time we accepted the food offered to us, and for the first time in over forty hours, I sat.

I sat, knowing that we were all safe and dry. I could hear Hazel giggle from across the room as she played with the other kids.

Britt made some sandwiches and brought us sodas. This time the food disappeared quickly without nausea. It could have been the finest five-star meal. I breathed deeply.

Britt insisted they had more than enough food to feed an army. Hazel would have a bed, as would we, that night. Noel confirmed we could stay for as long as we needed to.

I breathed deeply as I looked at Catherine sitting next to me. I reached out to her, and our eyes filled with tears as we grabbed each other in a deep, life-affirming hug. We were alive.

Image courtesy of Catherine Pyfrom

THE NEXT STEPS

In the hours following our rescue, we made countless tear-filled calls. We had only spoken to Charlotte and Pattie and Catherine's cousins at the Sailing Club to alert everyone of our safety. With all our immediate needs met at the Fortune Bay house, we excused ourselves from the group, leaving Hazel entertained by the kids. We phoned Catherine's other sisters and best friend. I called my parents and sister. We tried to reach out to friends on the island to learn who was safe and assure them of our safety. Those contacts all muddle together in my memory. Some of them might have been texts, and others emails. All were filled with "I love you," and so much gratitude for our safety. Relief washed over us both. We couldn't stop hugging each other in tight, bone-breaking moments, almost as though we needed to be sure that this aftermath was real. That we were, in fact, safe and alive and together.

The first evening at the Fortune Bay house was surreal. We sat in a strange place, surrounded by people we had only ever said hello to a handful of times. We ate the food and drinks they provided. We even had a small cocktail our hosts insisted we needed to calm our nerves after such an ordeal, though neither of us felt any of its effects. It is difficult to explain the emotions of settling Hazel into bed that night.

"Is the storm gone now?" Hazel asked as she lay in the bed, still clutching the purple stuffed dachshund, Ellie. She had a look of worry on her face.

"Yes, baby!" we reassured her. "It's moved far away now."

"So, the water won't come back again, right?" she pressed, wanting to be certain we understood her question.

I glanced up at Catherine over Hazel's head and tears filled my eyes. "No, sweetheart. The water is gone. Dorian is gone. It won't come back," Catherine told her, leaning down to hug and comfort her.

"I love you, Hazel," I told her as I rubbed her leg. "You are safe. We are all safe."

"I love you, too," Hazel responded, and then thought for a moment before asking, "What are we going to do tomorrow?"

It was a reasonable question but not one we had an answer to. In her young mind, she was asking to learn what to expect during a completely new and unpredictable time.

For us, her question was filled with heavy decisions we hadn't even had time yet to ask ourselves.

"We will probably find a way to go back to the house tomorrow, maybe..." I explained.

"I don't want to go," she jumped in, quickly making her feelings known.

"It's okay, Hazel. You don't have to go if you don't want to," Cath said, trying to calm her.

Sensing her anxiety ramping up, I got Hazel to sit up on the bed between us and spoke calmly to her. "Listen, Hazel. No matter what happens tomorrow or over the next few days or weeks, the only thing that matters is that we are all safe and we are all together, okay?"

"Okay," she spoke quietly, and leaned into the both of us for another hug.

As the three of us sat alone together on the bed, we hugged and kissed and spoke of how much we loved each other. We spoke briefly of our house and wondered aloud what would happen now. Hazel fell asleep relatively quickly that night, all things considered. And she miraculously slept through the night.

We excused ourselves from the group in the living room later that first night. Everyone was very sympathetic to our exhaustion. It had been forty hours since either of us had slept. I walked the dogs outside in the dark, calling to keep them close to me without leashes to restrain them. None of them seemed very interested in the dog food we offered them, and Copper seemed to be limping more and moving even more slowly than usual. Pearl whined desperately, arguing about being locked in the garage again instead of inside sleeping on a couch. The air was dry and cool with only a slight breeze. The rain had finally ceased. Dorian had finally left our island and was quickly moved up the eastern seaboard by the Gulf Stream.

The storm was over, but our new reality had yet to begin. We lay close on a queen-sized bed in the heat of our assigned bedroom. The windows remained shuttered, unable to let any of the cool outside air in. I lay in the dark, remembering not to be ungrateful as the discomfort pressed onward. A soft, safe bed covered in sweat was far preferable to the cold attic, counting the moments in the dark to our inevitable death. We were alive, not hungry, dry, and in an actual bed. There was no room for complaint.

In the darkness, Cath and I spoke of our next steps. With the storm surge floodwater having now receded, we knew we would need to find a way to get back to our house. Looting would begin almost right away. We knew this, and we worried about what might be salvageable from our home. We feared for the safe particularly, bolted to the floor of our bedroom closet. We wondered together what else might have made it through the storm. After exiting the attic, our time in the house was very brief, and anything we had seen was filtered through a lens of shock and trauma. It was hard to remember what we had seen and to comprehend what might still be viable. Together we decided that the next day's priority had to be going back to the house.

I feared particularly for our passports and documents, left sitting in the attic after our rescue. The process of replacing a passport in the Bahamas was excessively lengthy and would require at least two trips to Nassau. Without our passports, we would be stuck on the island without the option of leaving until they were replaced.

As I thought of the valuable things left in our home, now unsecured from possible thieves, my mind went to the hard drives. I could not remember in the chaos of the water's advancement into our house whether I had removed them from the safe and put them in one of our bags or if they remained inside the safe. With every photo we had ever taken stored on them, they were a physical manifestation of our love and life together. My stomach bottomed out at the thought of losing them.

With our phones charged with borrowed power cords, we learned that our SOS Facebook posts got over one hundred comments filled with prayers for our safety and advice on what to do to stay alive. Later the comments section was used by Charlotte and Pattie to confirm our rescue to our friends and acquaintances. We used the social media platform to send a mass thank you to everyone who had tried to keep track of us during the storm. And we posted updates on our whereabouts and our plans.

The following day dawned with anxiety and helplessness. Coffee with our hosts was a conversation filled with more stories passed through WhatsApp messages and early morning visitors. We found out that over a hundred of our friends, acquaintances, and strangers had a running WhatsApp chat to network our whereabouts and safety during our ordeal. This was humbling, to say the least, especially when considering that the circle of people we called friends was tiny. Some of the text messages following our rescue were read aloud to us and were filled with joy at the news of our safety. We struggled to hold back the tears of gratitude. In a tight-knit community, that we still felt rather ostracized from at times, more people than we would speak to in the run of a month had been praying for our safe return.

Eventually, the conversation turned to the day's plans. On the agenda at the Fortune Bay house was getting the super-sized generator up and running. It needed an unexpected part, and the men were headed out shortly to try to procure it. As they prepared to leave, we learned that the feared looting had begun. Police had been posted and were restricting access to our neighbourhood, only allowing homeowners to that side of the island. This news brought fear and relief at the same time. Surely things had already been removed from our home, but the police were at least attempting to prevent it. Noel left in search of the generator part with a sixteen-gauge shotgun in tow. It was a licensed hunting weapon, but open carry was illegal. The stories of brazen looters made everyone nervous, and the security it provided outweighed the risk of carrying the gun.

After the guys left, we explained to Britt that we very much wanted to get back to our house to salvage what we could. We spoke about logistics and inquired about how accessible the roads were. Now, all we needed was a vehicle. At that point, we had no idea where our car was, having last seen it two days before, underwater. We knew that after the ocean flooded it, the vehicle would likely never run again. Britt offered to drive us later in the day after a visit to secure her own oceanfront home and restaurant. We were frustrated. We didn't like depending on others. Our feelings were motivated less by accepting the charity and more because we were very used to our independence and doing things for ourselves. She promised to make some calls to see if anyone had an extra, functioning car we could borrow for a few hours.

Hazel happily played on the floor with the other girls. Hearing our story, neighbours generously brought over a large bin full of toys, including a dollhouse. We watched them play and we talked about their resilience as kids. Tears filled my eyes as I thought of how close we had come to death. We noticed how a toy ladder had been propped up against the dollhouse, and Hazel had a doll climbing onto the roof. We asked her what the doll was doing.

Hazel's reply hit us all hard. She said, "The doll needs to get on the roof to be safe."

"Oh, okay," I said to Hazel, and turned to Cath, with tears welling in our eyes. For a moment the whole room went eerily quiet. No one knew quite what to say when hearing the trauma through the mouth of a six-year-old. As I looked around the room, hoping for some insight from virtual strangers, I saw a tear roll down the cheek of the largest man in the room.

Without a word to one another, we walked over to where Hazel was playing on the floor and gathered her up in a family hug. As we held each other in our arms, I thought of how close we had come to losing our lives. Tears spilled out onto our cheeks as relief and fear, in an odd mix, swirled around us.

"We're safe now, babe," I mumbled into Catherine's shoulder near the back of Hazel's head as we hugged. The weight of the knowledge that this trauma would stay with Hazel for the rest of her life made my heart hurt in a way I didn't recall ever feeling before. I made an absentminded mental note to prioritize therapy for Hazel as soon as possible. I knew trauma could and would have long-term, often devastating effects if left untreated. We would all need help processing the nightmare we were still living.

By mid-day, we received visitors. A family whose daughter was in Hazel's class had learned where to find us. They came to offer to have Hazel come to their house to play for a few hours. It was a sparkle of normalcy in the chaos. We agreed, and Hazel went willingly and happily with a smile on her face. By then, we had also heard from our dear friend, Kent. He and his mother had made a daring escape early in the storm and drove through three feet of saltwater to higher ground to escape the rising ocean water. While several of his personal and business vehicles had drowned in the flooding as well, he offered us one of his older trucks that had made it through. Unfortunately, he couldn't bring it to us until later that day. We were grateful, nonetheless.

By early afternoon another acquaintance arrived at the Fortune Bay house, ready to drive us to our home to begin salvaging what we could. By that time, the stress and trauma of the last seventy-two hours had caused a raging migraine for me. The migraine made speaking difficult and bright sunshine excruciating. My medicine was in a Ziploc bag inside the attic at our house. Saving medicine was something we had managed to think of and hang on to during the race to stay alive.

Our acquaintance, Lyndah, arrived with a camera in hand, and we loaded into her small SUV. The drive to our neighbourhood was like something seen in video footage following the massive tsunami in Indonesia years ago. The roads were drivable but covered in seaweed, trees, random household items, and downed power lines. Personal belongings hung in pine trees that had been stripped of their bark at the maximum level of the storm surge, at least thirty feet off the ground in places. A clothes hamper sat upright on a street corner. Next to it lay a mangled lawn chair. As we drove, we could see directly into the living room of a home that had an exterior wall blown out. Flood water lines were visible in the wind-burnt forest and on the exterior walls of the homes as we drove. We passed Hazel's school. It would be weeks, if not months, before it would be repaired and usable. We drove by our old house in an area that had not flooded. The house was intact, but the tropical gardens we had spent many hours creating were stripped and broken, with the lawn covered in leaves reminiscent of a New England Fall.

As we got closer to the bridge and the canal system, we saw boats, big and small, taken from the ocean and tossed into the bushes and onto roadways. One boat caught my eye. I recalled noticing it in the pre-hurricane preparation. This was the boat we had watched as the owners crossed-tied it with multiple lines in a tiny, man-made cove just at the base of the bridge. Cath and I had commented days before that the owners had done quite an extensive job securing it. Now the boat, some fifty feet in length, sat in the forest several hundred feet from the last place I had seen it.

When we reached the top of the bridge to cross into our neighbourhood, the police stopped us, and Lyndah rolled down her window. We confirmed our names and where we lived for the officer. He was happy to take our word on our claim to be homeowners in the area. We had nothing to offer as proof, as our entire lives had been under ocean water for some thirty-six hours. Descending the bridge, we noticed the debris line of more seaweed, branches, and garbage. The line was just a few feet from the peak of the bridge. We would later learn that the bridge was thirty feet above sea level. The debris line showed hurricane surge had reached some twenty-five feet in that spot.

At the base of the bridge, we passed another vehicle that we quickly recognised as another friend. We pulled off the side of the road and jumped out. We melted into her embrace, and floods of tears fell. Our friend had been over to check on Charlotte's home, less than half a mile from ours, and to see if she could find anyone who had any information on our well-being.

Our conversation lasted a few minutes before my migraine pain led me back to the car ahead of Catherine. I worried I might pass out. It was hot and humid with the afternoon sun baking down on us. Catherine and Lyndah continued to talk to our friend for several more minutes, briefly recounting our survival and the stories of those who had not been as lucky. Our photographer friend asked permission to take some photos to document all that had happened. We agreed. Returning to the car, we began again to make our way into our neighbourhood.

8:29

Catherine Pyfrom-Tara Pyfrom

Catherine Pyfrom-Tara Pyfrom
Monday at 9:49 AM ·

Help

  Rosalie Pyfrom and 27 others   114 Comments

👍 Like   💬 Comment   ➤ Share

Catherine Pyfrom-Tara Pyfrom
Monday at 8:10 AM ·

Help the water won't atop rising

THE REALITY OF ALL
THAT WAS LOST

Entering Pine Bay was like entering the film set of a post-apocalyptic movie. Massive boats sat on the land, broken with gaping holes in the hulls. Houses were missing roofs and walls. Trees were twisted, snapped off, and hanging in the few power lines still attached to the electrical poles that had survived the monstrous winds. A garage door was torn off and lay in the front yard. Cars were upended and covered in debris. Much of what we saw looked like a bomb had gone off. Most of the buildings still standing had visible water lines with obvious seaweed attached near the top of the walls, in some cases halfway up the pitch of the roof.

We went to Charlotte's house first. The decision was just as logistical as it was emotional. Charlotte's house was closer to the neighbourhood entrance, but we may have been prolonging the inevitable pain of seeing our own home again. Pulling into Charlotte's driveway, her bright coral-coloured home came into view. The very first thing that caught our eyes was her detached garage. The concrete block walls remained, but there was no sign of the rest of the structure at all. The roof was missing, as were the garage door and windows. Charlotte's small blue SUV was still parked inside. The wind and ocean had managed to move the vehicle. Instead of sitting head-in as it would normally be parked, it was sitting catty-cornered so that the entire passenger's side of the car was visible in the opening left by the missing garage door.

Across the driveway lay the trunk of a Bismarck Palm, thirty feet tall, that used to stand next to the circular driveway. The other massive palms remained standing guard over the entry, though the fronds were gone entirely, leaving only bare sticks like dock pilings. Littered over the driveway were all of Charlotte's possessions. Some trinkets lay smashed while others sat perfectly upright as though someone had gently rested them in the now-brown grass as lawn ornaments. Her beautiful tropical oasis was now a collection of brown sticks missing leaves and upended trees crisscrossing the pathways. Most of her PVC fencing on one side lay in the neighbour's yard. The chain link fencing on the opposite side was twisted and leaning, with tree trunks weighing heavily on it in places.

As we made our way up to her front door, I noticed a McCormick's spice container lying gently in the boxwood hedge. This small item, obviously from Charlotte's kitchen, so light and buoyant, struck me. How and why had such an insignificant item survived and remained?

At the landing of the house, the front door was closed, but two other exterior doors were missing at the front of the house. One doorway led to what had been the laundry room. The washing machine had been forced out of the room and onto the front porch by the floodwater. Through the other exterior doorway leading to a guest bedroom, we could see broken furniture, clothes, picture frames, and insulation covering the floor in a pile no less than four feet high. We stood in the doorway, dumbfounded. The roof was missing, and we could see the blue sky through the bedroom door.

It was clear that just getting into the house was going to be a monumental task. However, we were highly motivated by our salvage mission. We had learned from Charlotte that in her second-floor master bedroom closet, there was cash, family photographs, jewelry, and dry clothes, assuming they had all survived the storm. We worried about looters and the cash. Charlotte's jewelry was valuable if it could be found and recovered.

Slowly and gently, we picked each step with care, fearful of the rubble that could easily slice open a foot or leg. Getting medical attention would be damn near impossible. None of us could afford to need stitches or a cast at that point. As we made our way into the house, we discovered that the roof on the right side of the first floor was completely gone. We never made it into the second guest bedroom on that side of the house, as broken furniture made accessing it impossible. Through the living room, we were able to pick our way through a fifteen-foot-long path over silt-covered books, couch cushions, and a desk chair to make it to the staircase to the second floor. Each step was like walking on a child's toy "Slip-n-Slide", covered in mud and random items. One wrong step and we both would've gone down.

From the pausing point at the base of the staircase, we could see into Charlotte's kitchen and dining room. Cabinets had fallen off the wall, the refrigerator was leaning precariously, and the china cabinet and dining room furniture were all smashed. The contents of the two rooms were lying everywhere, and just getting into those rooms was impossible without the help of a bulldozer.

We decided to attempt to reach the master bedroom on the second floor. The stairs were also covered in ocean mud and seaweed mixed with papers, clothes, and other miscellaneous items. It looked like the interior of the dining room and kitchen had experienced a washing machine of ocean water and over one hundred and eighty-five mph wind. The heavy wood furniture had smashed several hundred times into the side of the staircase, causing a portion of it to buckle and collapse. Climbing the stairs was dangerous, even more hazardous than just picking our way through the first floor.

The first step up the staircase held my weight, and my foot felt firm, not slippery. I took each step slowly. I tested each step with my total weight and ensured I secured my hands each time before attempting the next step. Catherine followed a few steps behind, taking care to step in my footprint with a sense of security that those places must be strong enough to get up the stairs.

Looking up the staircase, we could see the watermark of the tide's final level two steps from the landing. No water had reached the second floor at all. No wind had disturbed the contents, and the roof and windows had remained secure. The air in the upstairs space was stuffy and smelled wet with humidity. The damp smell was a forewarning of what would soon come. With the outside temperatures skyrocketing to nearly ninety degrees on the bright, sunny day, mold and mildew would blossom quickly even in places that had not been wet with the storm surge.

When we reached the landing at the top of the stairs, I leaned against the wall, my head pounding from the exertion mixed with the migraine. I squinted my eyes through the pain and looked around. It was as though we had instantly stepped through some weird pre-Dorian portal. The tiny home office on the landing was completely untouched. Everything was in its exact place, not so much as a book off a shelf. In the desk chair, there was a circular indentation covered in cat fur where Charlotte's cat, Nimbus, often slept.

We opened the door to the master bedroom and the hurricane and horror of the last seventy-two hours melted away for a brief second. Charlotte's bed was made neatly. Her laptop bag sat casually on the edge of the chest, situated at the end of her bed. Her dresser was lined with trinkets, and her bookshelves were filled with books. Mementos of her life were intact throughout the room. The entire scene looked just as it did when we had last been in that room during one of Charlotte's visits. She was safe in the US, but her life was in the things collected, just like ours. Most of it was now lost to the demons of Dorian on the first floor.

Regret hit me hard as I realized that our decision to remain in our home was a mistake. Looking around the untouched room, I imagined briefly what it would have looked like if we had chosen to shelter there. We would have feared for the security of the roof and windows throughout the storm just as we had in our home. We would have spent the long night fearful that the water would reach even higher and trap us, just as we had in the attic. However, we would have been far more comfortable riding out the storm in Charlotte's bedroom than in the dark discomfort of our attic. Regret tore at my heart briefly and tears filled my eyes, but I squeezed them away quickly and got to work.

In the master closet, Catherine dug through an unlocked filing cabinet for jewelry, cash, and photographs stored there. We were salvaging them for Charlotte and saving them from the looters that would eventually make their way upstairs to strip everything of value they could. In the corner of the large walk-in closet sat a black garbage bag, half-full of clothes that Charlotte intended to donate on her next visit. We dumped out the contents and began sorting for usable clothes. We had only the clothes donated to us the day before, already covered in mud and ill-fitting at best. We found t-shirts and elastic waist shorts, underwear, and socks, and even saw two pairs of old Croc shoes. It felt odd briefly, sifting through Charlotte's clothes, but the feeling was fleeting as this was still survival mode. We needed clothes and cash, and we had Charlotte's blessing to take whatever we could.

Once we loaded ourselves with whatever we could carry and deemed necessary or valuable, we made our way back down the treacherous staircase. At the bottom, we met Lyndah, and she helped us carry two garbage bags and several armfuls of things to her SUV. We all had to take care as we picked our way through the rubble again. At one point, I stepped on what appeared to be a stack of magazines outside what used to be the powder room. The stack gave way slightly, and I slipped. I was able to brace myself against one of the interior walls, still covered in soggy drywall. As I readjusted my footing, I stepped onto something else, and a god-awful glass-breaking sound echoed. I looked down to see a drinking glass, shattered underneath my foot. Instantly, Cath and our friend called out from ahead to make sure I was okay. Luckily, I was still sporting the sewage-soaked sneakers that I had weathered the storm in. They protected my feet from any injury. I made my way out of the house, leaving the same way we had entered, still marvelling at the missing roof in the guest bedroom.

Despite the horrible pounding in my head and the stabbing pain behind my left eye from the migraine that persisted, I helped lug the garbage bags into the car and got ready to leave for our next stop. When we were all situated in the car again, I put my head back against the seat and briefly closed my eyes. I had often had to function at reasonably high levels when suffering from migraines over the years. I was used to pushing through the pain, but this was taking that ability to a whole new level.

The physical pain I was feeling left no room to feel the emotions of what I had seen. It would be weeks and months before I even began to process it. At that moment, the physical pain was now causing nausea. Nausea only happened rarely when I got a migraine. I normally had access to the medication before it ever got this bad. I wondered how I would manage to climb back into the attic to retrieve the pills in the dark while in this much pain.

I felt the car begin to move. I opened my eyes for a second to see we were driving down the lane toward the cul-de-sac, inspecting the damages. As we passed the driveway of the construction zone of the neighbours' house, we noticed a truck parked outside and activity at the entrance. Pulling over, Catherine and Lyndah jumped out to check on them. I moved far more slowly, debating whether I could even muster the energy to get out, let alone have a conversation. I squinted through the sunlight that was shooting daggers through my brain.

The family was safe, having weathered the storm elsewhere. We shared more stories of survival and loss; more stories of people who drowned, pulled from their loved one's arms while trying to escape to higher ground. There were more tears shed for those who were still missing.

I sat on the edge of what would be the neighbours' garage one day, only listening half-heartedly. I held my head in my hands, and for another very brief moment, tears began to well in my eyes as the weight of the physical and emotional pain pressed down on me. The neighbour touched my shoulder and asked if I was okay. Before I could answer, Catherine explained that we were on our way to our house to retrieve my medication and to see what, if anything, could be salvaged. I would find out weeks later that our photographer friend had snapped a photo of me at that moment, overcome with pain both physical and emotional.

With our mission renewed, we returned to the car and drove toward our house. I recall looking at roofs torn open like tin cans with a dull can opener. Walls were missing on neighbours' homes and boats were tossed into the pine trees. As we passed another friend's home, we speculated on the state of their second-story garage apartment, wondering if the water had reached the inside of their meagre studio space. We hoped they were safe as they had sheltered at their parents' house, further inland.

When we rounded the corner to our street, we were struck by the stark and surprising sight of a brand-new Bahamian flag flying from our neighbour's house. It was a testament to the resilience and the plain stubborn nature of Bahamians: proud even in the face of complete and total disaster, optimistic in their ability to recover and rebuild. It was a beautiful sight: the bright blue and yellow in contrast to the black triangle. I wanted their optimism to comfort me. I wanted it to make me believe that we, too, could recover from this tragedy, that we all could recover. While the flag's beauty struck me instantly, its message was not as easily received.

The Butlers, to whom we had spoken during the storm and to whom we had hoped, unwittingly, to swim in the height of the wind and flooding, were busy dragging soggy furniture from the house onto the lawn. We paused and leaned out of the car windows to assure them of our safety and to hear of their fear for our lives as they watched our house go underwater to the roofline. They had escaped to their second-story bedrooms and spent much of the storm in ankle-deep water there. The exterior structure of their home appeared to be unfazed by the horrific winds. There were no holes in their roof, and all the windows we could see from the roadside were unbroken. Their spirit, too, seemed unbroken, and they expressed gratitude to God for seeing them through safely.

Image courtesy of Catherine Pyfrom

Image courtesy of Catherine Pyfrom

Image courtesy of Catherine Pyfrom

RETURNING HOME

Seeing our home as we turned from the Butlers' house and onto our street was anticlimactic. The structure looked remarkably normal to the point of being strange. There was debris, mud, and seaweed all over the exterior of the house. The windows were dotted with torn bits of brown organic material, and the driveway was covered in gray silt, several inches deep. However, the roof, windows, and exterior walls were in remarkable condition. Our beige sheet metal roof showed no sign that it had just withstood a Category 5 hurricane. The house had been built to withstand the worst that nature could throw at it. The structure had remained steadfast, saving our lives in the process.

We could take in most of the house and roof from the entrance gate, still propped open from hurricane prep before the storm. The yard was totally wrecked. Most of our large, tropical trees, grown from seedlings in many cases, lay in the yard or had disappeared completely. The trees that were standing were stripped of leaves and most of their branches. Piles of leaves and ocean debris were caught against the inside of the chain-link fence that surrounded the property. Miraculously, the entire chain link fence was still standing, only bent, or leaning in places where tree limbs weighed it down. The street was covered in the same gray ocean mud that was six inches deep in certain areas. Deep tire marks led almost to our driveway as evidence that we were not the first to pay a visit since the storm. Lyndah drove carefully, staying in the center of the road to avoid the deeper mud and risk of getting stuck.

For the first time since the car alarm blared as the ocean water reached its engine, we saw our vehicle. The silver Ford Escape sat at the bottom of the driveway, having crashed through the dog pen fencing. The purple crystal that hung from the rear-view mirror still twinkled in the sunlight. The car hadn't floated far from its original position, a mere twenty feet down from its spot on the elevated parking pad. At the peak of the storm, the ocean level would have submerged it entirely with at least another four to five feet above its roof. The car was fifteen years old, but we had taken good care of it, and it still ran great before Dorian. Now it sat dead, already corroding from the saltwater flood. I wondered briefly if I could even open the car door and whether ocean water would come rushing out if I did.

We slipped our way up the mud-covered driveway. I lost my footing in the mud and yelped as Catherine grabbed my hand to help steady me. Mud splattered up my right shin in the process. My level of cleanliness didn't matter much. Our pool bath had done little to make me feel clean the day before. I knew there would be more mud and muck as the day wore on.

We made it up the driveway to our kitchen door. The window in the door was open, and the memory of me opening it as the floodwater rose higher and higher came rushing back. In the chaos of survival mode, I had opened the window, fearing the thought of being caught inside the house, unable to escape. My mind had insisted that perhaps that open window might be a means of escape later. It was not.

I tried pulling on the doorknob, but the door did not move an inch. The ocean water had swollen the foam interior, making the door permanently stuck in the closed position. I cupped my hands around my eyes as I pressed my face to the window glass to see inside. I could not see the floor of our kitchen or dining room. One of our large blue couches from the living room remained perched haphazardly on top of our kitchen island. Hundreds of antique bottles that once lined the top of the kitchen cabinets were scattered everywhere, many broken, others intact.

We turned toward the backyard and made our way to the pool deck to enter the house through the back porch French doors. We noticed that our hundred-gallon propane tank, which once sat on a concrete pad and secured to the ground with a few bungee cords for the storm, was gone completely. It was nowhere to be seen in the yard or road. I didn't see Hazel's large wooden swing set and climbing frame either. To this day, we have no idea where either of them ended up. As we proceeded into the backyard, I sidestepped bits of our lives scattered through the muck and burned grass. A vintage *Star Wars* Princess Leia doll, a collector's item that once sat on a shelf in our master bedroom, lay torn and muddy in our path.

The pool deck was not covered in the thick gray silt, perhaps because it was elevated above ground level. So much effort had gone into raising our living spaces to protect us, all in vain. The pool, once blue and crystal clear, was now brown and opaque at the deep end. At the shallow end, we could see the bottom of the once-pristine space covered in more gray sludge. I realized then how easily I could have taken a misstep and ended up in the pool as we made our way to the rescue boat just the day before. An error like that could have meant being pulled away by the current during our rescue. For us to make it out alive and relatively uninjured, so many things had to go exactly right.

When I turned to look at the house, I noticed the missing patio furniture. Most of it had been only six months old, brand new, and just purchased in the spring. It had been stolen by the ocean monster as well.

One of the French doors swung in the slight breeze on our porch; the other pushed closed and jammed slightly. Stepping inside what was once the heart of our dream house, I was hit by an overwhelming wall of pain, grief, and loss. Nothing looked salvageable. It was hard even to discern what we were seeing. Mildew was already visible on the interior doors of the house. The furniture was upended and moved. Pieces from other rooms made their way into the main living room during the swirl of the hurricane throughout our house. Interior walls were stripped to expose the wooden studs, with bits of drywall that were torn and hanging precariously in places. Our solid wood dining room table sat in our foyer, piled high with god knew what. Couch cushions, the most buoyant thing in our house, were clearly the very last things to settle. Though saturated with salt water, they sat gently all over the room. Some had seaweed clinging to them. Others looked almost normal, as though someone had casually tossed them on top of the disaster that had imploded inside the house.

We stood there, in the doorway to our dream-turned-nightmare, for what seemed like hours. Each time I scanned the room, I saw something else that was once beautiful and carefully chosen to represent us, now smashed, broken, and waterlogged. The scene was like the hunt-and-find magazine pictures in which one must find the ten or so hidden objects. One could scan the same spot a dozen times and see something different each time. On one pass, my eyes caught sight of the decorative wooden oars hung high on the walls of the foyer, still in their place with just a bit of seaweed attached. That point was clearly where the water level had stopped. On the following scan, I noticed Hazel's toy sack zipped up and full of stuffed animals. It had floated out of her bedroom and now sat under a pile of furniture near the laundry room. When I looked again across the room, I saw our three-tier china cabinets all piled one unit on top of the other, face down, so we could not see the trinkets and mementos they held.

To my left, I noticed one of the oddest things about the entire scene. I had gifted Catherine two ceramic coral sculptures the Christmas before. They had a prominent place on the couch table that had once accented our living room wall. The two sculptures now sat upright on the tile floor against the same wall, unbroken. The couch table was nowhere to be seen. The coral had been hand-carried from Florida on a shopping trip out of fear of breaking them in shipping. Somehow, in the whirlpool of heavy furniture and countless other items churning in our living room, these fragile items had floated from the table and remained in the very same place. As the storm surge receded, they had come to rest gently in their rightful place, minus the table. It was weird beyond words.

As I continued to study the scene, instead of a bright, colourful, and whimsical scene in the usual hunt-and-find pictures, I saw a horror story in gray wash. Everything was gray. The floor, where it could be seen peeking from underneath the mountain of debris, was gray. The walls that remained were gray. The furniture was gray. The piles of our trinkets and Hazel's toys were all gray. Everything was covered in swamp mud churned up from the undercurrent of excessive tides combined with the waves and wind.

The counterclockwise spin of the Atlantic hurricane and the due east movement of Dorian meant that the storm's worst wind and waves had washed over us from north to south, from the swamp across the island to the beaches. As the storm stopped forward motion completely for some twenty hours, those waves had torn through the shallows of the silted seabed. It moved hundreds of thousands of tons of ocean-floor mud from the swamps and pushed it over the island.

This gray silt that covered everything we could see inside what was left of our home was mixed with even more slime. The nine feet of floodwater inside our house had compromised our septic system, pushing its content up through drains and toilets. When the ocean receded, what was left was a bacteria-filled paste of mangrove mud, seaweed, ocean water, and raw sewage. The house smelled like death, rotting organic material covered in century-old ocean silt and feces. It reeked. It cut our breath as we stood there, even with the doors and windows open to allow fresh air in.

At first glance, nothing looked salvageable to me as fear and hopelessness settled uncomfortably in the pit of my stomach. I had no clue where to begin or what to do. Then the stabbing pain in my face reminded me where my priorities needed to be. Catherine moved deeper into the living room, searching for anything sentimental or valuable that was worth taking with us.

I turned and moved toward our bedroom. I placed my feet lightly as I moved in that direction, stepping on a picture frame and broken glass as I went. I braced myself in the doorway and looked at the buckled door that Catherine had broken to reach the dogs two days before. I climbed over furniture and braced my hand on the bed, still sitting in the middle of the room, to steady myself when my foot slipped. Everything was covered in obvious sewage. There was no way to avoid the remnants of our makeshift bathroom facilities as I climbed the metal ladder into the darkness that had been our saving grace.

In the attic, I used my cell phone flashlight to illuminate the darkness. The space was humid and hot, not cold and damp as it had been during the storm. I snapped off a couple of quick photos of our safe space to show family in the future before grabbing the bag I needed with the medication. I held my breath as I reached inside, hoping the contents were dry. Thankfully they were. Catherine called up to check on me and offered help. I declined as I grabbed what I could and descended the ladder once again. Back on the porch, I took the water bottle we brought with us and took a big swig to swallow the tiny pink pill that would hopefully give me some relief eventually.

When I looked up, I saw Catherine rooting through the piles of photo albums we had tried so hard to save. Tears rolled down her face. Despite our best efforts to place the albums inside garbage bags and on our highest shelves, all the albums were ruined. Years and years of Catherine's life, her entire childhood, were held in those photos. Most of them migrated from her parents' home after her mother's death over ten years before. When we tried to remove the photos from the plastic sheeting, the ink remained attached to the sleeve and the blank photo paper came out. We tried to take photographs of the pictures in the albums, but we were not able to save any of the photos.

For years before Hazel's birth, Catherine and I had scrapbooked together. All our travels had unique books meticulously created over hours of creative evenings spent together. As I watched Catherine mourn the loss of her childhood photographs, I turned my attention to those scrapbooks, already knowing they could not be saved either. I looked in the direction of the cabinet where they had been stored. The six-piece furniture unit was piled on top of one another, all face down. I tried to move one, hoping to turn it over to inspect the contents. As I lifted, the wooden unit crumbled, and I couldn't move it but a few inches. It was too water-logged and broken to move without machinery or a few burly men. I stopped trying.

I moved back toward the master closet again, explaining to Cath my intention to check the safe. In the corner of our closet, bolted to the floor, was our small fireproof safe. As I pulled on the safe door and pressed buttons on the utterly dead keypad, fear rose inside of me. I tried to remember through the chaos of securing valuables and necessities two days before. I knew I went into the safe, grabbed our documents and passports, and stuffed them inside the blue backpack I had just brought down from the attic. The bag had been hefty to move. The clothing inside had absorbed saltwater as we lugged it around the flooded house before escaping to the attic. All the paperwork inside would be wet, but hopefully, it could be dried and saved. Had I grabbed the hard drives from the safe? I recalled placing them inside Ziploc bags as I had done with our cell phones. The cell phones remained with us and still functioned, but I could not remember if the hard drives were in the backpack as well.

Panic rose from my belly into my throat, and I felt nauseous again. I went outside and emptied the contents of the backpack onto the porch deck. The documents (birth certificates, marriage certificate, and passports) were all there, though sticking together and in need of drying out. The clothing that Cath had packed hastily for a dry rescue over forty-eight hours before was soaked as I expected and had the same terrible odour as everything else that was wet in the storm. As I dug through the bag, I found no hard drives. My eyes welled up with tears. I must have left them inside the safe.

Cath, Lyndah, and I debated how to get the safe open. We all knew that each night that passed would bring looters to the flooded and abandoned houses. It would not take long for an enterprising thief to find the safe and bring back enough muscle or tools to crack it. Inside the safe, we guessed to be thousands of dollars of antique jewelry. It was primarily gifts given to Catherine's mother by her father throughout their marriage. While it held significant sentimental value, it also held tremendous monetary value too. We had to get into the safe as soon as possible. We agreed that we would have to come back with tools and help to get it open.

As Cath continued to scavenge for items we could take with us that day, I searched for more valuables. Catherine had grabbed her wallet from the kitchen countertop during the chaotic packing of valuables and shoved it inside the backpack. My wallet had been on a small table near the door and had not been grabbed in the shuffle. As Cath had packed in knee-high water, I stuffed our two jewelry boxes from our bedroom into large black garbage bags. Without much thought at the time, I secured them inside the highest cabinets in our kitchen above our microwave. That spot was notoriously difficult to reach in our everyday use and was mostly empty. I shoved the two boxes in there and hadn't given them another thought until now.

As I made my way to the kitchen through the obstacle course of our living room, it struck me that moving around was incredibly difficult for an open-floor plan house. Every pile of crumbled belongings I stepped over or around, moved as I did. At the laundry room door, it became impossible to walk around things. The majority of our larger furniture pieces had come to rest in the dining room and kitchen. To enter the kitchen, I had to plot my path carefully and climb onto the upended couch. It was like a game of "The Floor is Lava." Don't fall in. Don't let your toe touch the floor, or you're out. Only this wasn't a game. It was our life, in shambles, and whether I wanted to get into the kitchen or not, I needed to retrieve the valuables there.

After each step, I stopped and picked my next move. As I paused, I studied the piles of furniture. I hoped to find my wallet wedged in between the dining room chair that was lying on the toppled china cabinet or under the igloo cooler that had floated out of a kitchen cabinet that was missing its door. At the end of the couch that acted as my gangway into the kitchen, I stopped and looked. I could see the hole in the ceiling that I pushed in to access the water on the shelf. The kitchen sink was filled with brown saltwater and broken antique bottles. The teal Kitchen-Aid mixer sat in its rightful place in the corner of the kitchen, too heavy to float.

My next move would be my most daring so far. The floor was littered with broken bottles, and I was scared to walk on it. I stood balanced on the edge of the couch and leaned off the end, hoping to have enough stretch to place a foot on top of the kitchen island. I did not want to slip on the slick quartz countertop we had loved so much. It had bits of what looked like seafoam sea glass embedded in the manufactured stone surface. Unfortunately, I was not agile enough to accomplish such a move. I lost my balance in slow motion, recovering just enough to land softly on the glass shards I had been trying to avoid. The crunching glass sounds echoed and yielded another call from Catherine in the living room to make sure I was okay.

Not wanting to waste more time, I reached up over my head on tiptoes and opened the cabinet door. Inside, precisely as I had left them, were the two jewelry boxes filled with years of gifts given to one another. They were both saturated as the floodwaters had reached the highest shelves in our kitchen, but at least the contents remained safe. I grabbed one and hauled it out, placing it on the island before reaching for the second. With a box under each arm, I climbed back onto the gangway couch and moved toward Catherine. She met me and took the boxes so I could climb back into the living room with the use of my hands to steady me. There was no sign of my wallet.

The heat, the smell, and the overwhelming nature of it all finally set firmly in, and our progress slowed considerably. We knew there was no way for us to access the safe without more help. Feeling exhausted, both mentally and physically, we decided that we had gathered what we could for now and set off back toward the car out front, moving slowly with arms full, through the slippery mud. It took several trips to move everything.

After the last things were placed safely in the trunk of the SUV, I stood on the porch deck and looked out at what was once a million-dollar view that few people on Earth were ever lucky enough to see, let alone own.

The Sunday morning alone on the deck, the calm before the storm, and mentally preparing for the coming chaos came rushing back to me. That moment, taken in haste but absorbed nonetheless, was of very little solace as I stood looking at the muddy canal over the no-longer-blue pool. The structures were all still standing, but the home was gone, taken by the cruel, evil beast that was Dorian. The peaceful summer evenings swimming under the stars. The radiant sunsets we photographed so often. The years of hard work to create the gardens. The memories of Hazel toddling around the house and dinner parties with friends. The house we decorated so perfectly over the years that every square inch of it screamed who we were and what we loved. It was all gone. I closed the glass door, hoping it would stay that way and that looters would leave the place alone at least long enough for us to return and get the contents of the safe.

252

Image courtesy of Catherine Pyfrom

Image courtesy of Catherine Pyfrom

FORWARD MOTION

That evening back at the Fortune Bay house, our friends Cindy and Mike arrived to offer hugs and reassurance. We gave them a much more detailed story of everything we had done to survive the storm, feeling more comfortable with our old friends than our new ones. They offered us their spare bedroom if we wanted it. We thanked them kindly, but they also had several dogs, and the logistics would have been complicated. The topic of our safe came up, and Mike offered to help us try to break it open the next day.

During conversation much later, there were more stories of Dorian. Everyone had gone their separate ways that day on errands, and the stories we all returned with were numerous. There was one I wish I didn't hear. The same story was told of the man in the tree. This time the story carried more gruesome details. He had been found with his arms and legs wrapped around the trunk in a bid for survival as Dorian tried to tear him away. He died this way with rigour mortis setting in, making removing him from that tree difficult. We learned that his wife, who had been with him, was swept away by the current, drowning in the process.

The stories of those who had died were hard to hear. There was empathy and sympathy for those who had lost their loved ones, of course. However, hearing the stories of people in Abaco and Grand Bahama who had tried to escape the rising water and crumbling buildings to seek shelter only served to highlight just how close we had come to death. Any decision could have gone horribly wrong. The tornado we spent the entire night fearful of could have stolen our roof and us with it. As we heard a tale of the father losing his grip on his young child as they tried to swim to safety and watching in horror as the waves took the child away, I blinked back more tears that filled my eyes and slid down my cheeks.

I turned to check on Hazel, playing not far away with the other girls. The story was whispered so the children couldn't hear, but during those first few days I'm sure they heard so much that would cause nightmares for a lifetime.

We also learned that most of the electrical poles throughout Freeport, almost all brand new and replaced after Hurricane Matthew just three years before, had stayed up for the most part, though many were missing lines. Then we found out that the massive diesel generators on the island that powered those lines had all been submerged in saltwater. The electrical components would need to be replaced entirely at the least, or at worst, new multi-million-dollar generators would need to be purchased, shipped, and installed before anyone on the island would have electricity again. Freshwater was going to be a problem as well. Electricity was needed to run the pumps that pull the water from the water table through wells and city pipes. No pumps meant no running water.

The airport apparently fared worse than other facilities. It was located on the northern part of the island, bordering the marsh. The building was standing but with gaping holes and, despite being elevated, still had six feet of ocean water inside. Crews were working desperately to clear the runway of massive piles of pine trees that had been uprooted and left there by the storm. The runways were still underwater because of their extremely low elevation. In a particularly heavy summer downpour, the runways tended to flood. This situation was something else entirely. There was even a story of the crews finding a shark that had been stranded on the tarmac with the receding tide.

Many businesses in town had ocean water, though traveling farther west on the island saw the stories of damage and death decrease. One of the major grocery stores also elevated, had suffered significant damage, and would take years to rebuild. Both hardware stores had tremendous damage and loss of merchandise to the storm and looters. Banks had been filled with ocean water. Many of the public schools would need major repairs.

Yet through the catalogue of loss, there were odd stories of those spared. Noel and Britt's apartment on the south shore beach had only a foot of water. I say "only" because while the interior walls would need to be dried out and replaced and all electrical would need to be repaired, the structure itself was fine. A popular beach bar and restaurant just next door had suffered only minor wind damage. All along the southern shore of Freeport, beachfront property and homes had fared far better than ours. The location of the storm and its path had left much of that area protected from the worst storm surge.

The conversation shifted to talk of relief supplies and volunteers' impending arrival. The moment the storm had passed and turned to miss Florida, relief agencies there and further abroad had begun to mobilize. We learned that a convoy of private boaters in Florida was loading up as we spoke and hoping to arrive in the next day or so once the governmental red tape had been crossed. Instantly a plan began to materialize for getting our five dogs and us off the island.

The idea of travelling by small boat from Freeport to Florida wasn't out of the ordinary. It's about sixty-five miles from the western tip of Grand Bahama Island to the east coast of Florida. Boaters do it all the time—it is a thriving part of our country's tourism. It is, however, not a fast means of travel. It would be as much as an eight-hour ordeal with a seasick child and five terrified dogs to get to Florida by boat.

Staying at the Fortune Bay house was the most comfortable hurricane shelter we could have dreamed of. We were grateful for the stable roof over our heads and all the food and drinks we needed. We would have electricity and air-conditioning that night with beds and privacy. It was nothing like the actual hurricane shelters currently overrun with people in cramped quarters with few supplies. Plus, none of those official shelters allowed dogs, and we had five of them. We knew we couldn't stay at the Fortune Bay house long-term even though we were assured that we could remain for as long as we liked. None of our friends or family in Freeport were able to put us up comfortably, even short-term.

Being separated from the dogs was wearing on us as well. They had been locked in a garage for a day and a half. We missed their constant presence and the love and cuddles they provided throughout our average day. In our current state, we needed their comfort more than ever but wouldn't bring them inside with us given we were guests in this home. We did sneak each of the little ones inside for some extra, individual love when we could. With a furry, warm bundle wrapped in our arms and wet kisses of love, we could almost close our eyes and pretend it was all just a nightmare. Almost.

We would walk the dogs frequently in the yard, but it was not secure, and it took two of us to keep track of them. Since we didn't have any leashes, we feared one or more of the dogs might run away in the strange, stressful place.

We were beginning to worry about the dogs' health as well. Copper and Pearl were showing signs of stress and physical deterioration. Both had been on medication for various ailments. We had not been able to rescue any of their medicines from the house. Copper was having a lot of trouble walking on his old injury and was wheezing and coughing often. He also looked like he was retaining fluid, a common issue for a dog with congestive heart failure with no medication. The dogs were all fed and loved, but they were pampered pets, and being locked in a garage for almost two days, separated from us, was an issue that needed to be addressed soon.

Then there were the looting stories. I think those stories were more terrifying than the rest at that point. Even as we sat in the living room that night with a loaded shotgun in the corner, I worried for our safety. Evil and vile people had been taking advantage of torn-open homes and businesses. We heard that Jamie's father, Colin, had stubbornly decided to sleep on his catamaran that they had found pushed half a mile inland during the storm. He was worried about looters stripping his prized vessel, so he alone protected it, shotgun in hand. A group of men tried to steal from him, but luckily, he scared them off by firing over their heads and calling for backup. Hearing this story, we worried about the remaining valuables in our safe.

Having nowhere else to go, our goal became getting out of Freeport. Utilities would be weeks or even months from repair, water shortages would be a continued problem, and the lawlessness was escalating. By some miraculous act, we did have another place to go. We had been at our Florida condo just a month before. It had been the last weekend of friends, shopping, and restaurants before school began again. Now the vacation home was the only home we had left. The condo was filled with clothing, toys, and things that were familiar and chosen with care. We just had to figure out how to get there. I was ready for privacy and quiet and comfort so that we could try to digest all that had happened and figure out what would happen next.

More conversations that night also gave us hope for a way out that did not involve an eight-hour boat ride. With the news that the runways were being cleared for the arrival of supplies came the brief thought that perhaps one of the aircraft bringing those supplies might be willing to take us back to Florida with them. Commercial flights in and out of the airport could be weeks away. Small, private airplanes would be the first to arrive and perhaps the only to come for some time. Our hosts knew of our desire to get ourselves, our daughter, and our dogs off the island as quickly as possible. They promised to inquire, as they had already become a big part of the community's grassroots efforts, suddenly mobilizing to network help from the outside. The government was nowhere to be seen, and the shallow pockets of the Treasury would not begin to make a dent in the need for relief supplies. The only way people were going to get the help they needed was if folks like Noel and Britt used their business contacts to get it done.

Despite our physical and emotional exhaustion, we stayed up with our new friends later into the night. We felt like it was polite to socialize given all they were doing for us, but the conversation was challenging in our post-traumatic stress state of mind. My mind was reeling with what we needed to do. Survival was accomplished, but, in my mind, there was no real rest. Little did I know that "rest" wouldn't come for many months yet.

The following day brought word that the supply boats were still caught in the bureaucratic red tape of import laws even in the middle of a natural disaster. They wouldn't arrive for another day or more at least. On the brighter side, Kent brought us the loaned truck. We were grateful for the independent transportation because it meant we could go back to our house again.

Another vital step to getting off the island to our condo in Florida was veterinary paperwork for the dogs. We knew that US Customs would require Health Certificates for each dog to gain entry to the country whether we travelled by boat or by plane. We worried that our vet would not be open for business so soon after such a natural disaster, but a quick Facebook message confirmed they were ready and able to help. Unfortunately, by that time, our rescue boy had been struggling more and more. Copper refused to walk on his old injury entirely and had gained considerable weight in fluid retention in just a few days. His eyes were pained, though his tail never stopped wagging.

Just three days without his medicine, Copper had begun to lose his battle. Our vet confirmed that he was likely suffering from kidney failure. The decision not to prolong the inevitable was heartbreaking. It would have been difficult under normal circumstances, but the overwhelming nature of our lives amid a massive natural disaster made everything painful and hard. We did not want to say goodbye after just saving his life, but we felt that was our only option. The vet agreed that we were nearing the end of his life, and so we left Copper in her very compassionate care. She promised to take care of everything for us. Through even more tears, we said goodbye to our good boy.

We didn't tell Hazel our plan to end Copper's suffering. In truth, the decision to tell a white lie was as much for her well-being as it was for ours. We couldn't fathom explaining the difficult decision while already coping with so much loss and destruction. We told Hazel instead that we were leaving Copper with the vet so he could get medicine and would come back for him when he was better. For us, it was easier to put off the inevitable explanation of euthanasia to our six-year-old than try to have it right then.

After we visited the vet, we dropped Hazel at her school friend's home, promising to return in a couple of hours. Hazel went willingly without fear. She had been at their house before and felt comfortable there. We were so grateful for their offer to have Hazel while we went back to the house to salvage more. Our discussion the night before, in hushed voices as Hazel slept, had concluded that it was too dangerous to take her back to the house. Additionally, we were unsure of the emotional impact on her to see it all again, completely wrecked. It wasn't worth it to test just how resilient she was so soon after almost dying.

We made our way back to our broken home and Mike met us at the house as we arrived. There were more tire tracks in the mud than had been there the day before and new footprints leading up to the house. Looters had visited during the night. We held our breath, both in anticipation and to avoid the odour, as we went straight inside to check the safe's security. The safe was still there, bolted to the ground. Mike grabbed his crowbar and sledgehammer and began beating at the hinges in hopes of cracking it.

The missing items taken by the looters were obvious. The alcohol bottles from our bar that had made it through the storm were gone, along with a few six-packs of soda. Several bathroom fixtures had already been removed. The five hundred-pound generator in the center of our living room that had weathered the storm, having moved only a few inches under nine feet of ocean water, was gone. The machine had wheels to move it more quickly but getting it out of the house through the mud would've taken several men. It had spent thirty-six hours in salt water. I couldn't understand how anyone thought it would ever function again.

As the sledgehammer echoed each time it slammed down on the hinges of the safe, we worked our way through the house again. We were trying to find more things to salvage. We made our way to our storage closet that housed Christmas decorations and years of special items. Part of the closet wall that bordered the foyer had been ripped away to the wooden studs, and we could see inside. Before the storm, the closet was full of Rubbermaid containers filled with CDs, shot glasses, and memorabilia collections from years gone by. It had Hazel's baby toys and newborn baby clothes saved for sentimental reasons, old journals, old artwork, and so much more. Now, peeking through the exposed studs, the interior of the room was a massive pile of wet, broken memories. Many of the

Rubbermaid containers had opened, spilling the contents into the swirling water and mud.

I stood looking at the items, dumbfounded. I could think of hundreds of very personal items in this eight-by-six room that could simply never be replaced. Many of the items in our house would never be replaced: things collected over a lifetime from around the world, gifts from friends, family, and each other. However, this room held particularly special items. Childhood things that had been saved by Cath's mother and left for her to pass down to Hazel. A bracelet that had been given to me by my grandfather just before his death. Hazel's first Christmas ornament was buried among the mountains of debris. There was simply no way to sort through the items in this small space except to bust down the water-swollen door and sort through items one by one to find diamonds in the rough that were not broken and could be cleaned with great effort. Tears welled up in my eyes.

The sledgehammer noise stopped, and it was suddenly calm. I made my way to the master closet to see how Mike was getting on. I found him sweating profusely, leaning on the door frame as he caught his breath. I looked down, and the door of the safe remained intact. I felt so defeated and overwhelmed.

"I'll get it open," Mike assured me when he saw the look of worry on my face. "The hinge is starting to give." He took a deep breath and began again at beating the safe. The difficulty Mike was having in getting into the safe did not ease my fears of looters. Criminals, when highly motivated, could be even more determined and ingenious than a retiree with a sledgehammer.

I went out onto the back deck and took a deep breath. I wondered briefly about our floating dock that had disappeared. We'd last seen it while we struggled to keep our heads above water outside. I walked down to the edge of the pool and looked back at the house. I noticed our BBQ grill lying in the grass against the side of the house.

When I looked down into the depths of the pool, I noticed a familiar object. Near the bottom of the steps in the shallow end lay a white urn with pink roses on it. The lid was still fixed to the top, unbroken. I was stunned. When I last saw this urn, it was sitting on a wooden shelf in the corner of our bedroom. Inside the jar, in tiny plastic bags, were the ashes of three of our dogs that had passed over the rainbow bridge years before. Tears filled my eyes as I thought of how close we had come to losing the four dogs that now waited for us in the garage. I retrieved a stick from the debris in the yard, maneuvered the jar up the first step, and waited for the water and mud to settle before repeating the process twice more. Finally, the urn was close enough to the surface that I could retrieve it by reaching in until the water was up to my shoulder.

With the jar in my hands, I sat on the pool deck, thinking about the item's weight. If it were full of ocean water, it would have been much heavier. As I turned the lid, I was amazed to find that the ashes were completely dry inside. I got up and went to see Cath and show her the miracle item I had found.

By then, Mike finally cracked the safe. It took forty-five minutes of banging on the hinges of the safe to pop the door off. Water and mud poured out of the one-foot square interior. We retrieved saturated paper envelopes of old coins collected by Cath's mother. We pulled out a bit of cash, also soaking wet. There were containers of expensive jewelry. As happy as Catherine was to retrieve the expensive, sentimental pieces, I was equally horrified to find the two hard drives filled with thousands of digital photos taken throughout our lives together. The two drives were inside the plastic Ziploc bags where I had placed them during the beginning of this nightmare, but inside the plastic was a lot of water, so much water that I poured at least several tablespoonfuls of ocean water out when I opened the bag.

At that moment, I cried. I cried for the loss of all our things. I cried for the ordeal and almost losing our lives. I cried for the unknown and the chaos that was still surrounding us. And I cried for the hard drives in my hand. In passing dinner party conversations over the years, the "what if" question had been asked, "If you could only save one prized possession from a fire, what would it be?" My answer was always, "Our photographs." Now I stood holding my prized possession in my hands, knowing that there would be no recovering the images on them after hours of soaking in corrosive saltwater. We did eventually send them off to be professionally analysed weeks later, to no avail.

As we gathered the few things we had managed to salvage and began stacking them in the borrowed truck, I paused to peek inside our garden shed to see what had made it through the storm. During the middle of Dorian, the garden shed had been completely submerged with only the very top of its slanted metal roof visible. Inside the small building, I stared in disbelief at the pile of unbroken glass floats mingled with rusted garden tools. Sitting on top of the pile of glass and metal was Hazel's eight-foot unicorn floaty, still inflated, and ready for a fun-filled pool day. The things that survived the ordeal were simply mind-boggling.

Image courtesy of Catherine Pyfrom

Image courtesy of Catherine Pyfrom

THE NEXT LEG OF
THE JOURNEY

n our Pine Bay neighbourhood, over the bridge, cell service had been spotty since Dorian, even though the service had stayed very reliable during the storm up until the point we retreated to the attic. When we left the remains of our home late that afternoon, we drove to the parking lot of Hazel's school. For some mysterious technological reason, we had been able to get cell service and data for internet access from this spot. When we arrived at the school, our phones began a series of various notification chimes as emails and voicemails began coming in. Instantly, we noticed multiple phone messages from Britt. We quickly learned that the first flights bringing relief supplies would be arriving on the island shortly. Our hosts had been making inquiries about a way to get us off the island through their connections. One flight that would be en route soon had confirmed that it would be going back to Florida empty and could transport three people and four dogs. We had to hurry to provide our travel documents and gather our things to be at the airport within the hour.

We rushed to pick Hazel up from her friend's house and hurried our way through thank yous and goodbyes, unsure if we would ever see these people again. Post-Dorian would see a mass exodus from Freeport that we were not yet aware of, but at that point, the future was entirely uncertain for everyone. Back at the Fortune Bay house, we threw some donated clothes and some of our salvaged items into a couple of suitcases Kent and Charlotte had given us. We made phone calls to friends and family with only the most basic of plans for our evacuation. We relied entirely on Britt and the arrangements made for us. I have never been one to give up control, especially in travel arrangements, but desperate, unknown times had me so overwhelmed that making plans was simply not something I could do at that time. We each grabbed a small snack from the kitchen and raced out the door with the three of us and the four dogs crammed into the front cab of the loaned truck.

We drove to the airport and were completely blown away by the scene. It looked like an image from some war-torn country, not the second largest city in the Bahamas. We hadn't ventured anywhere aside from the drive between the Fortune Bay house to our home and back. At the airport, we saw first-hand the stories we had heard about the destruction. Airport hangers were peeled open like tin cans with massive warehouse walls curled up or missing entirely. Several private planes left secured by wire cables for the hurricane were thrown around and ripped apart like matchbox toys. The main airport terminal, which we could see in the distance, was severely damaged and missing part of its roof. The tarmac was still covered in debris in sections, and large ponds of water made other parts inaccessible.

At the far end of the tarmac, next to the leaning gate of the private air terminal, were several cars and trucks. We pulled in, recognising several other acquaintances and our hosts, all awaiting the arrival of the supply flights. Folks were there with trucks to move supplies and prepare to distribute them where needed. So far, there was still no sign of government assistance or organization of relief supplies. These were just community and rotary members, and other people less affected by the storm, ready to help.

When we parked and got out of the truck to find out what was happening and where we needed to be, we found out that the flights had not arrived yet. I left the dogs waiting in the car with Catherine and Hazel and walked out to a group of people standing on the tarmac to find out what the plan was. It was getting close to dinner time, and a tired Hazel was becoming a handful. The dogs were crammed into the truck with Catherine, eager to get out as well.

After thirty minutes of waiting, we transferred Hazel to a different car with the girls from the Fortune Bay house to entertain each other with an iPad, and Catherine joined me on the tarmac. There were two other small planes already unloaded and various people I did not recognise milling around. I was getting very anxious about not being in control of the timeline and not having any information about when or if we would leave. We were all tired and hungry, and emotionally drained from the last two days. The more anxious I became, the more I pushed Britt for information they simply did not have. We were just waiting to see if the flight would arrive and if our evacuation would happen.

Finally, we watched a small single-engine plane land in the distance over the runway. As the aircraft taxied to our location, we learned that this was the flight we were waiting for. Once the pilot deplaned and volunteers began unloading the cases of water, diapers, and non-perishable food items on board, Britt left to speak with the pilot. She returned shortly after with bad news.

"They can't take you," Britt reported, though through my trauma haze she did not look disappointed by this news. My heart sank. "They had to take out all six seats on the plane to make room for the supplies."

Her lack of frustration at this news served only to exasperate my stress level, which was threatening to become unmanageable as more problems that needed solutions filled my already-packed brain. "Well, can't we just sit on the floor of the plane? We don't mind."

I was picturing the three of us sitting cross-legged in the tiny plane with dogs in our laps for the short flight to Florida. It would be much more comfortable than the eight-hour journey by boat that seemed to be our only alternative.

"The pilot says it's against FAA regulations to transport passengers without seats. I asked." Britt cut me off, answering my next question before I could ask if the pilot would make an exception to the rule. In that moment of desperation, the need to escape the "war zone" outweighed logical thought. I knew such an idea was ridiculous, but I was grasping at straws.

The rage, anxiety, and uncertainty that had been simmering inside of me since our rescue, just forty-eight hours before, came bubbling up and threatened to spill out completely. I swallowed back tears and harsh words as I threw up my hands and began to march away.

"I don't know why we bothered to rush out here if they can't take us," I mumbled to myself as I walked away, too disappointed to control myself within the group for much longer. The situation was no one's fault. I was grateful for all Britt had done trying to get us on that flight, and I understood that we were already privileged to be among the first victims of the storm to be searching for a way off the island. Hundreds of others were likely injured and needed to be evacuated far more than we did. We were just lucky enough to know the folks organizing these first relief supply runs.

Even still, my disappointment was very hard to cage among all the other emotions. It was like salt on an open wound. I was tired of problem-solving, and it was in my nature to control as much as I could. I had no control whatsoever over anything in the last seventy-two hours. The hours spent sifting through what was left of our home left me raw and broken. I needed food and sleep to recharge.

I was about to fall headfirst into a full-out panic attack when Britt stopped me with a hand on each of my shoulders. "It's going to be alright. Just wait a minute," she instructed and walked off in the direction of the planes once again without waiting for me to agree.

I took a few deep breaths. As she walked toward the other two planes we had met when we arrived at the airport, I walked several feet away from the group and closed my eyes, sucking back tears. I was tired, overwhelmed, hungry, and incredibly stressed. I knew that Hazel was hungry, and I knew the dogs were stressed, locked in the truck cab with a friend minding them. My patience was done, and I was ready for the day to be over.

When I turned back to the group, I found Britt speaking with Catherine and exchanging information.

"They need our passports," Catherine called to me.

One of the planes parked on the runway was a private charter out of South Florida carrying supplies and diapers bound for the orphanage on the island in the wake of the storm's devastation. The orphanage had been spared any major damage and flooding but would need goods, as supply chains following Dorian would be slow. The wealthy couple responsible for the flight and supplies had come along on the quick flight to drop off the much-needed goods. With them came a news crew for Fox News out of South Florida. The news crew, a single journalist and cameraman, had come along to take some video footage and head back to Florida to have a segment for the ten o'clock news that evening. After hearing our story from Britt, the couple agreed to take us back with them.

Tears of relief filled my eyes instantly. I rushed to provide our travel documents and passports to the pilot to amend his flight plan. Our passports turned out to be our most prized possessions, in the end. They were our ticket out of the disaster zone. If we had lost our passports in Dorian, it would have taken at least weeks, but more likely months, to get new ones. Once the pilot filed his amended flight plan, there was a rush to grab our bags, Hazel, and the dogs. The sun was setting quickly, and the pilot planned to be back in Florida before dark.

Our goodbye to Noel and Britt and other acquaintances waiting on the tarmac was hurried. Arms were thrown around necks in tight, heartfelt hugs. There were whispers of encouragement and well wishes made into our ears. Tears of relief spilled down my cheeks. We walked toward the plane, dogs in our arms and pulled along by a couple of leashes, frightened by the engine noise and chaos.

The wealthy couple, news crew, and pilot turned out to be another set of saviours in just a few days. All were well-dressed and had kind, friendly faces that expressed concern for our well-being. We were some of the very first, uninjured people to evacuate the island. As we loaded into the aircraft, the reporter asked, yelling into our ears over the roar of the engines, if we would be willing to be on camera and answer a few questions. It was difficult to be anything but grateful for their help at that moment. Catherine and I had no time to discuss the idea as we climbed into the aircraft. I nodded at Cath, thinking I could somehow muster the calm to be interviewed.

Once on the plane, we struggled to get situated. The pilot needed the small plane balanced for weight, and I was fighting with Sky, who had never been on an airplane before and was very frightened. I ended up plunking myself on a small bench seat near the back of the plane with the larger dog held tightly near my feet and Pearl tucked under my arm. Catherine and Hazel, with Nutmeg and Ginger, had been herded to the front of the small plane to sit on another bench seat. Everyone else was spread along the aisle between us as the cameraman set up to film.

Catherine pleaded to me with her eyes. She wanted a way out of being interviewed and in front of a camera, but lacked the mental strength to object. Given the huge favour these people were doing for us by getting us to Florida, she didn't feel she could say no to the questions. She resigned herself to be interviewed and confirmed our name spelling and fact-based details to the journalist, who fervently jotted the info down.

As the plane door was closed, locking out some of the engine noise, I could hear Catherine retelling our Dorian saga. "We got into the attic and stayed there for twenty-four hours. We didn't think we were going to make it, honestly." I could hear Cath's voice falter as they spoke about the goodbye video she had made. She was trying to maintain composure and not allow the tears in her eyes to fall down her face while on camera.

The newscaster was kind, but he saw an opportunity and was just doing his job. The drama of an interview conducted on what had become an evacuation flight would make for excellent evening news coverage.

The aircraft taxied toward the runway, and I tried to take several deep breaths and settle the dogs. I shifted on my tiny bench seat. My back screamed at me for the odd angle I had contorted myself into yet again. My body was exhausted, and my mind even more so. I told myself I only had a couple of more hours that I had to hold it together. Freeport is only eighty miles from Fort Lauderdale, Florida. On an average trip on a commercial airline, it is barely a thirty-minute flight, not even enough time for beverage service. On the small private plane, I guessed the flight might take forty-five minutes. From there, we would need to find a way to get to our condo, which I estimated might take another forty-five minutes or more.

At the front of the aircraft, I could see Catherine talking into the microphone as the journalist asked questions for the next fifteen minutes, though I couldn't hear her words over the engine noise. Hazel laid her head in Catherine's lap, with one dog cuddled in front of her and the other cuddled behind. I looked out the window to see a spectacular sunset dipping low on the horizon as the Florida coastline came into view. The reds and oranges were warm, familiar, and comforting on many levels.

I studied the ocean below us as we flew. With the sun losing its last bit of light across the surface of the Gulf Stream, I thought of the waves there. Still, their white-capped crests were being propelled by Dorian as it shot up the Eastern Seaboard, no doubt nearing Bermuda or even Canada by then. The water was angry, but at our height, it was nothing compared to being inside the storm. I wasn't angry with the ocean for all we had endured. In truth, I was too exhausted to be angry or feel much of anything just then. As I watched the ocean move below the aircraft, my mind flashed with images of mud-brown waves crashing into us as we swam outside our home under our covered porch. I took a sharp involuntary breath in as I recalled the ocean trying to pull me under before Cath grabbed me, and my pulse quickened suddenly at the memory. I took several more deep breaths as I reminded myself that we were safe. The ocean was not going to kill us today.

I wondered briefly if that sudden fear would be a constant companion now, and I worried about whether Hazel would now have a fear of the ocean because of our near-death experience. Only time would tell the answer. I thought of my fear and briefly analyzed whether I would be frightened by the power of the ocean now. However, as I studied the limitlessness of navy blue below me, dotted with white sea foam, I did not see a monster ready to swallow me as I had during the worst of the hurricane. I saw only the splendour in its vastness and even the moments of serenity garnered from years of viewing the ocean as a powerful thing of beauty. It surprised me in that moment of self-reflection, something I had had little time for just yet, that despite all the fear and anxiety that now crowded my psyche, the ocean was not a part of its root cause.

My attention returned to the front of the plane as the cameraman finally lowered his camera, and conversation at the front of the plane appeared to become more casual. I caught Cath's eye again, and she gave a slight glance at

Hazel with a tiny smile, grateful that she had fallen asleep. Then she gave a slight tilt of her head at the news crew and a well-hidden eye roll that would've been missed by anyone other than me. She was frustrated at having to talk and be interviewed for the flight. I mouthed the words, "Are you okay?" to her. She shrugged her shoulders and nodded slightly. I wanted to squeeze her hand, to offer a touch to say, "We'll be okay," but the seating arrangements made that impossible.

Before long, the plane's wheels hit the runway smoothly, just as the last of the sun slipped below the horizon. I looked out the window, trying to get my bearings before realizing that we had landed at the smaller executive airport and not the commercial airport to which we were accustomed. We unloaded and cleared US Immigration and Customs quickly with travel documents in hand. Once formalities were done, we loaded back into the plane and taxied to another building on the other side of the airport. The staff there gave us bottles of water which were much needed and much appreciated. It had been hours since any of us had had any.

The news crew generously ordered and paid for an Uber for us. We thanked them all profusely for their help as we loaded ourselves into the car with the four dogs. Hazel talked as we drove, energized by her brief nap. The song "We Belong" by Pat Benatar played on the radio. The ride to our condo in the dark took twenty minutes, but the air-conditioning and the comfortable seat made it seem like less. We spoke very little to the Uber driver, both because of our exhaustion and her less-than-friendly attitude.

When we reached our condo, we climbed the three flights of stairs to our unit, hauling dogs and our meagre suitcases with us. The key for the condo was long lost to the storm along with my wallet, but we had intentionally installed a coded lock for just this reason.

Once we were inside, surrounded by the familiarity of our possessions and furniture and smells, and the dogs had settled, I turned to Cath and smiled an exhausted sort of smile. Hazel sat quietly on the couch with Moxie, the stuffed toy that was now her constant companion, tucked under her arm.

It was the first time in almost four solid days that I felt like I could breathe. It suddenly felt like I had been holding my breath all that time and didn't even realise it. I took several deep breaths and relished in the familiar comfort of our second home. After constant problem-solving and fear, adrenaline-fueled decisions, exhausted conversations, and emotional overloads, we were finally at a real moment of self-reflection. Yet, somehow, there weren't tears at that moment. Perhaps it was my psyche protecting me by not allowing me to experience the full range of emotions that moment could have held. My mind knew my body did not have the stamina to feel the complicated waterfall of feelings that sat just out of reach in my subconscious mind. As I sat on the couch, sinking into its softness, I let it wrap itself around me in the protective hug I so desperately needed from the universe at that moment.

I looked down at my legs. From my upper legs down to my ankles were a patchwork of black, blue, and purple bruises of varying shapes and sizes. I raised my right arm and studied the inside of my bicep: from my elbow to my armpit was purple. As I studied the bruises I marveled at our luck. The bruise on my arm was from my fall into the kitchen, made worse by my repeated attempts to haul myself back out. I couldn't pinpoint when I had acquired the other bruises on my body. It didn't matter, really.

I was astonished that we had all made it out of our near-death experience without major physical injury. During our multiple trips back and forth across our flooded living room, our legs or feet could have become wedged in between heavy floating furniture causing at best, a sprain, or at worst, a broken bone. Catherine could have been knocked unconscious when diving back into the house in her rescue mission for the dogs. I could have cut myself severely while falling into the kitchen, swimming among broken bottles. Any of us could have been pierced with a stray, exposed nail in the darkness of the attic, or lost our footing and fallen through the drywall-covered ceiling. We could have slipped and cut ourselves when coming down from the attic after the flooding had receded. Being out in the elements while the storm raged on during our rescue could have resulted in any number of projectiles hitting us. The scramble into the bobbing boat could have knocked one of us out or torn Catherine's already injured rotator cuff to the point of needing surgery. The overexertion during the intense physical demands we made on our bodies could have torn, ripped, herniated, or otherwise maimed any of us in any number of horrific ways. Yet as I sat on the couch, looking at my meagre injuries, I was astounded that we were not so much worse off than we were. Somehow through all the horror, we were actually lucky.

In a moment of inspiration brought on by deep-seated gratitude, I jumped up from the couch and grabbed my cell phone. I hoisted Hazel up onto the back of the living room couch, so she was near our standing height. At that moment, I felt the need to take a photo of us together.

We had survived. Somehow, we had made it through the worst hurricane the Bahamas had ever seen. There were hundreds of people still missing and likely dead. Their story could easily have been our own. It suddenly felt extremely important to mark that moment with a photograph after losing so many other pictures of special moments to the storm.

In the photo, we are all smiling. None of those smiles are huge, jubilant smiles like those taken at birthday parties or Christmas. They are grateful smiles, filled with the joy of being together.

After our photo, I turned to Cath and said, "Do you hear that?"

"What?"

"Silence," I replied, and we relished the peace in that silence and the familiarity of a home.

It wasn't the home we had built over the years, filled with mementos of our lives. That was now lost to the ocean and raging wind. In the aftermath of near-death, homelessness, and uncertainty about the future, the condo was the only home we now had, and it was what we all needed now. We needed a place and the time to recover and regroup. There would be days, weeks, and even months ahead of chaos and fear. Massive and sudden life decisions would need to be made. Yet, at that moment, we had all that we needed. We had shelter, love, and peace.

CHANGES

Following Hurricane Dorian, massive changes came flying at us at hyper speed. Each day we woke up was a new day of decisions and logistical nightmares. Despite having survived the near-death experience of a Category 5 hurricane, we did not get the opportunity for a calm recovery period for a very long time. Chaos became our way of life, and everything felt more challenging than it should have. Minor life annoyances became the cause for tears and anger unrelated to the circumstances. Within the first week alone, our meagre plans for what the future might hold changed three times.

At first, we focused on necessities. Charlotte asked if we wanted them to visit Florida to be with us. Through grateful tears, Cath said, "Of course!" They made plans to arrive in a few days. We washed Hazel's precious stuffed toys to finally remove the sewage and bacteria she was still holding on to. We rented a car to get around. We spent time with Florida friends and purchased things we needed for everyday life in a home only stocked for weekend use.

One of our first priorities was to get Hazel into the water. The thought of her developing a phobia following the trauma of the flooding inside our house was a logical one, and we discussed it fervently in the first few days of being in Florida. Even in our altered mental state, the ocean was with us. The very idea that Hazel might now fear this innate part of who we were was not something we could imagine living with. We knew that therapy would be a priority very soon, but first, we felt that testing the theory of getting back on the horse following a fall was paramount.

As Cath and I talked of all that had happened to us, late at night from the darkness of our bed in those first few days, neither of us found fear of the ocean or swimming to be among the lasting impressions for us. Though the ocean and its monster storm had tried very hard to kill us, we did not take away a negative view of the ocean. For too long in our lives, and the lives of our parents and grandparents, the ocean was beautiful and powerful. A thing to marvel at, but also a thing to be wary of. Often in those first few weeks after Dorian, as I lay in the darkness at night, I felt the ocean waves moving me, though I was not moving at all. Even with this uncomfortable swaying that had settled into my brain as a symptom of PTSD, I wasn't afraid of the water.

Without a word to Hazel about it, we took her to the community swimming pool in our condo complex and watched with anxiety as we waited for signs of trauma as she went in quite willingly. Our fears were entirely unfounded.

Never fans of public swimming pools, Cath and I sat in the shade of a pool umbrella as Hazel happily splashed and swam. She dove into the quiet pool that afternoon as though she had not had a terrifying near-death encounter just a few days before. Relief washed over us. While we knew that therapy was still a must for all of us, it was a relief that this hurdle did not need to be crossed. The idea that our daughter, raised with the ocean in her soul, might suddenly be frightened by one of the things that were so solidly ingrained in us would have been very hard to cope with on top of everything that was coming at us at lightspeed. But there she was, relishing in the simple joy of swimming and playing imaginary games of mermaids and an underwater world. Those were the games we had played as children. And so, for just a brief few moments, we were able to rest in the knowledge that whatever permanent scars Dorian had in store for us, they did not include a fear of the ocean.

Our immediate plan was to remain in Florida for six months to access therapy and try to begin to recover. Leaving Freeport ahead of the storm with four dogs to shelter in the condo had not been an option for fear of breaking the Homeowners Association rule of only two small dogs per unit. In our current evacuated state, we hoped our story would garner sympathy from the Board if we were caught in the interim breaking the rules. As it was, we would only walk two dogs at a time from our third-floor walk-up. We wanted to avoid drawing attention and risk being evicted from our only source of stability. We decided to begin hunting for short-term house rental options in the area. We also started reaching out to friends to investigate school options for Hazel. Freeport was wrecked, and we could not bear the thought of returning to see it all, day after day. In Florida, we would have all the modern conveniences like running water, stable electricity, and fresh groceries. And we would be close to home for the inevitable trips back to deal with the remnants of our broken home.

Within the first week, though, it became clear that I would need to make a trip back to the Bahamas as soon as possible to replace my driver's license lost in Dorian. I was not happy about leaving Catherine and Hazel, even for just a day. The Post-Traumatic Stress Disorder was genuine, and everyone was still on edge with massive emotions. However, I was driving a rental car in a foreign country without a license, having rented the car in Catherine's name though I was the primary driver. I needed to fix that quickly.

My trip to the capital of Nassau, with a visit to my dad and stepmom, was planned for a single day. I left early

Wednesday morning, less than a week after being evacuated, and I planned to get my license reprinted and travel directly back to Florida that evening. The bad luck in that plan was twofold.

The first issue was that I happened to travel on September eleventh, the same day that then-US President Trump went on national television and called Bahamians "gang members and very bad people." As I read the news report on my cell phone while waiting anxiously for my flight to take off from Florida, I shook my head at the stupidity of a world leader making such a stereotypical statement about an entire country of people. I wasn't sure what the ramifications of such a proclamation would be for us in the future. At that moment, I had more than my fair share of anxiety about the day ahead of me. Hearing this news did not help.

The second issue was that the Bahamas, even before Dorian and the many storms before that, is a developing country. However, it is strategically packaged for the world to see as a first-world, luxury tourist destination. Governmental processes are snail slow, and I had to rush and beg officials to accomplish a near-impossible feat. It was necessary to use tears and my sad story to get my driver's license in a matter of hours instead of the days or weeks it might generally take.

I spent my few hours in Nassau running from one government office to another in ninety-degree heat. The entire time I was fearful that I would not get my driver's license or would not make my flight back to Catherine and Hazel that day. Being separated from my family even for a day was enough to induce a lot of anxiety, and I spent the day problem-solving in a full-steam-ahead situation.

In the wake of the natural disaster, many Bahamians were fleeing to America to be with family and friends there. Travelling back to the US and to Cath and Hazel meant clearing US Border Patrol in Nassau International Airport, who were now on alert to question and refuse entry to many Bahamian citizens based on the President's comments earlier that day. There was now fear that we all were planning to immigrate to the US illegally. By the time I stood in front of the immigration officer at the airport, I was sweating profusely, red-faced, and overwhelmed. I know I looked like a crazy person.

"Where are you headed?" the brunette, female officer asked as she flipped through the pages of my passport.

"Fort Lauderdale, Florida," I replied quickly, out of breath.

The officer looked up from my passport and studied me. "What's the purpose of your trip?"

"I'm going back to my wife and daughter. I only flew in for the day," I replied. When the officer paused and waited, I interjected, "Vacation." The word sounded like the afterthought that it was. I felt dizzy as my heart beat faster and my stomach growled. The small sandwich I had inhaled for lunch several hours before was long gone.

"And how long will you be in the United States?"

"About two months," I answered quickly without thinking. I didn't know exactly how long I was going to be in Florida, and I didn't have a return airline ticket. I didn't want to lie and say a random date, but I also knew I couldn't say, "Indefinitely."

"How long is 'about two months'?" she inquired quickly, and her tone told me I had chosen the wrong words.

I explained briefly that we had been impacted by Dorian and that my family and I were recovering in Florida. I hoped that I might have the woman's sympathy with my story. I did not.

"You'll need to go to secondary screening. Follow the signs," she said and indicated the sign on the wall to my right as she handed me back my passport.

Secondary screening turned out to be a closed room with a high counter on one side, behind which several US Border Patrol officers were working as they called individuals forward for further questions. I stood, waiting, in US Border Patrol Pre-Clearance for three hours, missing my flight in the process. While standing in a room crowded with other Bahamians trying to fly to the US, I felt like I was in some sort of county lock-up situation, except I had committed no crime. I was terrified of being permanently separated from my family just seven days after surviving a near-death disaster together. I leaned against a wall with my eyes closed several times per hour, trying to avoid a panic attack.

After multiple harsh questions ranging from my housing and employment status to my financial stability, the US Border Patrol denied me entry initially. They assumed that I had lost my job because of Dorian and was attempting to live and work in their country illegally. There was much back and forth, often with the officer repeating the same questions, though worded differently in hopes of catching me in a lie.

At one point, the Border Patrol agent, a tall, bald man who moved with an air of superiority, asked me to provide copies of my bank statements to show that I had some sort of savings and did not need illegal work in the US. I agreed quickly, though he would not allow me to show him my bank statement on my phone. Eventually, I managed to convince the very unsympathetic officer that my dishevelled appearance resulted from Post-Traumatic Stress Disorder and not an illegal immigration attempt. When I was finally permitted to travel, the officer was excessively clear that I must leave the country within sixty days. The airline thankfully rebooked me on the next flight out that evening.

During the ordeal I had refused to contact Catherine to unnecessarily disrupt her day with the arrival of her sisters, instead choosing to say simply that I had missed my flight and would arrive later than expected. Charlotte and Pattie flew to Florida from Connecticut to be with us for a few days. Catherine's other sister, Rosalie, was already in Florida, visiting from an unaffected part of the Bahamas. By the time I made it back to my family that evening, I met them at a restaurant for dinner. When I arrived, I immediately crumbled into Catherine's arms in uncontrollable sobs in the middle of a very public place. It was minutes before I regained enough composure to speak.

"I almost didn't make it back to you," I cried as I paused in my hug with Cath to lean down and hug Hazel tightly as well.

"What?" the entire table asked.

"Trump won't allow Bahamians back into the country because he thinks everyone is trying to immigrate illegally. The Officer in Nassau didn't want to let me through at all. I have to be out of the US in two months." My words spilled out in a disjointed, panic attack moment.

The incident with the US Border Patrol changed our initial six-month plan to remain in Florida. Suddenly, we needed a new plan. Freeport and Marsh Harbour were virtually unlivable following Dorian. People were desperately trying to find and keep the simple necessities of life like electricity, potable water, and food. The schools would not reopen for many months. We had no home there, and we quickly found out from insurance assessment and structural reports that our house was no longer structurally sound. Other parts of the Bahamas, like Nassau, were unaffected by Dorian, and so masses of people were migrating there. We had family there, but the capital of Nassau is crime-ridden and has a horrific traffic problem. Even in the short term, Nassau did not feel like the right option.

Of all the options, a completely new start was the one that checked the most wish list boxes. We spoke with several US immigration lawyers to see if there was any way we could immigrate permanently and remain in Florida. With its notoriously difficult immigration laws, staying in the US was only an option if we did it as illegal immigrants, and we were not interested in breaking the law. Now faced with nowhere to go, and our original post-Dorian plan shot to hell by the US government, we jumped sort of half-heartedly into an international move while our psyches were still reeling with PTSD. Within the four weeks following Dorian, we researched Canada as an option. We spoke to Canadian immigration lawyers and found there were immigration opportunities for us there.

Immediately following Hurricane Dorian, I began referring to us as "climate change refugees." I don't remember where I first heard the phrase. In the world of climate change studies, our situation is also called "environmental migrants." We were choosing to leave our home country partly because climate change had made living there increasingly challenging, even bordering on impossible. Rising sea levels and ocean temperatures create more frequent catastrophic storms that make living in the Bahamas more dangerous each year. That, coupled with homophobia and discrimination in our country, made leaving permanently a necessity rather than a choice.

Then came the inevitable question once we settled on a broad destination: where in Canada? The idea of moving inland was tossed out the window very early on. If we were leaving the Bahamas, we still needed to be close to the ocean. Neither of us could imagine living our lives in the middle part of any country, where the ocean was only reachable by a long airline flight.

We prioritized a need to be within easy driving distance of Charlotte and Pattie in Connecticut. Remaining as close to family as possible was important to us. We were moving to an entirely new country, sight unseen for the most part, so we needed to know that some sort of support system was at least reachable by car. Nova Scotia seemed too far to be considered driveable to New England, so we settled on New Brunswick. I had done a tiny amount of research on the area previously, thinking we might take a vacation one day to see the Bay of Fundy.

The terror of being hunted so relentlessly by the ocean left us scarred. Even still, our view of it remained unchanged at its core. From birth, the sea was a thing of beauty. Throughout our lives, the memories and interactions with the ocean, both directly and indirectly, held such a compelling place in our idea of righteousness. Even at its worst, we could not hold the ocean eternally accountable for our losses and grief. Much like a bully is only the result of their upbringing, so too were the actions of an ocean directed by abuse to create the monster that was Dorian.

With nothing in our lives seeming constant or tangible in our PTSD haze, we agreed, virtually unspoken, that we would never remove the ocean from our lives no matter where we lived. It was too important to who we are as people, both individually and as a family.

All those decisions led to researching schools for Hazel. Once we located a school near Saint John, New Brunswick that we liked, Catherine took on the job of house hunting. Real estate perusal became our evening pastime when Hazel went to bed. With only the most basic logistics organized, we set a date to have movers pack up the contents of our condo, all that was left of our worldly possessions, and ship it to a random storage facility in Saint John.

We had never been to the east coast of Canada, having spent only a few days in Vancouver years before. We knew precious little about where we were going and had only the most basic information gained from googling the area in the weeks leading up to the move. We were throwing a dart at a map. We crossed our fingers and hoped that we would have the stamina to make it work with massive amounts of emotional baggage, four dogs, and a six-year-old girl in tow.

Before leaving Florida on our long drive north, Catherine and I made a trip back to Freeport. Part of our initial processing of the trauma and loss involved Catherine's need to search for more salvageable things from our home. In my mind, it was all already gone, broken, and rotting from being left for weeks following the storm. Catherine needed to try, so we decided to leave Hazel in Florida for two days with our dear friends. Through connections with a pilot friend, we were able to secure seats on a small aircraft flying back to Freeport: our third and final heartbreaking trip back to what was left of our dream home.

In the three weeks since the storm, mold and mildew had grown in our home. To avoid respiratory illness, we had to wear face masks even to move around inside. Looters had spent considerable time and effort on our home in the few weeks we had been gone. More plumbing and electrical fixtures had been stolen. Quite a few windows had even been forcibly removed using what looked like a crowbar or even a jackhammer.

We spent two days, with help, salvaging more of our lives. Canvas paintings, trinkets, and seashells were among the things we saved and moved to a friend's garden shed for storage. Aside from the lost photos, the loss of years of collections from the sea was among the hardest losses to swallow.

A beachcomber her entire life, Cath's thousands of shells and pounds and pounds of sea glass were scattered throughout the house and out into the yard. We sifted through what we could. Most of the collections had been housed in massive floor-standing vases to showcase them in our beach-themed home. As the water rose, the vases floated. Even the heaviest ones, filled with tiny pieces of sea glass, had floated in the storm. The horrible swirling sent the vases crashing into heavy pieces of furniture only to shatter very early on. Much of the vases' contents would have floated. Even still, we were able to find pockets of shells collected in the corner of a room or wedged under the edge of a couch. Everything at ground level was mixed with broken glass. Collecting shells inside our home, with heavy garden gloves protecting our hands, was a low point. For so many years, we had taken the treasures the ocean had offered us. The ocean had decided, in one fell swoop, to take so much of it back like an angry child withdrawing their offer to share their favourite toys.

For me, the trip cemented the loss, but for Catherine, it reinforced that there were things we could still save. However, leaving Hazel any longer was impossible, and the logistics of another trip seemed unmanageable with plans already set for moving north.

By early October, we packed up the new car we had bought, and movers packed up the condo contents for shipping. We drove to Orlando and spent a couple of crazy days at Disney World with my mom, stepdad, sister, and family, who joined us from Georgia. It was an insane time for a family trip, but it took our minds off the chaos for a few days as we watched Hazel and my nephew melt into the magic of Disney World. We made our way up the East Coast and stopped in Connecticut to be with Charlotte and Pattie for a week. We were moving to another country and were unsure when we would see everyone again.

We were frightened, unsure, and suffering when we crossed the Canadian border in mid-October 2019, just six weeks after losing everything to Dorian. We found an Airbnb willing to take us with four dogs for a month. The first couple of weeks were a total nightmare. Having arrived in a new place and new country without knowing anyone and barely the most basic of plans, we muddled through.

Thankfully, the timing of our arrival in Canada allowed us a few months of cold temperatures that were manageable before the daytime high dipped below freezing in the long, snow-covered winter. It was absolutely a seasonal adjustment, but at least we weren't going into it completely unprepared, having vacationed regularly in the snow in the past.

Each day, we faced problems and logistics as we tried to settle and find a permanent place to live while tackling immigration. Paperwork, something I had always been good at, became a challenging task. Focusing on details when my brain was so filled with unaddressed emotions was a painful struggle. I researched colleges and universities in the area after being told that attending would be our fastest route to permanent residency, something that would still take up to five years to obtain. Moving money from the Bahamas to Canada for living expenses and eventually purchasing a home was another unnecessarily difficult challenge that I plowed through. The hassle of rebuilding our lives from a logistical level was infuriating and everything I did felt harder than it should.

Depression, anger, despair, and sadness were daily experiences. The month in the AirBnB was my lowest point: having forced myself to keep going, keep pushing forward, and keep searching for the point where we could feel stable and able to rest. Early in our first few weeks in our new country, I reached a breaking point before realizing that I finally had to address my mental health as a priority.

However, through the trauma-induced aggravation, fear, and hopelessness came a beacon of hope. Within a month of our arrival in New Brunswick, when we still knew precious few people, Hazel spoke of an observation she made. She piped up one day during a drive around the area as we tried to familiarize ourselves with our new home.

Staring out the window from the backseat of the car at the dusting of snow that had fallen the day before, Hazel stated, "I really like Canada."

"Oh? Why's that?" I responded absently, as the statement had interrupted some unrelated conversation we had been having in the front seat.

"They see us as a family here," she stated in a matter-of-fact tone.

The wisdom of our six-year-old in that moment was profound. While Hazel had certainly seen and heard many of our conversations as we hashed and rehashed the life-changing decisions that had been coming at us full tilt over the previous six weeks, her statement was not one either of us said out loud up to that point.

"You're right, Hazel," Catherine responded with an astounded tone, ever surprised at Hazel's ability to see the world so well for someone so young.

Having lived all her short life in a country which, though mostly subtle, made sure gay and lesbian people understood that they were inherently inferior, Hazel could immediately feel the level of welcomeness we experienced in Canada. Her words that day echoed in the months and years that followed and grounded us when we felt the most doubt about our decision to leave the Bahamas.

"They see us as a family here." That was the real, underlying motivation for our prompt departure, post-trauma. While neither of us could ever imagine living in the path of another Dorian, our need to give Hazel a better life, both physically and emotionally, was the motivation we clung to when the road ahead in our new country felt arduous.

Image courtesy of Catherine Pyfrom

RECOVERY

As part of my recovery, I took to marking the anniversaries of Dorian. Needing to write my emotions out as my form of therapy, I punctuated the first few months with Facebook updates of where we were in our emotional journey. It became a journal of sorts. The updates were as much about organizing how I felt on those anniversaries as they were about sharing with family and friends, though we would not likely see any of them again for a very long time.

October 2, 2019

It's been four weeks. One month since all hell broke loose. A month of tears, fears, guilt, anger, sleeplessness, heartache, and headache. Yes, we are so grateful to be alive. Yes, every single second of every day, we give thanks that we are safe and together. So many others are not safe or together or alive.

Time has not been our friend. There simply hasn't been enough of it. Time to mourn our losses. Time to make decisions. Time to plan logistics, lodging, and daily care. Time to stay connected with those who remain in the Bahamas and others who have become part of the post-Dorian mass exodus to begin building lives elsewhere.

Every step seems extra heavy as we carry huge baggage with us. Physical Baggage filled with the remains of our worldly possessions. Emotional Baggage filled with all the feelings brought on by the trauma.

Personally, I'm happy to leave the last month behind. And I truly hope that the month to come brings more time to process all that has happened and all that continues to unfold.

November 2, 2019

It's been two months since Dorian blew our lives away. Not our stuff. However, that's, for us, a big part of our lives. It blew our lives away. Yes, we are alive. But honestly, every day, or, at best, parts of every day, don't feel like living. It feels like existing. We are conscious. We are making decisions—hard ones. We eat, we sleep (sometimes), we walk, we talk. Shit, we even laugh though god knows how. And we cry. Often at the same time and not that good kind of laugh that makes tears of joy spout from your eyes. No, it's that bad kind where the laugh automatically gives way to tears because, in the middle of the laugh, you remember something or someone you've lost.

Just existing. I, for one, am the worst version of myself right now. To the point that my closest people would not recognize me. I know this. I'm keenly aware of it. Oh yes, the first step is admitting, etc. Hopefully, eventually, I'll find the time and space to work on it and work through it and find the better me still buried in there somewhere. But I'm too busy just existing and surviving right now.

The day-to-day is hard. Washing clothes was never this hard. Caring for our dogs and our child was never this hard. Sending emails and doing paperwork was never this hard. Minor setbacks in everyday life were just a small annoyance before Dorian. Now, if I can't find a misplaced object or an email response takes too long, it's all I can do to hold it together.

My to-do list before Dorian read something like brush the dog, sweep the floor, grocery shop, pay a bill. Now my to-do list has all of those things PLUS PLUS PLUS PLUS. I told someone recently that I have an unpaid evening job: answering emails and correspondence from friends and family worldwide. The time I could be spending trying to unwind, I'm spending with my nose in my phone showing support for the people close to us so we can remain connected. It's a part-time job for sure. But it is very important to us to do it. To be supportive of everyone who has been so supportive of us. To stay connected.

Everything was so easy before, to the point that I'm actually angry with myself for ever feeling stressed before Dorian. I had NOTHING to be stressed about before Dorian. Nothing! I didn't even know what stress really was. I guess that's what they mean when they say don't sweat the small stuff. That's what I should've been doing before when my front gate stopped working and needed to be fixed. Or I forgot to buy an item from the grocery store, and now I have to drive 15 mins back to buy it to cook dinner. Tiny things that didn't matter. Now everything matters A LOT.

Apparently, rebuilding your life is tough. I've never had to do it before. Not on this scale. I've watched others do it and offered empathy and help where I could. But rebuilding our life in many cases requires BIG decisions that must be made with very little time to process the pros and cons and ramifications. And rebuilding our life means finding a new house to call home when you damn well loved the one you had, and now it's gone. The house is gone along with the favorite T-Shirt you can't find until you remember that fucker Dorian took it. Rebuilding means making new connections while maintaining a hold on the old ones. It means changing our routine and trying desperately to put a new, more complicated one in place.

We are people who thrive on routine. That's really boring for a lot of people. And that's ok. But for us, there is a sense of calm in knowing that most nights, dinner is on the table at the same time. That bedtime routine is the same. That on Tuesdays and Thursdays between 4-5 we are at piano lessons. Or that on a hot Saturday afternoon, we could always be found in our pool swimming with the dogs. Rebuilding our lives involves finding new routines that fit into our new lives—and having trouble making those new routines fit because we had spent so long creating those old, perfectly planned ones. I miss our routines too.

The animals we have so lovingly raised to become a part of our family have become, in part, extra stress. They are confused and used to their routines that have suddenly changed. They are used to their home with an acre to run in and freedom to come and go from the house to the yard whenever they want. Our dogs were all raised with dog doors. Before Dorian, most had only been on a lead a handful of times. Walking four dogs on a leash 5-7 times a day is another part-time job in itself. And on the odd occasion, they are off lead, the risk of chaos multiplies as hard-headed dachshund owners can sympathize. New smells and sights combined with the courage of a pack make listening to us all but impossible for them.

We make decisions, and then we question them constantly. I, for one, can't figure out for the life of me what's the "right" decision. Before Dorian, decision-making was something that came relatively easy for me. I trust my instincts, but more importantly, I had the confidence in my ability to manage the fall-out of a bad decision. Now I can barely make tea in the morning, so fall-out is no longer on the list of things I can handle right now. This complicates every decision, from what to eat for dinner to how late we let Hazel stay up.

Hazel, bless her, seems to be so very pliable in all of this. Because she's a child? Because that's her personality? Because she's actually not ok in her head after almost dying and losing everything and is doing a great job of not letting it show? Thank god for professional therapists because I can't tell.

So it's still Step one, then Step two, then Step three through today. And tomorrow we start again....

I spent so much time, during the few months after Dorian, feeling responsible for everything. There was guilt in the decision to remain in our house instead of sheltering elsewhere. I felt that decision was mine alone since I adamantly maintained my belief that we would be safe, even as we watched the people in Marsh Harbour experience catastrophic flooding. I felt even more guilt about dragging us all outside as the water rose to the height of our windows. It took many months of therapy to accept that those decisions, and others, were not mine alone, and that I was reacting to an impossible situation clouded by terror.

In early January 2020, we decided to have the remnants of our dream home torn down. Thankfully we had almost full insurance coverage on our house, which included hurricane coverage. Once the structural engineers had assessed our home and determined that it was no longer structurally sound, we had professional advice that it could not be saved and rebuilt, even if we wanted it to. Leaving the shell of the house full of ruined furniture and piles of various personal belongings to be rooted through by looters daily was never going to be an option. The idea of leaving the house abandoned was more brutal to comprehend than facing its physical removal. With significant financial and emotional expenses, we arranged to have a construction crew tear down the house and remove the rubble.

January 7, 2020

We spent 7+ years designing and drawing and re-drawing the floor plan of our dream home. We started landscaping years before we broke ground. Before we even had water, we would cart buckets of water by car to water trees we had planted. Six plus months building and being on-site daily, sometimes for hours at a time, during construction. Almost five years of decorating and perfecting the interior so that every square inch screamed our lives, our joys, and our memories. Our dream house was our happy place.

What took YEARS of blood, sweat, and tears to create was destroyed in less than 48 hours. The shell looked intact to anyone passing by, but the reality is that the foundation and exterior walls were compromised, and a structural engineer determined the house a complete write-off and unrepairable.

Of course, we knew demolition was happening yesterday and today. There's a lot of anger and pain. It's a bit like a long-distance funeral for a loved one who passed away four months ago, and you've spent all this time missing them and trying to live without them. And now, all this time has passed to say that final goodbye without actually attending the funeral.

Opening Facebook last night and seeing an aerial view video shot by a drone of our dream house, our happy place, demolished by heavy machinery, was NOT something we needed to ever see. It was like having the stitches of a really large incision ripped out before healing is complete.

Life does feel a little like it's leveling out at times. New things to focus on to pass the time. 'Cause time is the only thing that will ever make this whole thing ever so slightly more bearable. Only not really...

Six months after Dorian, we found ourselves in our own new home. We purchased a nice house in a suburban town in Atlantic Canada and decorated it with our items from our Florida condo. We gained the stability of a home that was ours and a routine that, while different in many ways from our Bahamas life, was at least comfortable. We did everything we could to bring the Bahamas to Canada with us. Our condo in Florida had been filled with tropical-themed décor. The furnishings might have seemed out of place in our river valley, but they helped us feel closer to the ocean, which was still a part of who we were. As we slowly increased our possessions, after losing almost everything we owned, we continued to feel drawn to palm trees, shells, lighthouses, nautical items, and, of course, seashells and sea glass. We couldn't begin to replace the collections, but we slowly began collecting again.

March 2, 2020

We've both been trying to write about this milestone for over a week. Each time I try to compile the emotions and put them into words, I feel overwhelmed, and so I procrastinate and put it off. After much encouragement, I've also been trying to put down in story form what exactly we went through in Hurricane Dorian. I've only managed to get through the first 5 hours of the 36-hour ordeal.

It's been six months. Half a year. 183 days. Every single day of that, we've felt grateful. So incredibly grateful to be alive, have each other, and have access to immediate physical needs like food, water, shelter, and clothing.

But six months later, I still struggle to make a decision about a non-essential purchase in a store after losing everything. I struggle with an inability to sit still because if I sit still, I have to think. Then if I force myself to sit still, I struggle to get back up off the couch as hopelessness sets in. Anxiety is a daily companion. PTSD pops up if the wind picks up or a movie scene is too real, and art imitates life.

Neither of us feels like we can say it seems like a lifetime since Dorian tore our lives apart because it doesn't. We also can't say it seems like it happened only yesterday because that's not the case either. The passage of time is warped. As though time no longer exists at all. Only the waves exist that battered us inside of our home. They ebb and flow still, even thousands of miles away and six months later. The waves that broke us still move us along.

Each of our Facebook updates was met with a chorus of support. Some of that support was from friends and acquaintances offering positivity and encouragement. Some support was in comradery with others who had also lost everything but their lives in Dorian. Sadly, knowing that we were not the only ones trying to rebuild our lives after the storm did not help the long road feel any shorter.

A quick trip back to Florida in March of 2020 to sell the condo and liquidate the investment for expenses in our new home was followed by the world imploding again. Only instead of just our world imploding, everyone else's did as well. The COVID-19 pandemic arrived to complicate our PTSD, mental illness, and new country problems. After barely managing to begin to settle, an entirely new way of life began again. Stay-at-home orders, virtual school, social distancing, and mask mandates became normal. COVID delayed our immigration applications tremendously, further complicating our transition into our new life.

As we coped with the emotions of moving to an entirely new country, I felt responsible for putting my family into the situation of adjusting to unfamiliar surroundings while being treated for Post-Traumatic Stress Disorder. As the primary organizer and paperwork person in our family, I felt the process of stabilizing us in Canada sat on my shoulders because of my innate need to be in control. I managed to overwhelm myself with the level of responsibility I unknowingly and voluntarily placed on my shoulders. Therapy helped me see that and shifted my perspective about my need to control and accept responsibility.

For Catherine, the loss of years of collections and memorabilia that held so many of her childhood memories and connection to her deceased parents was one of her biggest hurdles to overcome. For her, there was a great sense of self in the items collected, and their loss was difficult to comprehend and surmount. Those feelings of loss were made worse by her belief that far more was salvageable from the house than we had the mental and physical stamina to accomplish. There was guilt in that. Acclimating to our new country and climate was hardest for Catherine, as the pull of the ocean and the beauty of our country called to her constantly.

Throughout those months of acclimating, we each spent time in therapy to sort out and feel the emotions of the trauma, loss, and grief. It was a long, multi-tiered process for each of us, and we were often at different stages of the process at different times. Hazel's recovery was the swiftest of us all. Perhaps because of her age or personality, she readily accepted therapy and easily talked about the emotions resulting from the storm. She settled into her new life, new friends, and new school remarkably well. Catherine and I continued to struggle to sort out our feelings, individually and together, into our second year post-Dorian.

We survived, and slowly, we began to feel more settled. There are so many others that did not survive. In the weeks and months following Hurricane Dorian, the final estimated death count in the Bahamas rested around seventy, with many more still listed as missing today.[iv] Poor, undocumented Haitian immigrants living in shanty towns in Marsh Harbour, Abaco made up a large portion of those numbers. As a result, accurate death toll statistics are virtually impossible to state. A friend and former employee of ours, living in Marsh Harbour during Dorian, was among those lost. His body was never recovered in the aftermath, and we think often of his family and their unimaginable loss even as we are grateful for our own lives.

My stepmom inherited an investment property in Abaco some years before Dorian that sat directly on the shoreline, its foundation made of a series of concrete pilings that kept it perched on the edge of a sharp embankment. Built in the 1970s, the house had seen and survived many hurricanes over the years. My dad and stepmom were safe in Nassau for the storm, and their cottage, located in the town of Marsh Harbour, sat empty when Dorian ran headlong into it. After the storm had passed, the house was nowhere to be found; only two pilings remained. Weeks later, a small portion of the roof was recognized among the debris half a mile away across the main harbour. The rest of the house and its contents were never found. Many other, older homes along the harbourfront disappeared as well. Some folks scrambled during the storm to seek safety. Many did not make it out alive.

Catherine's parents had a vacation home in Marsh Harbour as well. It belonged to one of Catherine's sisters when Dorian arrived. Her sister was living in Ohio at the time and was not in Abaco for the storm. There are aerial photos of the house in the aftermath taken by a drone. After Dorian was done with the house, it looked like a pile of matchsticks.

A childhood friend sheltered alone in her apartment during Dorian in Marsh Harbour. Having been through so many storms in our lives, weathering a storm alone in an otherwise strong building was not unheard of. She was not in the area that experienced heavy flooding. Instead during the worst of the storm, a portion of the roof gave way and was ripped off by the wind. Fearing for her life if she remained in the house, her instincts told her to flee to the neighbours'. She was found after the storm, under piles of palm fronds, unconscious. She was air-lifted to the closest hospital in Nassau where she spent four days being treated for lacerations and a broken neck. She survived. By some miracle, her spinal cord was not severed, and she made a full, physical recovery, though the emotional scars live on.

Our friends who owned a farm in Freeport, after whom we asked during our rescue, made it out alive but they lost everything as we did. During the worst of the rising flood waters, they had storm surges as high as their house walls like ours. They had been unable to lift their elderly mother into the attic during the storm since they did not have an attic ladder. The old woman was forced to wade in the water as it rose, holding onto the refrigerator with a rope tied under her arms to keep her from drowning for close to thirty-six hours. The three of them survived, miraculously. Their friend and farm hand who was sheltering in staff quarters on the property drowned in the storm. He had not been able to get to higher ground as the waters rose. Most of the animals, including horses, goats, chickens, pigs, dogs, cats, and rabbits had been placed in barns and closed-roof pens to keep them safe from the anticipated high winds. Not expecting thirty feet of ocean, almost all died.

Our friend Kent, who had evacuated himself and his mother from her flooded home during the worst of the hurricane, lost his pest control and CO^2 distribution business. His office and equipment were under six feet of ocean surge in the central part of Freeport's commercial industrial area. Hurricane Matthew had left his company struggling for business. Without the funds and motivation to begin again on an island that would eventually see another major storm, he and his wife and son chose to leave the island. They settled in the United States permanently.

It was estimated that Dorian left approximately twelve thousand homes damaged or destroyed.[v] Our stories are just a few in that staggering number. Staggering especially when remembering that the entire country only has a population of around four hundred thousand people.

The remoteness of our islands and the underfunded nature of our government meant recovery on the islands moved at a snail's pace. It was the opinion of many that the government's initial and subsequent response was slow, using antiquated procedures and insisting on abidance by unyielding red tape. The public response also lacked the resources to provide the needed aid on its own. Many international relief agencies and average people on the island and from around the world wanted to help. They all had to be coordinated by a system not set up for a disaster of the magnitude of Dorian.[vi] Grassroots organizations in Nassau, Marsh Harbour, and Freeport, much like those that Noel and Jamie were a part of immediately following Dorian, used their connections and determination to manage and coordinate inbound humanitarian efforts with the Bahamas National Emergency Management Agency (NEMA).

CORE[vii], a grassroots non-government organization (NGO), and several others like it, provided valuable recovery efforts. Often using WhatsApp as their main source of communication, the group can be attributed with coordinating large groups of pilots and aircraft for supply delivery and transport of evacuees, coordinating with NEMA and other similar NGOs to share information, and creating an evacuation shelter in Nassau that eventually received almost seven thousand people from Grand Bahama and Abaco. The group also helped arrange private housing for nine hundred people when there was no more shelter space, and they had no other support systems to rely on. CORE arranged, stored, and delivered more than four hundred thousand pounds of donated relief supplies.

In Abaco, a makeshift morgue utilizing a forty-foot refrigerated shipping container sat in the middle of Marsh Harbour, filled with the remains of fifty-one people until May 2020.[viii] The process of identifying the bodies was tied up in bureaucratic red tape by authorities for many months. With no DNA testing available within the country, all samples had to be sent abroad for processing. It is possible that the lack of expertise in the country resulted in such samples often getting lost long before making it out of the Bahamas. Authorities made matters worse by refusing to allow family members to attempt to identify their loved ones in the early days after Dorian, due mainly to the already-decomposing state of the remains when they were recovered days and even weeks after the storm. The situation highlighted missing key procedures and the government tried to mitigate that with a good deal of finger-pointing.

In Freeport, Samaritan's Purse set up a forty-bed field hospital that exceeded the original government-funded hospital there. World Central Kitchen provided hundreds of meals a day until the pandemic made it impossible to continue. Grand Bahama Disaster Relief Foundation in connection with several other NGOs mobilized in hopes of assisting with the rebuilding of hundreds of homes on the island.[ix] Mercy Corps and Mission Resolve Foundation installed a system to generate seventy-five hundred gallons of potable water per day after the storm surge that covered the island contaminated the well water systems. Potable water from home taps wasn't restored until two years later when new reverse osmosis systems were put in place. Funds for providing long-term shelters, removing tons of debris, and restoring utilities have continued to trickle in slowly, with the pandemic inhibiting progress.

We were blessed to have the financial stability and stamina to immigrate to another country to avoid ever living the nightmare of Dorian again. Those who could leave did. Friends of ours who used to live in the Bahamas are now spread across the United States from Florida to Texas. There are hundreds, if not thousands, of people in the Bahamas who would like the same opportunity but do not have the means.

There are just as many people who choose to remain in the country of their birth because of a strong pride in their homeland and their ability to recover. Bahamians are a stubborn but resilient bunch of people. They are proud to a fault at times, often not willing to accept charity until circumstances are dire. Their religious beliefs sustain them through hard times. The slogan "It's better in the Bahamas" is not just a tourism gimmick, it's an indoctrination, too. Even in the face of natural disasters ever more frequent, they believe in their ability to carry on. I wish I had the optimism that fills many of their hearts. Perhaps it's not optimism as it is a refusal to see the inevitable.

The Bahamas rebuilds after each of these monster storms, though with each direct hit, that rebuilding becomes slower and more costly. For the people that remain, it is not about if another storm of Dorian's magnitude will strike again, it's when. Global warming is very real, nonetheless. As the years go on, the effects of warming oceans and changing weather patterns will continue to impact low-lying countries like the Bahamas far more quickly than many of its larger, first-world neighbours.

The United Nations estimates that as much as forty percent of the world's population lives within sixty miles of the coast.[x] Living near the coast is one thing. Living in a place surrounded by the primitive, untouched ocean is another. For island people, the ocean isn't just about location. For those of us who have the ocean in our blood, it is part of our very souls. It influences us in a way we don't even realize. The ocean is in our every concept of beauty and power. It's in the decisions we make about how we raise our children. The ocean affects how we see the world and our place in it.

Many will say simply, "Move away from the coast. Get to higher ground." If international refugee programs in first-world countries ever do catch up to assist with the resettlement of future climate change refugees, moving, for island people like us, will still mean contending with the pull of an ocean becoming too volatile to live with. Even today, knowing the storms grow larger and more destructive, there are millions of people throughout the world who choose to remain at the edge of the ocean. That choice has as much to do with soul needs as it does with financial and immigration restraints. Many, given the money and the pathways to move to a new, safer place, would choose to remain as island people. The need to be near the ocean is ever-present.

Millions of people around the world, but more particularly in first-world countries, have seen a documentary or two about the ocean and its connection to all things. Between Netflix and Disney+, there are several dozen at least. Before Dorian, I would watch a film and admire the breathtaking cinematography and be awestruck by the statistics and claims about climate change in each one, rarely remembering much of what I'd seen within a week. They were, after all, for mindless entertainment. Since Dorian and our firsthand experience of the cause and effect of climate change, I see these documentaries in a new light. My eyes have been opened to the reality of people's relationships with nature. Climate change drastically affected my life; it's not just content for government forums and filmmakers for me anymore.

It is up to average people to sympathize and understand the connection between how they live to how the earth reacts, in some cases, thousands of miles away. Natural disasters are becoming more and more frequent. It is only a matter of time before the forces that created our own personal worst nightmare find themselves on the doorstep of everyone on planet Earth.

By the first anniversary of Hurricane Dorian, we felt no closer to recovery than the six-month mark.

September 2, 2020

"How do you find the will to press forward when you don't even know what you're pressing towards?"

I've been trying to corral the emotions surrounding the lead-up and importance of this date for over a month. Each time I take a few minutes and allow myself to truly feel the still-raw pain and sadness and grief on what this date will now forever hold, that part of me that knowingly tries to avoid pain kicks in. That coping mechanism demands that I find something physical to do to avoid feeling that pain.

A year on, with 365 days and some 1,500 miles of physical distance between Dorian and us, life remains fragile. We have all taken steps toward recovery. Some of us have gotten emotionally further on than others. In just our little bubble, the stages of grief, recovery, and PTSD vary daily and quite literally change with the wind: pun intended. As with the death of a loved one, time makes the loss more bearable but not easier.

A year later, we do not truly know how we survived, but we are grateful. We often think about the people who did not survive and those who lost loved ones to Dorian, who have no closure. Their stories could easily have been ours. We think of all of the people who saved us, and our gratitude is overwhelming. I won't name them. You know who you are. Thank you again. And for all the support and love and encouraging words from family and friends and random strangers over the last 12 months, we are grateful.

Words fail in properly describing how it feels to try to live fully following a near-death experience and a total rollercoaster of a life change in the immediate aftermath. It's raw stress and anxiety and second-guessing every single decision and each step forward while constantly replaying the events that brought you to that single moment in time. Go to bed. Try to sleep. Wake up and do it all again. Watch a commercial or TV show, see a wave or a flood or a hurricane, and relive it all again. Walk into a store and see something you used to own and remember that Dorian took that special item along with so much else.

All of this just to say: there is still A LOT of sadness. Sometimes we who lived through Dorian zone out in Netflix to forget for a few hours. Occasionally we drink, some of us more than others. Or use pharmaceuticals, prescribed or otherwise, to dull the sadness and add a bit of cheer. We find pure joy in the blueness of the summer sky or our children's laughter, or the kindness of a stranger. We hold onto those moments so tightly as a lifeline to the actual happiness that will come again one day in weeks or months at a time, instead of just moments.

But we are strong. We were strong before Dorian and didn't know it. Post-Dorian, we know we are strong and can survive everything because we survived this monster. And we didn't just survive. Now we thrive. In a place that is exactly right for our family, especially Hazel, during an unprecedented time in world history. All things for a reason...

The Facebook posts marking the anniversaries were sugar-coated. Often this was my need to remain positive and suggest to the world that our decision to leave the Bahamas was the right one. We needed to convince ourselves of this often, as moving is complicated, but moving to another country is even more challenging. We battled with the loss of familiarity and the home we had so meticulously built. And we missed the Atlantic Ocean, the white sand beaches, and the beautiful turquoise waters of our home.

We learned, unexpectedly, that the Bay of Fundy, while fed by the Atlantic Ocean, is not the same Atlantic Ocean that fills our hearts. It's hard to explain that one body of saltwater is different from another, but it is. Visually, of course, any layperson can see the differences. The Bay of Fundy is dark and filled with muddy red silt from river runoffs, while the Atlantic Ocean of my birth is full of more vibrant blue colours than anyone can even count and is so crystal clear one can see the ocean floor.

It smells very different, too. The Bay of Fundy smells like northern seaweed and river sand. When standing on any shoreline with the Atlantic Ocean, the clean salty smell of wind that has travelled miles and miles over the open ocean to arrive in your nose is obvious. The smell of the ocean is filled with the hopes of sailors long past and the life-giving breath of the creatures that call it home.

On a trip south to visit relatives in New England, we took a drive to the Connecticut coast. I smiled as I drove along the waterfront, feeling a warm sense of nostalgia as the deep blue ocean came into view; a couple of sailboats motoring toward the open sea. I was happy to be close to the Atlantic in a way different from our frequent trips to the Bay of Fundy. When I climbed out of the car, after the longest I'd ever been away from the Atlantic Ocean, smelling it made me burst into unexpected tears.

This ocean was MY ocean, and I had missed its presence in my daily life. It was like being reunited with a treasured friend who had moved far away years before. There was so much happiness in being near the ocean of my birth; happiness I had thought I was learning to replace with things like meadows filled with deer and snowy hillsides.

Leaving the constant presence of my ocean behind has been an exercise in learning to live without.

Slowly, Catherine began painting again after an artist block that began pre-Dorian and lasted years, this time with an art studio in our new house. Her muse had always been the tropical place we called, and still call, home. Now living in a place decidedly not tropical, she lost herself for hours in creations of flamingos, turtles, stingrays, and fish. At times, her subject choice was a mix of both catharsis and depression. Being so far from the ocean has been the hardest transition for her, most of all.

Despite being only six years old during the experience of living through Dorian, Hazel has many vivid memories of the storm. She remembers being outside and screaming to go back into the house. She remembers sleeping inside the plastic bin in the attic and the hole that the wet dog bed created in the drywall ceiling. She remembers our house and her life before Dorian, but bits and pieces of friends and acquaintances and places visited less often in Freeport are muddy in her mind. We tease her about how Canadian she is now. She has acclimated well to our new country.

Few of us remember details of early childhood very well as we grow. Usually, the big events are the ones that stick with us. Most notable recently is Hazel's discomfort with larger waves. She is perfectly happy swimming in the ocean or swimming pool, but a recent encounter at a water park wave pool left her visibly unnerved. The scars are there, though well-hidden now, and likely always will be, for us all.

During most of the two years following Dorian, Catherine and I existed alongside one another but were rarely in the same mental space simultaneously. How trauma affects each of us is as unique as a fingerprint. Despite surviving the ordeal together, we were never at the same place in our recovery. We had to work harder at communicating than we had ever had to before, all while trying to comprehend our reactions and new needs, post-Dorian. While the storm nearly killed us, it also changed us in so many ways. How we each react to life and how we see the world and our places in it has changed. We have had to make a lot of strides toward knowing ourselves again.

I've thought often about that last day before Dorian arrived. The few moments of solitude and peace I had on our porch deck before starting the day come back to me in moments of extreme stress. At the time I had hoped that moment would see me through until the storm and aftermath were over. Now when I think of that time, my heart aches with longing and my eyes fill with tears as I come to terms with the fact that I will never have that moment again. The porch is gone. The gardens are gone. The feeling of peace is still elusive.

Some days feel like Dorian and our Bahamas life were just yesterday, still painful and fresh, but those days come in waves now, often few and farther between. We are very much like the coral sculptures in our living room that had floated during the storm and come to rest gently on the floor, unbroken by Dorian. Our foundations were moved, and as the ripples of the aftermath of the storm evened out, we came to rest gently in the exact right place for us, though we were all changed as a result.

On the second anniversary of Hurricane Dorian in 2021, I posted an update to our Facebook friends and family. For so many, progress was tenuous following Hurricane Dorian. For us, it was finally starting to feel attainable.

September 1, 2021

Two years ago tomorrow, we woke up at 4:00 am to the ocean coming into our home and 185 mph winds blowing outside. Throughout September 2, 2019, we fought to survive, facing death and miracles in equal doses. And survive, we did.

For a long time, being grateful was all we really had to hold on to. We felt grateful to be alive and together. We felt grateful that our circumstances allowed us to try to restart life when many could not. But the open wound of near-death, loss, grief, and resulting mental illness made the first anniversary of Dorian no less painful than the experience itself.

On the second anniversary of Hurricane Dorian, wounds now feel like scars: raw and red and angry. Not open and bleeding but still hurts at times and is still visible most days. There are days now when Dorian is not the center of every conversation, emotion, and response. There is healing, even on the days when it really doesn't feel that way at all.

The biggest difference from last year to this year feels like our ability to start looking to the future instead of just living each day individually. Dreams can again be built, and we can look forward instead of just back, and that feels like progress.

"There is no real ending. It's just the place
where you stop the story."

~ Frank Herbert[xi]

APPENDIX

Map of The Bahamas

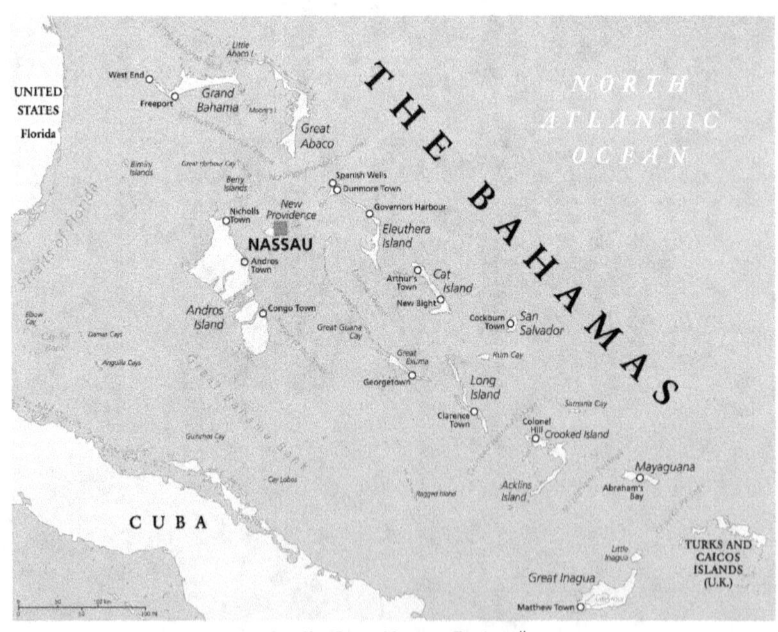

Credit: PeterHermesFurian[xii]

The Pyfrom Home

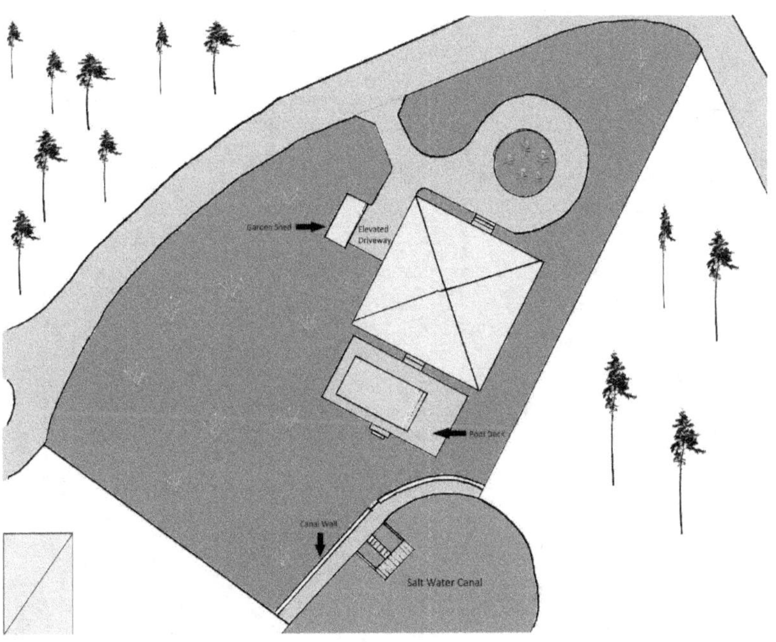

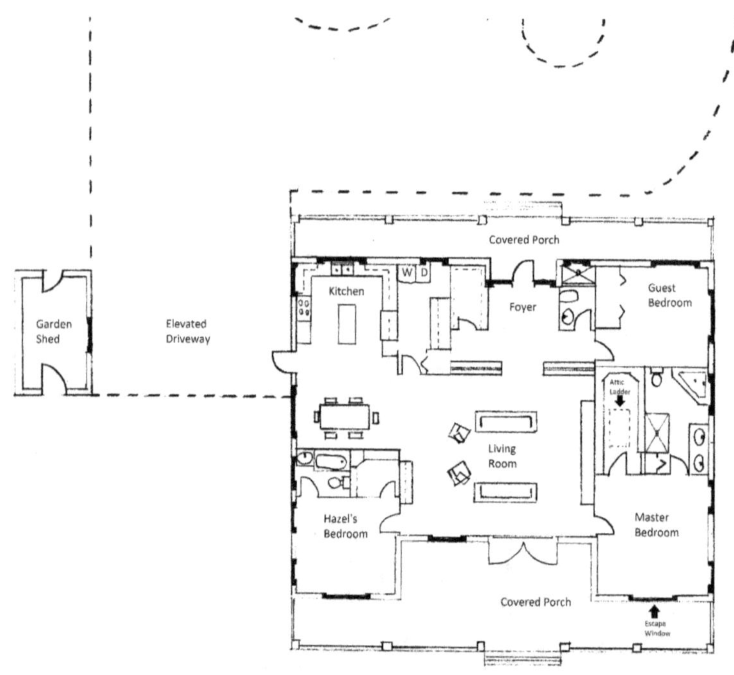

Covered Porch
Garden Shed
Elevated Driveway
Kitchen
W D
Foyer
Guest Bedroom
Living Room
Attic Ladder
Hazel's Bedroom
Master Bedroom
Covered Porch
Escape Window

SOURCES

ⁱCartwright-Carroll, T. The Nassau Guardian. January 31, 2023. Retrieved March 30, 2023. https://thenassauguardian.com/tourist-arrivals-back-at-7-million/

ⁱⁱ *Bahamas, The*. Climate Change Knowledge Portal. The World Bank Group. Retrieved September 9, 2022. https://climateknowledgeportal.worldbank.org/country/bahamas/climate-data-historical#:~:text=Mean%20temperatures%20have%20increased%20by,%C2%B0C%20per%20100%20years.

ⁱⁱⁱ *Bahamas, The*. Climate Change Knowledge Portal. The World Bank Group. Retrieved September 9, 2022. https://climateknowledgeportal.worldbank.org/country/bahamas

^{iv} Copeland, K. (2020). Disaster displacement: Examining the post-Dorian experience on Eleuthera. *Policy Point, Issue XVII, March 2020.* p. 1.

v Copeland, K. (2020). Disaster displacement: Examining the post-Dorian experience on Eleuthera. *Policy Point, Issue XVII, March 2020*. p. 1.

vi Thomas, A., LeGrand, C., Larson, S. International Journal of Bahamian Studies Vol. 27 (2021). https://journals.sfu.ca/cob/index.php/files/article/download/417/pdf_88

vii CORE. Retrieved March 20, 2023. https://www.coreresponse.org/the-bahamas/hurricane-dorian/

viii Smith-Cartwright, T. (2020, May 25). *Abaco concerns remain over burial*. The Tribune. http://www.tribune242.com/news/2020/may/26/abaco-concerns-remain-over-burial/

ix Grand Bahama Disaster Relief Foundation. (2020, February 25). *GBDRF Collaborates with GBPA, Local and International NGOs to help rebuild 400 Grand Bahama homes.* https://gbdisasterrelief.org/gbdrf-collaborates-with-gbpa-local-and-international-ngos-to-help-rebuild-400-grand-bahama-homes/

x The Ocean Conference. (2017, May). *Factsheet: People and Oceans.* UN.org. https://www.un.org/sustainabledevelopment/wp-content/uploads/2017/05/Ocean-fact-sheet-package.pdf

xi Frank Herbert interviewed by W. E. McNelly, 1969-02-03, 988-T, Carton: 23. Willis E. McNelly Science Fiction collection: Willis E. McNelly papers, SC-06-WEM. CSUF University Archives & Special Collections.

xii https://www.istockphoto.com/vector/the-bahamas-political-map-gm470836642-62729588